ACCLAIM FOR JAMES PATTERSON'S WOMEN'S MURDER CLUB THRILLERS

THE 17TH SUSPECT

"Patterson and Paetro blew this latest installment out of the water!...What's not to love about 4 strong and independent leading ladies with their own awesome and custom personalities?"

—TouchMySpineBookReviews.com

"The Women's Murder Club series...never gets old. James Patterson and Maxine Paetro have combined a familiar structure that houses ever-new and changing stories, which, as the series closes in on its second decade, has made these books a mainstay on the must-read lists of countless readers."

—BookReporter.com

16TH SEDUCTION

"16TH SEDUCTION is a fast-paced read from one of the world's most prolific writers. There are twists and turns...and the explosive climax brings the white-knuckle read to a satisfying conclusion."

—TheGremlin.co.za

15TH AFFAIR

"Filled with pulse-pounding international intrigue, 15TH AFFAIR proves that all is fair in love, war and espionage." —BookReporter.com

"Each chapter races by at a fast and furious pace, snatching the very breath from your lungs."
—NightsandWeekends.com

10TH ANNIVERSARY

"Short, pulse-pounding chapters come at you like bullets…a whirlwind of a ride…Don't miss this one."
—NightsandWeekends.com

"Verdict: Patterson and Paetro spin a fast-paced triple mystery that expertly weaves the stories together…Highly recommended." —*Library Journal*

THE 9TH JUDGMENT

"Another great Patterson/Paetro novel for those of us who can't get enough Patterson—ever!"
—TheReviewBroads.com

THE 8TH CONFESSION

"The ending was so mind-blowing…I immediately wished I had another Patterson novel to pick up."
—Bookalicio.us

"Mystery, mayhem, and murder most foul."
—*Publishers Weekly*

"Vintage Patterson…a must-read."
—TheNovelBookworm.com

7TH HEAVEN

"An ideal Patterson read for long-term fans and newcomers to the series."
—TheRomanceReadersConnection.com

Patterson chalks up another suspenseful outing for his Women's Murder Club."   —*People*

"A fast-paced thriller by the page-turningest author in the game right now."
                                        —*San Francisco Chronicle*

"Prime Patterson: first-rate entertainment...ripples with twists and remarkably strong scenes."
                                        —*Publishers Weekly* (starred review)

1ST TO DIE

"I can't believe how good Patterson is...He's always on the mark."   —Larry King, *USA Today*

"Patterson boils a scene down to the single, telling detail, the element that defines a character or moves a plot along. It's what fires off the movie projector in the reader's mind."
                                        —Michael Connelly, author of *Nine Dragons*

"His clever twists and affecting subplots keep the pages flying."   —*People* (Page-Turner of the Week)

"Delivers a sharp punch."   —*Chicago Tribune*

"That rapid-fire, in-your-face, you'd-better-keep-reading-or-else format will make you finish 1ST TO DIE in one sitting."
                                        —*Denver Rocky Mountain News*

BOOKS BY JAMES PATTERSON
FEATURING THE WOMEN'S MURDER CLUB

The 17th Suspect (with Maxine Paetro)
16th Seduction (with Maxine Paetro)
15th Affair (with Maxine Paetro)
14th Deadly Sin (with Maxine Paetro)
Unlucky 13 (with Maxine Paetro)
12th of Never (with Maxine Paetro)
11th Hour (with Maxine Paetro)
10th Anniversary (with Maxine Paetro)
The 9th Judgment (with Maxine Paetro)
The 8th Confession (with Maxine Paetro)
7th Heaven (with Maxine Paetro)
The 6th Target (with Maxine Paetro)
The 5th Horseman (with Maxine Paetro)
4th of July (with Maxine Paetro)
3rd Degree (with Andrew Gross)
2nd Chance (with Andrew Gross)
1st to Die

A complete list of books by James Patterson is at the back of this book. For previews of upcoming books and information about the author, visit JamesPatterson.com, or find him on Facebook.

THE 17TH SUSPECT

JAMES PATTERSON
AND MAXINE PAETRO

VISION

NEW YORK   BOSTON

Copyright © 2018 by James Patterson

Hachette Book Group supports the right to free expression and the value of copyright. The purpose of copyright is to encourage writers and artists to produce the creative works that enrich our culture.

The scanning, uploading, and distribution of this book without permission is a theft of the author's intellectual property. If you would like permission to use material from the book (other than for review purposes), please contact permissions@hbgusa.com. Thank you for your support of the author's rights.

Vision
Hachette Book Group
1290 Avenue of the Americas, New York, NY 10104
grandcentralpublishing.com
twitter.com/grandcentralpub

Originally published in hardcover and ebook by Little, Brown and Company in April 2018
First oversize mass market edition: March 2019

Vision is an imprint of Grand Central Publishing. The Vision name and logo is a trademark of Hachette Book Group, Inc.

The publisher is not responsible for websites (or their content) that are not owned by the publisher.

The Hachette Speakers Bureau provides a wide range of authors for speaking events. To find out more, go to hachettespeakersbureau.com or call (866) 376-6591.

ISBNs: 978-1-5387-1381-5 (oversize mass market), 978-0-316-41226-1 (ebook)

Printed in the United States of America

OPM

10 9 8 7 6 5 4 3 2 1

To the friends of the
Women's Murder Club

PART ONE

CHAPTER 1

JUST AFTER 4 A.M. under a starless sky, a man in a well-worn tweed coat and black knit cap crossed Broadway onto Front Street, humming a tune as he strolled south to Sydney G. Walton Square.

The square was a cozy one-block park, bounded by iron fencing with an artifact of a brick gate set at a diagonal on one corner. Inside were paths and seating and garden beds, cut back now at the end of the growing season.

During the day Walton Square was crowded with office workers from San Francisco's Financial District, eating their take-out lunches near the fountain. At night the streets were empty and the park was occupied by homeless people going through the trash cans, sleeping on the benches, congregating near the gate.

The man in the shapeless tweed coat stopped outside the iron fencing and looked around the park and surroundings with purpose. He was still humming tunelessly and gripping a 9mm gun in his right-hand pocket.

The man, Michael, was looking for someone in

particular. He watched for a while as the vagrants moseyed around the park and on the sidewalks that bounded it. He didn't see the woman he was looking for, but he wasn't going to let this night go to waste.

As he watched, a man in a ragged layering of dirty clothing left the park and headed east, in the direction of the Embarcadero and the piers, where the garbage in the trash cans was more exotic than discarded office worker sandwiches.

The ragged man was talking to himself, scratching his beard, and seemed to be counting, touching his right thumb to each of the fingers on his right hand and pensively repeating the ritual.

He didn't notice the man in the tweed coat standing against the fence.

Michael called out to him. "Hey, buddy. Got a smoke?"

The ragged man turned his bleary eyes to the man pointing the gun at him. He got it fast. He put up his hands and started to explain.

"No, man, I didn't take the money. It was her. I was an innocent—"

The man in the coat pulled the trigger once, shooting the bum square in the chest. Pigeons flew up from the adjacent buildings.

The bum clapped his hand over his chest and opened his mouth in a wordless expression of shock. But he was still standing, still staring at him.

Michael fired another shot. The ragged man's knees folded and he dropped without a sound.

He said to the corpse, "Worthless piece of shit, you asked for that. You should thank me."

He looked around and ducked into a section

of shade in the park. He placed his gun on the ground, stripped off his gloves, jammed them into his pockets, and shucked the old coat.

He was dressed all in black under the coat, in jeans, a turtleneck, and a quilted jacket. He transferred the gun to his jacket, gathered up the coat, and stuffed it into a trash can.

Someone would find them. Someone would put them on. And good luck to him.

Michael slipped out from behind the copse of trees and took a seat on a bench. Screams started up. And the crummy vermin poured out of the park like a line of ants and surrounded the body.

No one noticed him. There were no keening sirens, no "*Dude,* did you see what happened?"

Nothing.

After a few minutes the killer stood up and, with his hands in his jacket pockets, left the park and headed home.

There would be other nights.

One of these times he was bound to get lucky.

CHAPTER 2

ON MONDAY MORNING, assistant district attorney Yuki Castellano was in the San Francisco DA's conference room, sitting across the mahogany table from a boyishly handsome young man. Yuki was building a sexual abuse case that she thought, if brought to trial, could change the face of rape prosecution on a national scale. An executive at a top creative San Francisco ad agency had allegedly raped an employee at gunpoint, and Yuki was determined to try the case.

After she quit her job and spent a year at the nonprofit Defense League, district attorney Leonard "Red Dog" Parisi had asked her to come back and try an explosive case as his second chair—but they had suffered a humiliating loss. Now Yuki wanted very much to have a win for herself, for Parisi, and for the city.

She asked, "Marc, can we get you anything? Sparkling water? Coffee?"

"No, thanks. I'm good."

Marc Christopher was a television commercial producer with the Ad Shop—and the victim in the case, claiming that Briana Hill, the head of the agency's TV production department and his boss, had assaulted him. The Sex Crimes detail of SFPD's Southern Station had investigated Christopher's complaint and found convincing enough evidence to bring the case to the DA's office.

After reviewing the evidence and meeting with Christopher, Yuki had asked Parisi to let her take the case to the grand jury.

Parisi said, "Yuki, this could be a glue trap. You're going to have to convince a jury that this kid could keep it up with a loaded weapon pointed at his head. That a woman could rape him. You really want to do this? Win or lose, this case is going to stick to you."

She said, "Len, I'm absolutely sure he was raped and I can prove it. If we get an indictment, I want to run with this."

"Okay," Len said dubiously. "Give it your best shot."

In Yuki's opinion, nonconsensual sex was rape, irrespective of gender. Women raping men rarely got traction unless the woman was a schoolteacher or in another position of authority, and the victim was a child or, more commonly, a teenage boy. In those instances the crime had more to do with the age of the victim than a presumed act of brutality by a woman.

In this case Briana Hill and Marc Christopher were about the same age, both in their late twenties. Christopher was Hill's subordinate at the Ad Shop, true, but he wasn't accusing her of sexual harassment at work. He claimed that Hill had threatened to shoot him if he didn't comply with a sadistic sex act.

Would Hill really have pulled the trigger? For legal purposes, it didn't matter.

It mattered only that Marc Christopher had *believed* she would shoot him.

As Len Parisi had said, it was going to be a challenge to convince a jury that this confident young man couldn't have fought Hill off; that he'd maintained an erection at gunpoint, against his will; and that he'd been forced to have sex with a woman he had dated and had sex with many times before.

But Yuki would tell Christopher's story: he'd said no and Hill had violated him anyway. Yuki had seen the proof. The grand jury would have to decide if there was enough evidence to support that version of events. Once this case went to trial, win or lose, Marc would be known for accusing a woman of raping him. If Briana Hill was found guilty, she would go to jail—and the face of workplace sexual harassment would change.

CHAPTER 3

GLASS WALLS SEPARATED the conference room from the hallway, with its flow of busy, noisy, and nosy foot traffic.

Yuki ignored those who were sneaking looks at the broad-shouldered, dark-haired agency producer slumping slightly in his chair. He was clearly wounded, describing what he claimed had transpired two months before, and seemed very vulnerable.

Yuki stepped outside the conference room to have a word with a colleague. When she returned to her seat, Christopher had turned his chair so that he was staring out through the windows at the uninspiring third-floor view of Bryant Street.

Yuki said, "Marc, let's talk it through again, okay?"

He swiveled the chair back around and said, "I understand that I have to testify to the grand jury. I can do that. I'm worried about going to trial and how I'm going to react when Briana's attorney calls me a liar."

Yuki was glad Marc had dropped in to talk about this. He was right to be apprehensive. Briana

Hill's attorney, James Giftos, looked and dressed like a mild-mannered shoe salesman, but that was just a disarming guise for an attack attorney who would do whatever it took to destroy Marc Christopher's credibility.

Yuki asked, "How do you think you might react?"

"I don't know. I could get angry and go after the guy. I could break down and come across as a complete wimp."

"It's good to think about this in advance," Yuki said, "but Giftos won't be at the grand jury hearing. We're just asking the jury for an indictment based on the facts of this case. I think the jury is going to believe you, as I do.

"If Hill is indicted," Yuki continued, "we go to court. She'll be there to contest your testimony and present her version of this attack. James Giftos will do everything he can to make you look like a liar and worse."

"Oh, God. Can you walk me through that?"

"Okay, I'll give it to you straight. Because you dated Briana, you won't be protected by the rape shield law. Giftos could ask you about your sex life with Briana in detail—how often, what it was like, what made you invite her to your apartment. Nothing will be off-limits."

"Wonderful," said Christopher miserably. "Piece o' cake."

"The press will cover the trial. Public opinion may favor Briana, and you may be verbally attacked. It could get very ugly, Marc. And when we win, your life may never be quite the same."

The young man covered his face with his hands.

"Marc, if you don't want to go through with this, I'll understand."

"Thanks for that. I'll be ready. I'll *make* myself be ready."

"You have my number. Call me, anytime."

Yuki walked Christopher to the elevator, and as she shook his hand, he said, "I thought of something."

"Tell me."

"You should talk to Paul Yates. He's a copywriter at the Ad Shop. We're only casual friends, but I think something happened with him and Briana."

"Really? Something sexual?"

"I don't know," said Christopher. "I'm pretty sure they dated. They seemed friendly around the shop, then the big chill."

"There's no record of him speaking to Sex Crimes."

"No, I don't think he talked to them or anyone. I would have heard."

"Paul Yates," Yuki said. "I'll get in touch with him. Marc, stay strong."

His smile was shaky when he got into the elevator car.

Yuki stood in place as the doors closed, then headed back to her office. She wasn't confident that Marc would hang tough, and she couldn't blame him. In his place, she would feel conflict and fear, too. But the key facts in the case against Briana Hill were incontrovertible: Marc had recorded the rape, and Briana always carried a gun. Marc's testimony would bring those facts to life for the jurors.

CHAPTER 4

TWO DAYS AFTER her last meeting with Marc Christopher, Yuki got a call from James Giftos, Briana Hill's defense attorney.

"Ms. Castellano. James Giftos here. My client wants to speak with you. By chance do you have a gap in your schedule sometime this week?"

"Oh? What's this about?"

Yuki's laptop was open and she began making notes as Giftos spoke.

He said, "Ms. Castellano, uh, Yuki—my client wants to tell you her side of the story. She hopes that when you hear what really happened, you'll see that Mr. Christopher's allegations have no basis in fact. She's willing to apologize if there's been a misunderstanding, and then, she hopes, Marc can drop the drama and they can go on with their lives."

So James Giftos wanted a "queen for a day" interview, a proffer agreement. In this meeting Ms. Hill would attempt to convince Yuki that she should drop the case because of insufficient evidence.

The rules of engagement for these interviews

were clear. Briana Hill and her attorney would come to Yuki's office, where Hill would be sworn in, then submit to Yuki's questions, her answers transcribed by a court reporter. Hill would not be allowed to invoke the Fifth Amendment, and most importantly for Yuki's purposes, if the DA decided to proceed with the case, nothing Hill said could be used against her in the grand jury hearing or at trial.

However, and it was a big *however,* if Hill took the stand and her testimony differed from what she'd told Yuki under oath, all bets would be off. Her formerly privileged testimony would no longer be privileged, and Yuki could use anything she'd said in her proffer interview against her.

It was a good deal for the prosecution.

Briana Hill would give her side of the story, meaning that Yuki would learn the basis for the opposition's case.

Yuki said to Giftos, "Turns out I have an opening at two today."

"Sold," he said.

Yuki hung up with Giftos, made notes to add to the file, and then walked down the hallway for a pickup meeting with Len.

CHAPTER 5

YUKI GREETED BRIANA Hill and James Giftos at two that afternoon and walked them to the conference room where the court reporter was waiting.

Hill was petite, her dark hair blunt-cut to her shoulders, and she wore a modest silk blouse and sharp gray suit.

She was very pretty, and Yuki knew that she was also plenty smart. Born and raised in Dallas, Briana Hill had a film degree from USC and an MBA from NYU. She had gotten her first job at a production company, and a few years later was hired by the Ad Shop, where she rose quickly to head of TV production.

As head of TV, Hill reported to the agency president and was responsible for millions per year in TV commercials for big-name clients.

Briana looked the part of a highly placed young executive. She appeared cool and confident, but Yuki noted the dark circles under her eyes and the way Hill clutched at the silver crucifix hanging from a long chain around her neck.

Giftos turned off his phone, Hill was sworn in,

and the court reporter typed at her console in the corner of the room.

Yuki said, "Ms. Hill, do you understand that this interview means that we have a binding agreement, that you are required to answer all of my questions truthfully, and if you don't tell the truth, our agreement is void?"

"I sure do," said Hill. "I asked for this meeting. I want to tell you what happened. I swear to tell the truth."

The conference room door opened and Len Parisi entered. The DA was a big man, tall, over three hundred pounds, and had coarse red hair. He was known for his sharp legal mind, his tenacity, and his impressive record of wins.

Parisi was taking special interest in this case, among hundreds under his purview, because *The People* v. *Hill* would be a media supermagnet: a sex scandal with radical social implications. Before his office asked for an indictment, Parisi wanted to get his own sense of Briana Hill.

He shook hands with Hill and Giftos and sat down heavily in the chair next to Yuki. He clicked a ballpoint pen a few times with his large thumb and tapped the point on a pad of paper in front of him. He looked across the table, smiled, and said, "Ms. Hill, this is your meeting. As long as you tell the truth, nothing you say can be used against you."

"I'm aware," said Hill.

Yuki kept a poker face, but she was excited to be facing off against James Giftos on such an important case. This was why she loved her job with the DA.

CHAPTER 6

BRIANA HILL CLASPED her hands in front of her and said, "This is a pretty grim story, but it needs to be told. Where should I start, James? With the so-called incident—or with what led up to it?"

Her attorney said, "Give us the background first."

"Okay. Mr. Parisi. Ms. Castellano. The first thing you should know is that Marc had been working for me for about six months when he let me know he was interested in me. He sent flowers to my apartment on my birthday, and I wouldn't say he was stalking me, but he was just there when I'd leave the office, go over to Starbucks, like that. He bought me coffee, and the next time I bought coffee for him. Takeout.

"Then he asked me out.

"I said no. I wasn't thinking of him that way. If the thought even crossed my mind, I shut it down. It was possible that going out with Marc could screw up the chain of command and make people in the creative department uncomfortable."

Yuki said, "What changed your mind?"

Said Hill, "I'm getting to it. Coming right up.

Anyway. I fended Marc off, but he persisted and I realized that I was starting to like him. He was funny. Very charming, and by the way, a good producer. So I said okay to lunch. It's just lunch, right?"

Yuki noted a couple of things as Briana spoke. One, she was an accomplished presenter. Two, according to Hill, Christopher had made the advances. That meant nothing in terms of her guilt or innocence, but it was good for the defense version of the assault.

"I liked Marc," Hill said, "but this was just a flirtation until—cue the dramatic music—the Chronos Beer shoot in Phoenix four months ago. It was a great shoot, big budget, terrific director, and all of us, the production company and the agency people, were staying in a nice hotel. So we wrapped the shoot and went for dinner and drinks at the hotel bar and grill at the end of the last day.

"I was very happy," Hill said. "Everyone was. It was a celebration, and Marc and I closed the bar. It was like we were alone on a desert island. He invited me back to his room. I went."

Hill clamped her mouth shut. She swallowed hard. She seemed to be remembering what had transpired that night. It looked to Yuki like she was unhappy with the memory.

Giftos said, "Go on, Briana. What happened when you came back to town and reentered the atmosphere of everyday life?"

Hill sighed, then seemed to steel herself for the sordid tale of her new relationship with Marc Christopher.

CHAPTER 7

BRIANA HILL HAD been talking for half an hour, and her confident demeanor was starting to sag. She sounded resigned when she said, "Marc and I started dating.

"I wasn't in love with him, but I wasn't seeing anyone else. Eventually, though, I started losing interest, and Marc was getting the message. He got needy and borderline aggressive. One night he stopped by my office at the end of the day, and when he said, 'Let's grab a bite,' I said okay. I thought we'd have a discussion about how the relationship wasn't working out and probably agree to call it off.

"But that's not what happened.

"We went to our usual place, a restaurant called Panacea, a short walk from Marc's apartment. I started with a predinner drink. Actually, I was drinking before, during, and after dinner.

"I think Marc was talking about politics, but I wasn't really listening. I was trying to decide whether to break up with him that night or to give it more time, weighing the pros and cons. After dinner we moved to the restaurant bar. That's when Marc pitched his big idea."

"It was *his* big idea?" Len said.

"Yeah. He knew I carried a gun, and he said that it really turned him on. He said that he wanted me…to pretend to rape him. He said I should hold the gun on him and order him to tie himself to the bed and follow my directions, or I would kill him. Something like that.

"It was ridiculous, but I'd never played out a fantasy like that. He kept saying it would be fun, with this big grin on his face. And he said it would be good for our relationship—he wanted me to 'gut-feel' how much I wanted him. I think that's how he put it.

"We went to his apartment. That's where we always went," Hill said. "I unloaded my gun, put the shells in my bag, then I followed his script and tried to get into the role. It was kind of fun, but also kind of weird, what I remember of it.

"After the sex was over, I fell asleep. We both did. Passed out is more like it. I woke up at about five and untied his hands. He was still sleeping, so I went home. I didn't like how I felt and I didn't like him, either. I knew that we'd crossed a line. There was no way back.

"I avoided him at work," Hill continued, "but he called and left messages saying he wanted to get together. I told him no. 'Sorry, Marc, but it's over.' He didn't like that, but I thought he'd move on. Instead he came to my office after work a couple of days later and shut the door. That's when he told me that he'd recorded our sex play—recorded it! And that he wanted a quarter of a million dollars or he was going to post the video online."

Yuki asked, "You took this to be a serious threat?"

Hill's expression crumpled. "Yes," she said. "It was believable that he had a hidden camera. He's a film producer. He knew that my grandma had died and that she had left me a big pile of money. I told him to go to hell, but I was scared.

"I was also in shock. I'm *still* in shock."

Yuki found Briana utterly credible. Was she a world-class actress? Or was her version of the story true? One of them was lying.

Giftos put his hand on Briana's shoulder and told her to take a minute.

After she'd collected herself, but still noticeably distressed, she said, "I remembered some of what we did in his bedroom but very little of what was said. Still, I'm positive that everything I did and said was entirely scripted by Marc. I never ever thought of rape as a turn-on. And I surely never knew that he was recording…this game."

Hill went on, "I've always known the only way to defeat a bully is to stand up to him. Marc Christopher is a bully. He's also insecure and vengeful, and that's being *kind*. I did not rape him. It was all his idea. He set me up. And that's the whole truth."

CHAPTER 8

YUKI HAD QUESTIONS. Lots of them.

Sitting across the conference table from Briana Hill and her attorney, Len and Yuki fired away.

Yuki stuck to the workplace relationship between Hill and Christopher.

Did management at the Ad Shop prohibit relationships at the agency? Was Ms. Hill in a position to influence Mr. Christopher's promotions and raises? Why was his performance review poor after the incident in Mr. Christopher's apartment?

Hill told them that there was no explicit rule prohibiting relationships within the agency. Yes, she could influence his raises, but she explained that after the so-called rape incident, "Marc was defiant and threatening. He walked away from an assignment, leaving the team to scramble and endangering an account. Naturally, his crummy attitude and insubordination were reflected in the one performance review I conducted with him."

Len's questions were about the gun and the sex. Was her gun registered? Did she have a concealed carry permit? Where exactly did she keep the gun? Did she ever have it out during sex with

Christopher—or anyone else—prior to the event they were discussing? Would she describe her sexual preferences as nontraditional or "kinky"?

Hill asserted that she lived alone, traveled often, had obtained a concealed carry permit, and had carried a gun for most of her adult life. Her gun was registered, and she kept it in her handbag at all times for protection.

She added, "I don't know what you would call kinky, Mr. Parisi, but until this encounter with Marc Christopher, I'd never experimented with aggressive sexual role-playing."

Len said, "And you claim you don't know what you said or did during this sex act?"

"I remember enough," she said. "I remember the pitch he threw me in the bar but not much of what I said or what he said during the act itself. It was role-playing. We were having *sex*. I'd had a lot to drink. I wasn't trying to remember what we said. Wouldn't that have been crazy? When I think about it, I see flash images, as if the bed was under a strobe light. As soon as it was over, I wanted to forget it had happened.

"I have some questions for *you*, Mr. Parisi. Why didn't Marc grab my gun? Run for the hills? Call the cops? Did you ask him?"

Parisi said mildly, "If you know, had Marc been drinking, too?"

"Sure. I don't remember what or how much."

Parisi asked, "Before or during the sex, did Marc tell you to stop? Did he say no to you at any point?"

"He may have," said Hill. "But that was the point of the script he laid out for me. He was supposed to be the victim and I was supposed to take him by force. That was his game."

Yuki said, "Ms. Hill, can you prove that Mr. Christopher set up this game?"

"How? We had a conversation in a bar."

"I have the recording Mr. Christopher made of your sexual encounter," said Yuki. "We'll have a copy sent to Mr. Giftos's office this week. It's video with sound, Ms. Hill. You can see and hear it all."

After Briana Hill and James Giftos left, Yuki went to Len's office. They sat at right angles to each other in his sitting area, surrounded by bookshelves, in view of the clock with a red bulldog face on the wall behind his desk.

"What did you think of the defense?" Yuki asked.

"Hill is credible," said Len, "and a very accomplished presenter. But her defense of the rape, saying that Marc gave her the script and she performed to his direction, that's her word against his. We don't have the script discussion recorded. The video only shows and tells what happened in the bedroom, and even then, while the act was in progress."

Yuki asked, "Does the fact that they'd slept together before the rape hurt his case?"

Parisi said, "Not legally, but it could make a juror wonder what the hell he was complaining about. Unless you can turn up more evidence, we're pinning everything on the video. He said no and she kept the gun on him. He says it was loaded. She says it was not. He said, she said.

"But she asks good questions," Parisi continued. "Why didn't he call the cops when he woke up?

Why did he wait two weeks to do that? That's going to come up. And I don't like this story that he tried to blackmail her. Did that ring true to you?"

Yuki said, "This is the first I've heard of extortion. I'll ask him."

"Unless he puts that in writing, it's more of his word against hers."

Yuki nodded in agreement. "They have colleagues in common. I interviewed three people at the Ad Shop. I'll review their notes again."

Yuki went back to her office and made notes to file on the meeting with Briana Hill. Hill had sounded truthful, but Yuki had seen the video. Marc Christopher said no, and Briana Hill didn't stop. And that was what mattered in the eyes of the law.

CHAPTER 9

AT A QUARTER to eight on a hazy Friday morning, I parked my Explorer in the All-Day Parking lot on Bryant Street across from the Hall of Justice, where I work in Homicide.

I crossed the street between breaks in the traffic and jogged up the steps to the main entrance of the gray granite building that housed not only the Southern Station of the SFPD, but also the DA, the municipal courts, a jail, and the motorcycle squad. I was reaching for the handle of the heavy steel-and-glass front door to the Hall when I heard someone call out, "Sergeant? Sergeant Lindsay Boxer."

I turned to see a middle-aged woman with graying blond hair, who was wearing a dirty fleece hoodie and baggy jeans, hurrying up the steps toward me. I wasn't surprised to be recognized. My last case had been high profile. A murdering psycho had blown up a museum, killing and injuring dozens of people, including my husband. For weeks after the bombing and all during the bomber's trial, my picture had been on the front page of the San Francisco papers and on the local

TV news. Months later memories of that unspeakable crime still rippled through the public consciousness.

From the woman's dress she looked to me like she was living on the street. I had change from a ten in my jacket pocket, and I pulled out some bills, but she waved them away.

"I don't need any money. Thank you, though. What I need is your help, Sergeant. I want to report a murder."

I looked at her. The assertion sounded like the opening to an old episode of *Murder, She Wrote,* but I had to take it seriously. The woman was distressed. And I'm a cop.

We were blocking the entrance to the Hall. Attorneys and clerks and other cops were trying to get past me, some rudely, some urgently. I stepped aside.

"What's your name?" I asked.

"Millie Cushing. I pay my taxes."

I let that one go. If she lived in San Francisco, she had a right to ask me for help.

"This murder," I said. "What can you tell me about that?"

"Well, I didn't see the murder happen, and I didn't see the victim's body, but I knew him. Jimmy Dolan wasn't the first one to get shot dead on the street, and he's not going to be the last, either."

Was Millie Cushing of sound mind? I couldn't tell.

I said, "You know what? The morning shift is just starting and our squad room is going to be noisy. Let's go someplace where we can talk."

CHAPTER 10

I LED MILLIE to Café Roma, a small chain coffee shop on Bryant, up the very long block and across the street from the Hall. We found a small booth near the plate-glass window, and the waitress took our orders; coffee for Millie, tea and dry toast for me.

I said, "Millie, order whatever you want."

Millie took the cue and ordered eggs, toast, potatoes, sausage, and bacon. She laughed, saying, "I guess that will hold me for the weekend."

When the waitress left the table, I asked Millie to tell me everything she knew about the murder that had brought her to the Hall that morning looking for me.

She leaned across the small table and began her story.

"The murder happened outside Walton Square," she said. I knew the park well. It was in the Financial District, not far from Southern Station's beat.

Millie said, "It happened very early on Monday morning. This nice man named Jimmy Dolan was shot on the sidewalk on Front Street. Right here," she said, tapping the center of her chest. "Two and done."

"How did you learn about this?" I asked.

"You wouldn't think so, but we're a tightly knit community. Jimmy was shot at four fifteen or so in the morning, and three hours later it was common knowledge on the street. And that's by word of mouth and very few cell phones, you know."

"Community?"

"Homeless," she said. "For some it's temporary. For others it's a permanent way of life. The point is, we know one another. We keep tabs. We exchange news at the shelters and places we go on the street."

Breakfast came and Millie tucked in.

I excused myself while she was occupied to call my partner, Rich Conklin, to tell him that I was running late but would be in soon.

I went back to my seat and sugared my tea. Millie was well into her scrambled eggs.

I said, "Millie. The police were called?"

"What I heard is they came, but they never asked around or did anything but wait until the meat wagon arrived. Jimmy deserves more than to be shoveled up and stuffed into a box. He deserves justice. The man was a poet. A good one. And before the voices got to him, he was a college professor. To the cops, he's *trash*."

I murmured, "Sorry to hear this," and asked Millie to go on.

"Like I said, shootings are happening all over. Jimmy was one of I don't know how many of us who have been killed, and I tell you, Sergeant, being with you is the safest I've felt in a year."

"A year?"

I resisted an impulse to reach across the table and take her hands. If she was delusional, I was buying right in.

When the table was cleared, Millie said thanks to a coffee refill and picked up where she'd left off. It felt like she'd been waiting a long time for someone to listen to her. To help her.

"It's obscene," Millie said. "I can't be exact, but I can count three other killings, Sergeant Boxer, and none of them have been properly investigated. I saw your picture in the paper after the bombing, and I felt something for you. Like a connection."

As we stood to go, I told Millie I would follow up, giving her my card.

"Do you have a phone?"

"Sometimes I forget to charge it," she said. But she pulled an old flip phone from her pocket and showed me.

I forced some small bills on her, then told her I'd look into the case of Jimmy Dolan. I paid the tab and headed back to the Hall.

I thought about Millie as I walked. She was well spoken. Seemed educated and sane. Her story and Millie herself were believable.

I wondered how she'd ended up on the street.

As I climbed the Hall of Justice steps, I felt light-headed. I had lied to Millie when I said I'd had breakfast. I'd gulped coffee and kissed my family good-bye, expecting to have another cup of coffee at my desk. Honestly, I hadn't felt hungry, which wasn't normal for me. I took the elevator to the fourth floor and entered the Homicide squad room.

After saying "hey" to Conklin, I went to the break room and snagged the last donut in the box. Someone had hacked off a piece of it. In my humble opinion, that was an irrelevant detail.

It was chocolate-glazed chocolate, the very best kind. I bit into it. It was good.

CHAPTER 11

THE HOMICIDE SQUAD room is a square gray bull pen with our receptionist just inside the door, our lieutenant's glassed-in office in the back corner with a window onto the freeway. In between, on both sides of the narrow center aisle, are a handful of desks used by the other Homicide inspectors. There has been some talk that we'll be moving to newer quarters within the decade, and I hope it's more than gossip.

Conklin and I have facing desks at the front of the room, equidistant from the entrance and the break room. I shucked off my jacket, threw it over the back of my chair, and dropped into the seat.

Conklin said, "You have chocolate right here."

He pointed to the right side of his mouth.

I sighed, grabbed a tissue, and, under his direction, rubbed at the spot.

"Okay now?" I asked him.

Conklin and I have known each other for years. He was a beat cop who told me he'd like to be in Homicide. When positions in our department reshuffled, my former partner, Warren Jacobi, got a promotion and Rich Conklin and I became a team.

Known around the Hall as Inspector Hottie, Conklin is in his midthirties, brown eyed, brown haired, good lookin' and good doin', altogether just about the perfect American boy next door. We love each other like siblings without the rivalry, complement each other's strengths, and shore up the other's weaknesses.

In confrontational situations, interrogations for instance, I'm the one throwing fastballs and Richie is the "good cop," telling me to take it easy. Wink-wink. He's especially good with women. They trust him on sight.

Conklin gave me a thumbs-up after assessing the chocolate. He said, "You going to tell me about your mystery breakfast?"

Phones were ringing. The overhead TV was on low, but not mute, and people were talking over the ambient noise.

I said, "A homeless woman named Millie Cushing tagged me as I was coming through the door. She wanted to tell me that a series of homeless people have been shot to death over the last year or so, and that the cops haven't done anything about it."

"First I've heard of this," Rich said.

"The shootings have been happening in Central Station's beat, that's why."

"Aw, jeez," my partner said. "This isn't good."

While the citywide Homicide Detail is located here at Southern Station, a vestigial Homicide Detail operates out of Central Station, the result of a redistricting before my time. Officially called a station investigative team, Central Homicide sweeps up homicides that are called into their district during the graveyard shift.

That's fine with me. God knows we have enough crimes to solve right here in our own house.

I told my partner what Cushing had told me: that a man named Jimmy Dolan had been shot sometime in the wee hours down on Front Street. Since I hadn't heard about any killings of street people on our beat—and I would have—it could only mean that *all* of these shootings had happened in Central.

"I promised Millie I'd look into what she says is an ongoing pattern of homeless shootings, no arrests," I concluded.

Rich was already tapping on his keyboard, searching for a report of a homicide outside Sydney G. Walton Square.

"Got it," he said. "Victim: James Dolan, white male, fifty, shot twice in the chest at approximately four a.m. No witnesses to the shooting. Investigation ongoing. Body at Metro Hospital morgue."

I said, "That's the guy. Who was assigned to the case?"

"Sergeant Garth Stevens and Inspector Evan Moran. I don't know them. You?"

"I know of Stevens," I said. "He's been on the job for twenty-five years."

"Stevens and Moran work graveyard shift," Conklin said.

I called Sergeant Stevens before Conklin and I clocked out for the day, and was put through to his desk at Central. He knew my name, said he'd even worked with my father, Marty Boxer, back in the day. My father was a bad-news cop and a worse husband and dad, but I let the comment slide with a "No kidding."

I said, "Sergeant, you're investigating that shooting at Walton Square?"

"Yeah. Vagrant took a couple of rounds to the chest. Killed instantly. Why do you want to know?"

"A citizen got hold of me and said there may have been several incidents like this one. Does that sound right?"

"You have a suspect in this shooting?" he asked, answering my question with one of his own.

"No."

"Then don't worry about this, Sergeant. Moran and I are on it. Nice chatting with you."

And then he hung up.

I put the receiver back in the cradle and said to Conklin, "Stevens blew me off."

"Typical," said Conklin. "Old-timer. Get offa my cloud."

I had a bad feeling about it. It wasn't just that the old-timer had been rude; maybe he had a reason for blowing me off. Maybe there was something he didn't want me to know.

CHAPTER 12

YUKI WAS HUNCHED over her computer rereading transcripts of her interviews with some of Marc Christopher's associates from the Ad Shop.

Parisi had warned her that their case pretty much rested on the video, and she agreed. The recording was powerful. Yuki thought that if it was true the DA could get a grand jury indictment with a ham sandwich, then Marc Christopher's rape video was a five-star seven-course meal with a vintage wine.

No doubt she could get a grand jury indictment; if they went to trial, the rape video had to go into evidence and had to be shown to the jury.

Giftos would try to get the video excluded. That way, if he put Hill on the stand, the jury would hear both versions of the sex act. Only one juror had to agree that the rape was staged, and Briana Hill would not be found guilty.

Yuki had to find more evidence to shore up her case if the video was thrown out, but how?

No one else had been in the bedroom with Hill and Christopher. The cops had photographed fading bruise marks on Marc's wrists and ankles, but apparently, Marc hadn't told anyone that he had been raped until two weeks after the fact.

Now she wondered if anyone else had had a sexual encounter with Briana Hill that could be called rape.

As she reread the interview transcripts, she was looking for something that she might have missed, a comment that she should have probed, a tell that she had let slide.

She called up the transcript of senior art director Lyle Bevans. He was forty-two, had worn red-rimmed glasses and an untucked plaid shirt over his jeans, had long hair, and had smelled like weed. He had seemed to enjoy the meeting with the ADA and been willing to spend as much time as she would allow.

She had interviewed him because he had frequent and recent experience working with both Christopher and Hill.

Yuki highlighted the relevant parts of the transcript, including the part where Bevans told her that Briana Hill was hot and demanding. "She's a sex bomb."

Yuki: Mr. Bevans, did Ms. Hill use inappropriate sexual advances to manage or manipulate her staff?

Bevans: I would say that she's all woman with a masculine determination to git 'er done. You looked at her, you thought about sex, and she carried a gun. That was sexy, too.

Yuki: You say that you heard about Marc Christopher's accusation that she'd raped him. What was your reaction to that?

Bevans: You're asking me if I think she could have done it? Yeah, if I had to make a wager. I'd bet she made him her bitch.

Yuki: Did you ever *see* her make inappropriate demands on Marc Christopher?

Bevans: They were dating. You know that, right? So, did she slap his butt once? Yeah. Sure. I saw that.

Yuki opened the next transcript, the interview with Bill Keely, CEO of the Ad Shop and Briana Hill's superior. She remembered that Keely's wardrobe was gray, his haircut was Republican, and his work history was account management, not creative. Briana Hill had a dotted-line reporting relationship to him. He had made the final decision in hiring her, and recently he had put her on waivers.

Keely: I didn't want to suspend her. But this situation is a distraction, and our clients don't want any association with her.

Yuki: How would you describe her worth to the firm?

Keely: A+. Hardworking. Corporate values. Delivered a great product. I don't know her personally. So, is that all?

Yuki: Almost. Were there any complaints about her being sexually provocative or aggressive with agency staff?

Keely: I heard some hallway gossip that I put down to sexism. She was a good-looking woman in a power position. But no complaints came to me officially.

Yuki opened the transcript of her interview with Maria Cortes, the production department assistant. Cortes had worn tight jeans, a black shirt, and great lace-up boots, and had tattoos on her hands and neck. If Keely would be the last to know if Hill was guilty of sexual harassment, Cortes would be the first. She reported directly to Hill and was the go-to person for the whole production staff.

> Cortes: Briana is tough. She has to be. She's not a rapist, that I can tell you. Men like her. She likes them. They flirt with her, too. But she's honest and has a good heart.
> Yuki: You like her?
> Cortes: I do. And I like Marc, too.
> Yuki: What do you think of the rape accusation against Ms. Hill?
> Cortes: I'd like to say it was all a misunderstanding.
> Yuki: Thanks, Ms. Cortes. I appreciate your time.

Parisi called Yuki on her private line. "I thought you'd still be there."

"I'm reviewing my notes now," she said. "I have another interview in five minutes that could be a decider. I'll have a point of view in the morning."

"I'll be standing by," said the DA.

CHAPTER 13

PAUL YATES WAS about thirty, lanky, with thinning hair and a thick beard, conveying an over-all pleasant good-guy appearance. He shook her hand.

"I'm Paulie."

She offered coffee and Yates asked for orange soda.

"Coffee or water. That's what I've got," she said with a laugh. "Your choice."

He said, "Water would be great."

"Hang on a sec," she said.

She went out to the kitchen, got a glass bottle of water out of the fridge, and returned with it to her office.

"Premium H_2O," she said, passing the bottle to Yates. "Comes from the heart of a glacier, I think. Or else the Hetch Hetchy Reservoir. I don't really know," she said with a grin.

He grinned back and thanked her, and Yuki showed Yates the tape recorder.

"I'll be taping. Any problem?"

"None that I can think of."

Yuki switched on the small recorder. Yates got

comfortable in the chair across the desk from her and then reached over the desk and turned one of the framed photos toward him.

"Nice-looking guy," said Yates. "Your husband?"

Yuki took the photo out of his hand, put it back under her desk lamp, and said, "Let's talk about you."

"If we must," he said.

Paul Yates had come to San Francisco from Spokane five years before. He currently had a girlfriend, Amy, and they shared a rescue dog, Bosco. Yates was a copywriter at the Ad Shop and had won an award for last year's Skipperoo dog food campaign. He knew Marc, but they didn't hang out together.

Yuki said, "Paulie, I need to ask you about Briana Hill."

"Okay. Shoot."

"Did Marc tell you that she had raped him?"

"No. I only heard about it when the police started interviewing people at the agency."

"And what did you think when you heard there had been a sexual assault?"

"I try to ignore gossip and office politics. I've never known of anything good to come out of either."

"Good call," Yuki said with a smile. "Why do you think Marc thought I should speak with you?"

"Probably because I went out with Briana. Before Amy. Before Marc, too."

Yuki asked, "Can you tell me about dating Briana?"

"There's not much to tell," said Yates. "I only went out with her once."

"Did you have sex with her?"

"Christ. You want me to talk about that?"

"Please."

His expression tightened. He scowled.

He said, "What happens if I tell you? You're going to ask me to testify, aren't you?"

"Paul. I can't say at this minute. Tell me what happened with you and Briana Hill. You're in my office of your own volition. You're here to help me, but you aren't required to talk to me unless you committed a crime. Did you commit a crime?"

"Hell no. Unless going out with a psycho is a crime."

"You're saying that Briana Hill is a psycho?"

Paul Yates started shaking his head. Then, "Look, I don't know you and this is embarrassing. I've never told anyone, and I don't want to ever tell anyone else. Not for any reason."

"What happened, Paulie? Did she threaten you?"

"It was...terrifying."

"I'm listening," Yuki said.

Yates reached over and pressed the Stop button on the tape recorder. Yuki had to let him do it.

"I'll tell you, but I am not going to testify," he said.

"Okay. Okay, Paulie. Just tell me."

CHAPTER 14

YUKI AND MARC Christopher were taking the elevator to the fourth floor of the Civic Center Courthouse, where she would be making her case to the grand jury within the next twenty minutes.

The grand jury hearing was a trial run for the prosecutor. Yuki would present the case against Briana Hill, her few witnesses would testify, and she would introduce her evidence. All of this would be done fairly quickly, and with absolute secrecy.

There would be no judge, no defendant, no other attorneys. Yuki would be entirely in charge of this presentation. Unlike with a petit jury, where the jurors had to be convinced beyond a reasonable doubt, here the grand jurors—or twelve of nineteen of them—had only to find probable cause that Briana Hill had raped Marc Christopher.

If they found probable cause, they would indict and the case would go forward to trial.

The pressure was on Yuki, and on Marc.

While Len Parisi had always shown confidence in Yuki, she had lost big cases. But for the most part, the losses were not because of error, lack of preparation, or poor skills. Once, a star witness for the prosecution had committed suicide; another had choked on the stand and changed her testimony; and in one case the defense had sprung a surprise witness who landed a crushing blow to the prosecution's case.

Still, Yuki had notched several important wins. Although Parisi was skeptical about the Hill case, he had given her the green light to go to the grand jury. She was sure she was right to have fought for the case.

The elevator lurched and stopped at the third floor. People got out, replaced by others squeezing in, and once the doors closed, the car continued its ascent.

Standing beside Yuki, Marc Christopher was dressed in a navy-blue suit and blue-patterned tie. His hair was recently cut and he'd had a good shave. Yuki was wearing a blue suit, very much like the one Marc was wearing. No tie for her, but a strand of angel skin coral beads Brady had given her as a wedding gift. Unlike Yuki, Marc looked completely numb.

Yuki suspected he'd popped a Xanax or two. If so, he'd made a mistake. Yuki needed him to bring the story of the sexual assault to life for the jury. He had to emote. He had to be able to describe the damaging effects of what he had been through.

Yuki wanted to ask him again if he was feeling okay, but at this point it no longer mattered.

Unless Marc said in the next few minutes, "I've changed my mind. I want to drop the charges," the show would go on. She was ready. She could only hope that Marc would be ready, too.

The elevator doors slid open on the fourth floor. Yuki and Marc exited the elevator and walked down the hallway toward the grand jury room.

Her three other witnesses were waiting in the corridor outside the courtroom door.

Phyllis Chase, the arresting officer in the case, was in uniform. Paul Yates, the copywriter who had had one date with Briana Hill, wore denim and a panicked look. And Frank Pilotte, the tech specialist who would run Marc's homemade rape video for the jury and testify to its authenticity, had the calm presence Yuki had hoped for in an expert witness.

Yates and Christopher acknowledged each other with nods. Pilotte held open the heavy wooden door for Yuki, and she entered the grand jury room. It was a modern courtroom: wood paneling and white-painted plaster under a drop ceiling lit with embedded fluorescent fixtures.

The judge's bench, at one end of the room, would not be in use. Instead a massive wooden table had been set up facing the jurors. Yuki took her place behind the table, and her four witnesses sat alongside her.

The nineteen jurors had been impaneled for almost a month and had heard a hundred cases in that time. And still Yuki was pretty sure they hadn't ever heard a case like this one.

Yuki felt almost calm. She was prepared. In just a little while she would know if she would be putting Briana Hill on trial for sexual assault in the first degree.

CHAPTER 15

YUKI MADE HER succinct opening remarks to the jurors, each word carefully chosen.

"It may be hard to imagine a woman forcing a strong young man into an act of sexual intercourse against his will.

"Now imagine that this woman is his boss, that she had a gun in her hand, and that she threatened to blow him away if he didn't perform. In a few minutes Marc Christopher, the victim, will tell you exactly what happened to him. But first I want you to hear from Inspector Chase, of Sex Crimes, who investigated this case."

Yuki called Inspector Phyllis Chase. The foreperson swore her in, and the forty-year-old police investigator, appearing motherly and calm, took the witness stand.

Yuki asked her to tell the jurors how she became involved in this case. Chase explained that the victim had called to report a sexual assault and then came to the police station to make a statement.

"He told me that he had been raped. He was very emotional, and he said that he was afraid there would be workplace ramifications if he reported this rape to the police. He showed me what looked like ligature marks, bruises that had faded to a light brown color, on his wrists and ankles. That would be consistent with bruising after two to three weeks. He told us that it took him a couple of weeks to get his mind around the fact that he had been raped."

Chase went on.

"My partner and I investigated this charge. There were no eyewitnesses to this sexual assault, which is true in nearly all the rape cases I have handled in the last fifteen years. But in this case the victim had a spy cam clock radio on his night table, and soon after the beginning of this attack, he recorded the event."

Yuki said, "Did you ask why he had this hidden camera?"

"He explained that he'd bought it years before when he had a roommate. He suspected the roommate of bringing women home and having sex in Mr. Christopher's bed. The roommate denied it, and after Mr. Christopher caught him in the act, he didn't use the camera function again until the night in question. Based on the recording, we made an arrest."

After Chase's testimony Yuki called Frank Pilotte, the police tech specialist. Pilotte had been with the SFPD for ten years, had a degree in electrical engineering, and was a specialist in computer science.

Pilotte testified that he had reviewed the digital recording, and while the lighting and sound were not the best—"think nanny cam"—he'd concluded that the recording had not been doctored.

After Pilotte left the room, Yuki called Paul Yates, copywriter at the Ad Shop. Yates took the stand. He fidgeted, sighed, and generally looked as though he wished he were *anywhere* but on the witness stand in front of a jury.

Yuki couldn't afford to worry about Paul Yates's nerves.

She said, "Mr. Yates, please tell us about your experience with Briana Hill."

He mumbled, "I'd be more comfortable answering questions. I'm not much of an extemporaneous speaker."

"That's okay, Mr. Yates. We can do it that way. Did you date Ms. Hill during June of this year?"

"I went out with her once. We had dinner."

"And what happened after that dinner?"

Yates spoke directly to Yuki, averting his eyes from the jury.

"We were in my apartment making out. It was getting heavy, and I got very nervous. I started to worry about how going out with her would be seen at the office. And I didn't really know her well at all. I told her I had to stop."

"What happened after that?"

"She took her gun out of her purse and told me to get undressed. I was terrified. At the same time she held out a couple of blue pills and told me to take them. I guessed that the pills were Viagra."

At Yuki's questioning, the reluctant Paul Yates described slapping the gun out of Hill's hand and running downstairs to the basement, where he waited until he thought it safe to come out.

"Did you report this incident to the police?"

Yuki asked her witness. Yates was sweating profusely and no longer meeting her gaze.

"No, I didn't call the police or anyone. Briana called me later that night and told me that she had only been joking. That I was taking it all wrong."

"Did you believe her?" Yuki asked.

"I only cared that it was over."

"Thanks very much for your testimony, Mr. Yates," Yuki said. "You can step down."

"Can I leave the courthouse?"

Yuki said that he could and called Marc Christopher to the stand.

CHAPTER 16

THE GRAND JURY foreman asked Marc Christopher to place his hand on the Bible, and after he was sworn in, Yuki said, "Marc, I realize this is hard for you, but will you please tell the jurors what happened to you on the night in question."

The young man rubbed his palms on his pant legs, then, grasping the arms of the chair, he began telling his story.

"I was crazy about Briana Hill. She was my boss at the ad agency," Marc told the jurors. "I really liked her, and we had been going out for a couple of months when she did this horrible...when she raped me."

Yuki asked, "You and Briana had been having sex during the two months you were dating?"

"Yes. Of course. I was very happy with our relationship. I didn't think we were getting married, but we had a lot in common, and working together while dating was great, or at least I thought so. I felt like we were basically *always* on a date, and I liked getting to know her in different ways.

"But then," Marc continued, "I got the feeling Briana was becoming uncomfortable with the attention we were getting at work. People calling us a couple. She started getting a little short with me when we were working together.

"I asked Briana out for dinner one night after work. I wanted to talk about it, but I was afraid she'd just say, 'It's over,' so in the end I didn't bring it up. We were both drinking in the restaurant bar. Panacea, it's called. I said something like, 'Let's go to my place and sleep it off.' She said, 'Why not?' We almost always went back to my apartment after a date. It's only up the hill a couple of blocks from the restaurant.

"So," Marc told the jury, "we went to my apartment. I stripped off my clothes in the living room, kept going to the bedroom, and threw myself facedown on the bed. I was falling asleep. I thought Briana had called my name, and then she said my name again, louder. So I turned over to see what she wanted.

"She had her handgun pointed at me. I laughed. I said something like, 'My wallet is in my pants on the floor.' She said, 'Pay attention, Marc. Tie yourself to the bed with these.'

"She was standing at the foot of my bed. She had the gun in one hand and a bunch of my ties in the other. My ties. Good ones. I said, 'Come on, Briana, that's goofy. Come to bed.'

"She said, 'I'm not joking, *bitch*. Do what I tell you, or I'm going to blow you away.'

"She pulled back the hammer. I suddenly believed her."

Marc stopped speaking and lowered his eyes, and it looked to Yuki as if he might cry. Yuki asked him if he needed a minute, and he shook his head no.

But he didn't speak.

The jurors were also in a kind of stunned silence. None coughed, shifted in their seat, or averted their eyes. Their attention was locked on Marc Christopher.

Yuki broke the silence. She said, "Marc, what did you do?"

"I tied my ankles to the footboard like she told me to do. When I was tying up one of my hands, she was checking the ties on my feet, and I hit the Record button on my clock radio camera. She didn't know that I was doing that. I finished tying up that hand, and she tied up the other one. I did what she said to do."

Yuki asked, "You'd had sex with Briana many times. Why, in this instance, did you think you were being assaulted?"

"Because this time she threatened to *shoot* me."

Yuki thanked Marc and asked him to step down from the witness box and return to the corridor outside the courtroom.

Only fifteen minutes had passed since Yuki introduced her case to the jurors. She was ready to produce her evidence.

Yuki recalled Frank Pilotte, the police computer specialist.

Pilotte set up his laptop on the big wooden table.

"Frank," Yuki said, "please run the recording."

CHAPTER 17

FOR LUNCH I met Claire at MacBain's Beers o' the World Saloon, where we had a small table between the front window and the peanut barrel, hemmed in by the lunchtime crowd. As usual at the crack of noon, our favorite watering hole near the Hall of Justice was packed with attorneys, cops, and courthouse staff. Owing to my long-standing status as a regular customer (and pretty good tipper), Sydney MacBain, our waitress, had given us the only empty table without making us wait for our entire party of four to arrive.

Claire Washburn is my closest friend, as well as San Francisco's chief medical examiner. Claire is black and bosomy and calls herself a "big girl." Despite all the death she sees every day and year, she's a compassionate woman, a loving wife, and a mom to three.

Her office and morgue are a short walk out the back door of the Hall, so we had trotted over to MacBain's together. We were saving two chairs at our table. One was for our tenacious, effervescent friend Cindy Thomas, top crime reporter at the *San Francisco Chronicle.* She was in a cab from her office, which was ten minutes away, traffic permitting.

Our fourth was ADA Yuki Castellano, a rising-star prosecutor. Yuki had texted me to go ahead and order lunch, leaving me to assume that the grand jury hadn't yet arrived at a verdict on her current case.

Meanwhile, I had Claire all to myself, and she was outraged about the death of a young man who had been delivered to the morgue overnight. It was the second time in a month that a customer had left a bar a short distance from where we were sitting now and had been shot dead on the street.

It wasn't my case, but I knew the details and understood Claire's frustration. A kid about the age of her own boys, in otherwise perfect health, was lying inside a drawer with bullet holes punched into his body. No one had claimed his body or called the police looking for him. And no witnesses to his killing had stepped forward.

"I like the Second Amendment as much as anyone," Claire was saying, "but seriously. Kids shooting each other outside the saloon like in an old spaghetti western? What is the point of that?"

Syd came over with two mugs of draft, and at that moment Cindy blew in, cut through the crowd, and slid into a chair between Claire and me. She looked adorable with a sparkling headband holding back her irrepressible golden curls.

"Hi, guys," she said, shrugging off her jacket. To Syd she said, "I want what they're having."

"Gotcha," said Sydney. "If you order now, I can get you in before a party of six."

"Another minute," I said. "Yuki's on the way."

I looked at my phone to see if I'd missed a travel update, but no. I said to Claire and Cindy, "I hope when Yuki gets here, she's got that true bill under her belt."

"Who wants to guess?" said a voice behind us.

Claire jumped up and pulled out a chair for ADA Yuki Castellano, the woman of the hour.

Yuki looked great as always, the streak of blue in her glossy black shoulder-length hair matching her impeccable suit of the same color. She was also wearing her courtroom face, and I couldn't read her mood.

We three spoke in nearly perfect unison. "Well?"

"Sorry you had to wait," said Yuki. "As you know, the grand jury has been known to turn in the verdict the second you're out the door. But I had to wait out in the hallway. Ten minutes went by. Twenty."

"Yuki, *tell us,*" Cindy shouted over the barroom clamor and the sound of laughter at the next table.

Yuki grinned.

She said to the waitress, "Sydney, I need a drink with a little kick to it. Surprise me. And I think we can order now."

"The usual dietary restrictions?" Syd asked. She looked at each of us and we all nodded, affirmative.

"Four burgers," she said deadpan. "Medium, medium rare, medium well, well done. Extra fries for the table. Surprise drink for ADA Castellano. With a kick."

We all laughed, including Yuki—the joke being that she can get drunk on iced tea. Cindy, known among us as Girl Reporter, grabbed Yuki's shoulders with both hands and shook her.

"Talk," she said. "And cut to the freakin' chase."

Yuki's phone rang, and despite Cindy's grip on her, and all of us yelling "No phones!," she went for her bag.

She took the call, listened, said, "Me, too, Marc. You're very welcome."

As Yuki clicked off the call, Sydney placed a fruity-looking drink in front of her. Yuki thanked her, then said to us, "As I was about to tell you— Briana Hill was indicted on the charge of rape. That was the victim calling to say he was overwhelmed and very grateful."

She smiled broadly. Glasses clinked across the table. Yay for Yuki. And a freaking great moment for the Women's Murder Club.

CHAPTER 18

JOE MOLINARI, MY huggable and exceedingly durable husband, cooked dinner for us that night. I love his cooking, but I had no appetite. I managed a little of the shrimp scampi and broccoli rabe and half a glass of the Cabernet.

"What's wrong, Linds?" he asked me.

"Nothing. Really. Dinner is delicious. I had a big lunch with the girls."

"Mrs. Rose has the flu," he said, speaking of our neighbor and occasional nanny. "Are you getting sick?"

"I don't have a fever. I'm just a little tired," I told him. While Joe read to Julie, our two-year-old, who was reveling in the replacement of her crib with a real bed without "fences," I cleared the table and loaded the dishwasher.

I went into Julie's room as the puppy dog in the story found his way home because the porch light was on. I kissed Julie good night, told her to have sweet dreams. She said, "More kisses, Mommy."

Right after smacky-kisses and huggy-wuffles, we locked the front door, turned off the lights and the electronics. Then Joe and I went to our sky-blue corner bedroom for the rare early night to bed.

Minutes later Joe was lying facedown in the bedding and I was massaging his bum arm. This was only one of his healing injuries from that explosive blast four months ago that killed dozens of people.

I warmed the massage oil in my hands and worked his muscles, gratified by the happy groans coming from my big, handsome man. I worked on his back and then turned my attention to his leg, which had been broken in two places.

He was walking fine now but still had pain, so we were keeping up with the physical therapy techniques.

Joe sighed. "That's all I can take, Lindsay. Thank you."

He rolled over onto his back and reached for me, and I went into his arms. He kissed the top of my head, and I held on to his chest and listened to him breathe.

We'd come so close to losing it all.

First there was Joe's marriage-splitting, government-sponsored escapade that involved a professional femme fatale. Whatever had happened between Joe and the mystery blonde, I would never know and now I didn't want to.

She was out of our lives. And Joe had promised nothing would ever come between us again.

Then there was the explosion that broke his bones, cracked his head, and almost made me a widow and Julie a fatherless child. But Joe was back. In many ways he was better than ever, and I thought I was growing, too.

But.

Well, there's always a *but,* right?

Having come so close to death, having reordered his priorities, Joe had told me that he wanted to have another child. We barely had enough time for the child we had. My job was dangerous and had never been nine-to-five. Joe wasn't working full-time. He had been Mr. Mom when Julie was tiny, and he was there for her when I needed him during the eight months when we lived apart and our marriage was a very tenuous thing. So Joe got top marks for Great Dad.

But another child?

How would that work? Even now he was working as a freelance risk management consultant in a laptop-at-home capacity.

That could change.

He had once been deputy director of Homeland Security. He had worked for the FBI and the CIA. He was trustworthy, experienced, cleared for classified everything. And in the current climate of terrorist attacks breaking out at random, I could see him being ripped out of his home office and pressed into service. The very qualities that had sent him into a bomb-struck and unstable building looking for survivors could be activated again.

Joe said my name.

I said, "I'm here."

He'd rubbed massage oil on his hands and now used them to stroke me, warm me up, and my God, I was responding to his touch. I wanted to tell him to wait. Was I ovulating? I wasn't sure. And before I could protest, reach for protection, it was too late.

I loved him.

He was dying for me.

And the feeling was mutual.

CHAPTER 19

YUKI WAS ON the phone with Claire, both of them at their respective desks, two floors and three hundred yards apart.

Yuki said to Claire, "I'm pretty sure a juror is going to question how a man can have sex when he's afraid of getting shot to death. You have any thoughts on that, Dr. Washburn?"

"You think I'm a sex therapist?"

"I think you may have a free and informed opinion."

"Hmmm," Claire said. "Well. My opinion may be worth what you pay for it, so by all means, talk to an expert. But here are my thoughts. There's a wide spectrum of sexual response, and some men may actually find the threat of violence exciting. S and M, bondage, for instance. There's an element of that in your case, right? Maybe the defendant knew or surmised that her victim might find rape a turn-on."

"I see," Yuki said. "That's possible. Or maybe she didn't care if he would like it, but *she* did and thought it would turn him on."

Claire said, "Okay, so let's say he wasn't into it.

At least, not consciously. So he was saying, 'No, no, no,' but his body, especially if he was responding to touch, was saying yes."

Yuki said, "And therefore, if he told her, 'No, no, no,' and she didn't stop, that's not consent and that's the definition of rape."

"So there's your answer. What else?" Claire asked.

"What do you mean?"

"I have a feeling you have something else on your mind."

"Oh, you're good," Yuki said. "It's Brady."

Jackson Brady, Yuki's husband, was lieutenant in charge of the homicide squad, one floor up from where Yuki was sitting at her desk. Brady was hot, but that was the least of what anyone would say about him. He had put himself in the way of danger many times, including the heroic save of too many lives to count when their honeymoon was interrupted by a terrorist attack.

Claire said, "What *about* Brady? Is he all right?"

"Oh, he's fine. What worries me is that he's working sixty hours a week, and I'm spending every working hour on the rape case prep by myself.

"When we're at home together, he's wiped out. I start talking about Marc Christopher because I can't talk to anyone else about it—you know?"

"I know. I understand."

"And he falls asleep while I'm talking."

"Two-career family, this happens," said Claire. "Speaking from experience, last thing my husband wants to hear about is dead people. It's not dinner conversation. Not pillow talk, either."

"So, what about sex?" Yuki asked.

"You just have to make time for it, that's all," said Claire.

"You'd think that sleeping in the same bed would do it," Yuki said. "But it's been a while. A month, anyway. And a month before that."

"You've brought this up with him?"

"Hah. No. Neither one of us is into talking about squishy feelings."

"Yuki, I know you can figure this out if you try. Maybe less talk, more see-through nighties?"

"Okay, Claire. Thanks for, you know, that."

"Maybe this drought has nothing to do with you, sweetie. Could be he's just bone tired. But listen. Do *not* bring a gun into the bedroom, hear me?"

Yuki let loose with a long peal of laughter. The idea of pulling a gun on Brady was just hilarious. He would pull *his*.

"You sound better," said Claire, laughing, too. "As for Brady, you're both working at the top of your careers, right? Don't make yourself crazy. That man loves you to death."

Yuki said good-bye to her friend and thought about what she hadn't said to her, what she was afraid of most. That Brady had lost interest in her. She had to be wrong about that.

Just had to be.

She went back to her case file and turned her mind, as best she could, to *The People* v. *Hill*.

CHAPTER 20

CINDY WAS IN her office at the *Chronicle,* writing a short follow-up piece on the indictment of Briana Hill for the Criminal Justice Calendar section of the paper, when she got a Google Alert about Marc Christopher.

She clicked on the page and saw that the article she had written after yesterday's lunch at MacBain's had spawned countless other articles. As it got picked up, the story was doing a fast and good job of blanketing the internet. The first story on the Google list had a thumbnail of a previously unpublished photo of the alleged rape victim, Marc Christopher.

The photo of Christopher showed him in his prep-school football uniform, holding his helmet under his arm, grinning widely. It looked like a yearbook shot.

Cindy scrolled down the page, reading the lead paragraph of the new stories, thinking that this topic of woman-on-man rape was more explosive than she had expected. It had equal billing with a contentious election, a horrific category-four hurricane in Florida, and a devastating terrorist attack in the Middle East. It was as if they were celebrities.

Even as Cindy scrolled down the Google list, new stories about Marc Christopher were being added to the queue, crossing the country, jumping the pond.

The subject of female-on-male rape was controversial, for sure. She went back to the story she had posted on her crime blog and skimmed the new comments. Opinions ranged from the assertion that men couldn't be raped, to the dismissal that women who were charged with rape were lying, to the outlier opinion that women had been raping men for centuries and the men had never been believed.

Cindy grabbed her phone and speed-dialed Yuki.

Yuki picked up, said, "Please only good news, Cindy. I'm swamped with phone calls, e-mails, interoffice mail. It's just crazy."

"I called to tell you that this Marc Christopher case has struck a nerve," Cindy said. "I'm surprised."

Yuki said, "Me, too. If this doesn't die down, I wonder about finding an unbiased jury. I'm worried that the defense will ask for a change of venue."

"Yeah," said Cindy. "Calling all people who live under rocks."

Yuki laughed and said, "That's not funny." She laughed again. "Thanks for giving me the redundant heads-up."

The two friends said their good-byes.

Cindy's computer rang out with each new alert until she turned off the sound. She had scooped other media with the story, but now *The People* v. *Hill* was taking on a life of its own.

CHAPTER 21

YUKI OPENED CINDY'S crime blog and read the impassioned reactions to the case against Briana Hill, which hadn't yet been brought to trial.

After that she googled *Briana Hill*.

When she had read enough articles and commentary to gather the points of view that would very likely be reflected in the future jury, she went down the hall to the cubicle belonging to Arthur Baron. Baron was about fifty, and he had just joined the DA's office from the in-house legal department of BW&T, a huge utility company.

When Yuki was in her late twenties, she had made a similar move, leaving a cushy corporate job for a lower-paying job with the district attorney. She had worked harder and longer for less, but this work for the people of San Francisco made her feel that her time and labor were worthwhile.

Arthur had e-mailed her that morning, saying he wanted to talk to her about the Hill case. Now she knocked on a wall of his cubicle, and Art looked up from his computer. He was wiry, average height, gray at the temples. He wore wire-rimmed glasses, a plain blue shirt, a tie, and dark slacks, and his jacket was neatly hung over the back of his chair.

"Yuki. Come in."

"Got a few minutes, Art?"

"Sure. Thanks for coming by."

Yuki took a seat next to the desk in the small work space and asked Arthur what he knew about the case against Briana Hill.

"What I've read in the press and overheard in the hallway."

"What do you think?"

"Congrats that you're going to trial. I'm jealous."

"Why?" she asked.

"Let me make some room here for you, why don't I?" Baron said, moving files and pens away from the desk next to the side chair. Then he said, "Why? Because it's a terrific case. Are you looking for help with the trial?"

"Might be," said Yuki.

"I hate to be presumptuous, but if you're looking for a second chair, I'm raising my hand." And then he did it.

Yuki smiled. She had spoken to Arthur Baron a few times since he came to the DA's office. She knew he was smart. She knew he had a background in litigation. He was straightforward and had a sense of humor. She just plain liked him.

"You can put your hand down now," she said. "What have you heard about our case?"

"What I've read is that Hill and Christopher were dating. Things went strange and she pulled a gun and forced him to have sex with her. According to what I've gathered at the water cooler, there's a video of this sex, and in the recording Christopher is telling her to stop and she does not stop. Is that about the gist of it?"

"That's right, Art. What are your thoughts?"

"The words *slam dunk* come to mind. But I know you can't count on that. The video could be excluded. The defense will certainly try that. Other thoughts: I've never litigated a criminal case. I'm a long shot for second chair, but I don't think you'll be sorry if you give me the chance."

"Okay," Yuki said. "I'm taking all of that on board."

"Something else," he said. "I have personal experience with...this."

Yuki sucked in her breath. "How so?"

"When I was ten, my babysitter assaulted me. Seduced me. I didn't tell anyone at the time, but I suffered with it, and once I went to college, I got some therapy. About twenty years of therapy. I finally told my wife about the assault when we'd been married for five years."

"Oh, man, Art. I wasn't expecting that. You really want second chair?"

"You don't have to ask twice."

"I'll clear it with Red Dog."

Twenty minutes later she had.

CHAPTER 22

YUKI CALLED HER husband from her office, telling him that she was about to leave for the day.

"How about you?"

Brady said, "Can't, Yuki. I've got some fires to put out. You should get dinner without me."

"Again? Okay. Wake me up when you get home."

He said he would.

Yuki finished the dregs of cold Earl Grey, shut off her computer, and headed out. She passed Parisi's office and waved to him, and by the time she was in the elevator, going down to the lobby, her head was back in her case.

She was thinking about Art Baron's story of sexual abuse and was glad that he had asked to be second chair. He was going to be a great number two.

Yuki passed through the imposing garnet-marble lobby and out the front door that opened onto Bryant across from Boardman Place. She was hit with a cold wind that had not been there when she'd stepped out to get a sandwich at lunch. She buttoned her coat, took a scarf from her pocket, and wound it around her neck.

As she walked down the steps to Bryant, she saw a group of women gathered at the base of the staircase. They, too, were being buffeted by the wind, hair blowing wildly, hands in pockets—then one of the women recognized Yuki.

She pointed and called out, "Yuki Castellano. What the hell is wrong with you, Yuki? You're betraying your own sex."

Yuki kept on moving down the steps. Her car was in the lot across the street. And then the women were coming toward her, intent on blocking her way.

"Marc Christopher is twisted and a liar," said another of the women. "Briana Hill is a strong woman, a woman like you. She *made* him have sex with her? Give me a break."

Yuki stopped in front of the group of seven angry women who were determined to confront her.

"I wish we could talk about this," Yuki said. She was composing a couple of reasonable sentences—that she couldn't comment on the case, that Marc Christopher deserved his day in court—when a man with white-blond hair jogged down the steps.

"Yuki," her husband said with authority. "I'll walk you to your car."

He said to the women, "Y'all break it up now. You're harassing ADA Castellano, bordering on assault. You're blocking a public area. Hear me?"

Brady took Yuki's arm and walked her across the street.

"Brady, where'd you come from?"

"The planet Wonderful."

"No, really."

"I called you back and you'd gone. I just wanted

to say I'm sorry if I was stiff with you on the phone. I had three people in my office."

"Okay. It's okay."

They reached the All-Day Parking lot, and Yuki handed her ticket to the attendant along with a twenty. The man gave her change with her keys and shut the window to his booth.

Southern gent that he was, Brady opened the car door for his wife. He leaned into the car, kissed her, made sure her scarf wasn't in the way when he closed the door.

"See you later," he said.

She turned on the ignition and the lights and watched him as she drove out of the lot, his pale hair all stirred up by the wind, making a halo around his head.

God, she was confused.

She wished he hadn't run off that group of women. She could have handled them. And yet he was showing her he cared.

She let out a sigh as she headed home to their empty apartment, the empty chair in front of the TV, the empty spot next to hers in their bed.

What good was flimsy nightwear if there was no one home to see it?

CHAPTER 23

I WAS IN the shower when Joe pulled back the curtain, showed me my cell phone, put the mouthpiece against his chest, and said, "Millie Cushing?"

I took the phone and said, "Millie. I'll call you back."

I muttered to myself as I toweled off, something about the sanctity of my rain box, and then I got over myself. After dressing in pj's, I returned Millie's call.

I knew what she wanted. She was checking up on what if any police progress had been made in the shooting death of Jimmy Dolan, who'd been shot dead outside Sydney G. Walton Square. I had nothing for her.

It was not my case. Not my beat. I would apologize, of course, but I'd done what I promised to do. I'd followed up and had been told by the detectives in charge to mind my own business.

I tapped out her phone number and waited for her to pick up. The ringing was going on too long. I was a nanosecond from clicking off when Millie said my name. I had my apology all teed up, but I never got the words out of my mouth.

"There's been another murder," she said. "And before you ask if the police were called, they were, but no one has arrived. You have to see this, Sergeant. You really have to see this. In the name of God, something has to be done."

My partner and I had spent the day in court, testifying for the prosecution on a carjacking homicide that had taken a year to get to trial. I was tired. I knew Conklin was dragging his back end, too. But I called him anyway and summarized Millie's call.

"We can just kick it to Brady," I said. "He can call Central. That may be enough."

Conklin said, "Fisherman's Wharf, near the museum. I'll meet you there."

I told Joe the breaking news while I changed out of my jammies into jeans, a sweater, and flat-heeled boots. I explained that I had a bit of a moral debt to Millie and that I would call home as soon as I had scoped out the situation.

He was very understanding, but he said, "You're skipping dinner again."

"I have PowerBars in the car. Save a plate for me?"

"Be careful," he said.

"I will."

I strapped on my gun, hung my badge on its chain around my neck, and grabbed my keys, and after I had buttoned up my jacket, I went for the stairs. I had just started the downward jog to the street when a wave of light-headedness and nausea swept over me.

I clutched at the railing, stopping my fall, and I sat down on the staircase. What was going on?

Was it the hot shower and rushing to dress compounded by an empty stomach?

I put my head between my knees until the feeling passed, then got to my feet. I walked down the last flight of stairs, steady as she goes. I was okay. I thought I was okay. Out on the street I got into my vehicle and switched on the ignition. I did a personal systems check, too. I was *fine*. Much better now.

I warmed up the engine, then called Richie to say that I was on the way.

CHAPTER 24

AT EIGHT THIRTY that night I drove to Fisherman's Wharf, a neighborhood best known for Pier 39, attracting tourists with its rambunctious sea lions and tours of the bay. Within walking distance were Ghirardelli Square and the cable car turnaround at Hyde Street, which took visitors across Nob Hill to Union Square on the other side.

I made a turn off the Embarcadero and onto Pier 45, busy with foot traffic. The restaurants were open, street vendors sold Dungeness crab from their steaming cauldrons, and tourists mingled happily in the seaside-resort atmosphere.

I also noted the shadow population of street people who had set up their carts and sleeping bags in gaps between buildings, begged from tourists, and searched trash bins for food.

Millie Cushing had told me that the murder had taken place next to the Musée Mécanique, a museum of antique penny arcade games and musical instruments.

I saw the museum up ahead.

It was closed for the night, but still, red lights winked inside the arcade. I turned onto the road to the parking area at the side of the museum but didn't get far before I was stopped by two uniformed officers standing beside a police cruiser that partially blocked the entrance to the pier.

I buzzed down my window and badged the patrolmen, explaining that I'd gotten a citizen call about a homicide, and asked to be pointed to the first officers on the scene. I was told that Officers Baskin and Casey were just inside the perimeter.

I drove into the desolate parking area, bounded on both sides by the rear walls of buildings, open to the Embarcadero on one end and to San Francisco Bay at the other. Panhandlers were known to use this area after hours to gather and sleep.

I expected my headlights to illuminate a scrum of law enforcement vehicles around the crime scene. Instead I saw one other solitary cruiser. Two uniformed cops had taken up positions near a taped-off area enclosing an inert, lumpy form on the ground. A small gaggle of homeless people loitered in the vicinity, some of them taunting the cops.

A horn honked behind me. It was Conklin in his ancient Bronco. We parked and greeted each other, the cold wind coming off the bay blowing the words out of our mouths.

My partner looked around the gray, dimly lit scene. "Where is everyone?" he said.

"My question exactly."

We approached the beat cops and the small, restive crowd and exchanged introductions with Officers Joseph Casey and Donald Baskin from Central Station. Casey looked seasoned and unaffected, while Baskin looked green and anxious.

Casey said, "We just got here. We taped off the area as best we could but haven't had a chance to secure any witnesses."

I said, "I got a call more than a half hour ago. What took you so long to get here?"

Casey said, "Who are you again?"

I told him that I was from Homicide, and he understood that for the moment I outranked them. I asked, "Have your investigators given you their ETA?"

"We're waiting for them. They're on another case."

"Did you call CSI?"

"For this?" Casey asked incredulously. "A hit on a vagrant?"

I snapped, "Call them. Do it now." The two cops didn't report to me, but that didn't mean I'd stand by and watch them not do their jobs.

I walked over to the body of a woman who was splayed out faceup on the asphalt. She was wearing a hippy-style multicolored cloth coat over a long blue sweater and leggings with holes in them. Her hair was dark, and blood had puddled around her upper torso. It looked to me like she'd taken a couple of shots to the chest. So she'd seen the shooter. Had she known the person?

I turned back to Casey and asked, "What about bystanders? Did anyone see something? Say something?"

Baskin found his voice. "I talked to one guy who said he saw the doer. Described him as a tall white man wearing a nice coat."

"You didn't want to bring him in and get a statement?"

Casey said, "Shit, Sergeant. There were thirty-forty bums walking around when we got here. Until our backup showed up, it was the two of us trying to keep people from walking through the blood and stealing the victim's stuff."

I got it. It wasn't their fault that they were virtually alone at this scene. But forty-five minutes had gone by since Cushing called me. Meaning the shooting could have gone down long before that.

I pressed on, regardless.

I asked Casey, "Was there any ID on the victim?"

"I didn't actually pat her down. Mostly, I just checked to make sure she was dead."

I told Casey and Baskin to expand the perimeter. As they looped crime scene tape around parking stanchions, then blocked off the bay end of the area with their cruiser, Conklin and I walked a few of the onlookers into the shelter of concrete building walls.

Someone in this crowd we'd gathered up might know something. Hell, for all we knew, one of them could be the shooter.

CHAPTER 25

AS CONKLIN TOOK statements, I called Brady and brought him up to date on the untethered murder scene on Pier 45.

"Four uniforms are here, Brady, and a half dozen homeless people. No investigators, no one here from CSI. We don't have an ID on the victim. Conklin and I are doing interviews now."

Brady said, "Do I need to tell you, you're on Central's turf?"

"I'm not looking for a war, but I had to step in, Lieu. This isn't right."

"I'll put in a call to Central Homicide," he said.

I rejoined Conklin and the individuals shifting around him at the side of the museum.

My partner said to me, "Sergeant, this is Bettina Strauss. She knew the victim. Ms. Strauss, tell the sergeant what you know."

With that, Conklin took off with Officers Casey and Baskin to canvass the immediate area.

I said hello to Bettina Strauss. She looked to be forty, had piercings, and had tattoos on her neck and hands. She wore an old leather jacket over denim overalls and had a fluttering red chiffon scarf around her neck. Her face was red and swollen from crying.

"That's Laura Russell," she said of the victim. "She was the sweetest person. She wasn't hard-core homeless. More like displaced. She used to teach third grade, I think. Got laid off last year, as I remember it, and she started, you know…" Strauss acted out guzzling from a bottle, then went on.

"She had a family, but she didn't talk about them. I got the feeling she ran off, but I didn't push her, you understand. We all have stories."

I asked Strauss a slew of questions: Had she seen the shooting? Did she know who the shooter was or if there had been an incident before the shooting that had set the gunman off? Did she know anyone who wanted to hurt Laura?

She told me simply that she hadn't been here when the shooting happened.

"Laura and I were going to meet here and then go over to Pier 39," Strauss choked out between sobs, "but when I got here, oh, my God, she was on the ground. I shook her. I pressed on her chest."

She showed me her bloody hands. Tears sprang from her eyes, and she covered her face with the crook of her arm.

I told Strauss that I was sorry, but still, I asked once more, "Do you have any idea who may have wanted to hurt Laura?"

"God, no. But *someone* is shooting people, Officer. Laura and I were both scared."

"Bettina, if I want to show you pictures or ask you more questions, how can I find you again?"

She said, "I'm staying at the Green Street Shelter right now."

I thanked her just as Conklin came toward us saying, "Baskin and I went through a few trash cans around the corner. We didn't find the gun, but we've got this."

He held up a man's three-quarter-length coat, gray wool, with an intact lining.

"It's not new, but I'd still call this a 'nice' coat," said Conklin. "Knit gloves are in the pockets."

A freaking lead. *O-kay.*

"If it belonged to the shooter, he just ditched it so he wouldn't be recognized. This coat wouldn't have been in the trash for long."

Headlights swept the parking area. I looked up to see a van coming around the one-cruiser barricade to the crime scene at the side of the antique-mechanical-game museum.

It was CSI's mobile forensic lab.

Thank you, God. The cavalry had arrived.

CHAPTER 26

THE CRIME SCENE investigation van was parked outside the barrier tape, which enclosed a sixty-square-foot area of asphalt, a dead woman, and a double handful of cops and vagrants.

CSIs and techs poured out of the van and began setting up lights and an evidence tent. Moments later an SUV rolled up to the outer perimeter across the parking area on the Embarcadero side and stopped.

I heard shouting and saw Casey and Baskin try to block a gray-haired man and a teenage girl who had emerged from the vehicle. But they broke past the cops and ran toward the body on the ground. And now every gory detail was illuminated by professional-grade halogen lights.

A third person got out of the SUV. I recognized her from a hundred yards, and she saw me. From her gestures and body language I gathered that Millie Cushing was telling the cops at the barrier that she knew me.

I called out, "She's okay."

The tape was lifted. Cushing skirted the inner perimeter, sticking close to the museum's stucco wall, and crossed the parking area quickly. When she reached me, she said, "I phoned Laura's husband. I had to let him know."

The teenage girl screamed, "Oh, my Gooooood, oh, my Gooooood. Mommy, noooo. Get up, Mommy, get up. Oh, my God, Mommy. Pleeease."

The shrieks and cries coming from Laura Russell's daughter pierced the ambient sound of police radios, traffic on the Embarcadero, crowd noise coming from beyond our crime scene out on the pier.

The man I took to be the young woman's father grabbed her into a tight hug as a CSI forced them away from the body of someone they loved.

I was shaken. What had happened here? Why was a former schoolteacher with a family living on the street? Why was she murdered? Was this killing personal or circumstantial?

Was Millie Cushing right that someone with a beef against the homeless was picking them off one by one?

My phone rang in my pocket. I looked at the screen. It was Brady.

He said, "Boxer, Sergeant Stevens and his partner, Moran, are on the way."

"The family of the victim is here, Brady. They should be brought in for questioning."

"Step back, Boxer. You hear me?"

I heard him. Central Homicide's turf.

I stood with Conklin and Millie Cushing outside the tape at the boundary of the crime scene. I leaned against a patrol car and watched as the CSIs took photos of the murder victim and began to process the corrupted crime scene.

At long last an unmarked car came through the barrier at the Embarcadero end of the parking area and slowed to a stop near the CSI van. Two men in sports jackets got out.

Stevens and Moran had arrived.

CHAPTER 27

CONKLIN AND I watched Stevens and Moran, the two detectives from Central Station, approach Gene Hallows, a senior CSI on the graveyard shift.

My partner said, "Let's give them what we've got."

He held up the crime scene tape and we ducked under it, then crossed the parking area to join the cluster of CSIs and the pair of detectives. Thanks to the bug Millie Cushing had stuck in my ear and my own eyewitness account, I'd already indicted our colleagues for lateness and a lackadaisical attitude, until proven otherwise.

I would try to be diplomatic.

I said to Stevens, "Sorry to interrupt, Sergeant. I'm Lindsay Boxer. My partner, Rich Conklin."

Stevens said, "I recognize you, Boxer. You look like your father."

"I guess I do."

"I met you when you were this high. Marty used to bring you to Robbie Crusoe's, sit you on the bar top while we watched the games outta Candlestick. You didn't like beer."

I smiled. "I do now."

"Like I said, you take after your father."

I didn't recognize Stevens and I didn't want to think about Marty Boxer. My father hadn't been the worst cop in the world, but he had been a degenerate gambler and worse. He had left my mother with terminal breast cancer when I was thirteen, my sister six years younger. He didn't reenter our lives again until I was out of college. I'd seen him a couple of times after that, and he'd been in touch with my sister; but just when I might have forgiven him for past crimes and misdemeanors, he stood me up for walking me down the aisle at my wedding.

As far as I knew, Marty Boxer was dead. At any rate, he was dead to me.

Conklin told Stevens, Moran, and Hallows, "We've been here for about an hour and can fill you guys in on what we found."

Stevens said, "Okay, shoot. But before you do, what brings you to our crime scene?"

I jumped back into the debriefing.

"Same as when I spoke to you the last time," I said. "A citizen phoned me about a street person who had been shot dead and left for the buzzards."

Conklin shot me a warning look. Stevens smirked and said, "Maybe your informant was the doer. Didja think of that?"

My partner cleared his throat and continued with his report.

"Boxer and I arrived at eight thirty to find four uniforms holding down the scene—two at the western perimeter, two standing watch over the body. They had a witness statement but no ID on the witness, and he left the scene. One bystander identified the victim as Laura Russell. Her family members are right over there, by their SUV.

"I did an area search with Officers Baskin and Casey. We found a perfectly good man's coat in a trash can on the Embarcadero. A witness who may have seen the shooter told the uniforms that he was wearing a nice coat. So the coat we found qualifies as nice, and there were gloves in the pockets. Maybe it was dumped by the shooter. We handed it off to CSI Hallows."

Moran asked about the victim, and Hallows told him that she had been shot twice in the chest. No casings on the ground. No ID on her person. No phone. Twenty-two dollars and thirty-eight cents in her coat pocket.

"I'll have more for you after the lab goes over her clothing and after the ME signs off."

Stevens said to Hallows, "You've got my number."

I told Stevens I'd send him a copy of my report. He said, "Okay, Boxer. You've done your good deed. We can take it from here." He turned his back.

You're welcome.

Conklin and I headed to our cars, making way for the coroner's van, which was just rolling through the perimeter. We stood outside the tape as the ME's techs moved in and prepared to remove the body.

We could hear Stevens joking with Moran, saying that it was a good night for an unsolvable murder. That maybe the seals had seen the action go down.

Moran said, "Yeah, but no one is barking."

Their banter gave me a headache. Someone had been murdered in a tourist area. The crime scene had been contaminated by passersby. The shooter and any witnesses to the crime had fled.

Stevens and Moran just didn't care.

CHAPTER 28

THE WIND WAS to our backs as Conklin and I unlocked our cars.

I said across the roof, "Here's a thought, Richie. They're padding their time sheets. I wonder how many hundreds of man-hours they can bury in a case with no witnesses. The more dead ends, the better."

"Like a factory slowdown, you're saying. Could be."

"What should we do about it?" I asked him.

"We should go home, Lindsay. I'm gonna have a couple of beers and grab some quality time with my woman before she falls asleep."

I felt a pang from a promise I hadn't kept. I told Conklin I'd see him in the morning, got into my vehicle, and turned on the engine. While the car warmed up, I called Joe.

When he picked up, I said, "I'm sorry I didn't call you earlier. We got involved here in a conflict that didn't quite melt down into a dispute. Is everything okay at home?...Good. I'll be home in twenty minutes. Tops."

I made it home in less.

I opened the front door, expecting Martha, my old doggy, to charge at me with her trademark welcome-home woofing. But instead Joe was waiting inside the doorway.

He helped me out of my coat and holster.

"You look like you need a drink," he said.

"Do I?"

"Did you eat?"

"I didn't even think about food."

"You're in luck, Blondie. Big bowl of beef stew is coming right up."

"Yummy," I said with enthusiasm I didn't feel. I wasn't hungry at all. "Where is everybody?"

He told me, "Julie is curled up with Martha, both of them snoring."

I threw myself down on the sofa and toed off my shoes. Joe headed to the kitchen, an open-space galley separated from the living room by an island. He talked about TV news while heating up my dinner.

Then he said, "Come sit at the table and tell me all about what happened tonight."

I dropped into a chair and watched Joe taking care of me. He uncorked the wine and set down two glasses. The oven pinged and Joe brought my dinner to the table, sat across from me, and gave me that most wonderful of gifts: his undivided attention. I swear, it brought tears to my eyes.

"Let's hear it," Joe said. "Start talking."

I told him the four-word headline.

"Dirty, no-good cops."

CHAPTER 29

IN THE LIVING room of their apartment on Telegraph Hill, Yuki was sitting at her desk, fully dressed in comfortable pants and a pullover. She was typing on her laptop, with cable news on in the background, while waiting to hear Brady's key in the lock.

When Brady finally came through the door at ten fifteen, he leaned over the back of her chair and kissed her cheek. He shed his jacket and gun belt and was heading toward the bathroom when Yuki called out, "I have an idea. Let's go out."

He turned to look at her and said, "Now? I'm a dead man walking."

"I made a reservation at Renegade."

"You did?" He looked genuinely pained. "Jesus, Yuki, I'm sorry. Why didn't you remind me that today was your birthday?"

"They close at midnight," she said. "I'm not taking no for an answer."

Yuki let Brady's assumption that it was her birthday stand. It was a brazen lie of omission, but whatever it took to get her husband across a dinner table from her was worth the small stain on her conscience. She really couldn't take the silence and the distance and the small talk in their marriage anymore. She had questions, and she was good at getting answers out of people.

She hoped she could handle the truth.

They were quiet in the car on the way to Renegade, a special place where she and Brady had made some history together. The police radio was blatting and squawking, and as usual Brady was tuned in to the job.

Yuki looked out the window as they drove to SoMa. After Brady parked the car, she took his arm as he walked her to the restaurant.

He said, "We had our first date here, right?"

"Uh-huh."

She loved this restaurant. In the entrance, behind the hostess, was a floor-to-ceiling copper wall with a sheet of water falling into a pool. The hall led into a dining room featuring a million-dollar view of the dazzling lights on the Bay Bridge.

Yuki still remembered everything about that first date. Sitting in a booth close to Brady, a handsome stranger then; tamping down her desire to touch his shoulder-length white-blond hair, gawk at his impressive build, lock in on his lake-blue eyes.

That night he'd charmed her without trying. First there was the Southern comfort of his voice and the offhanded way he described the everyday violence of working in the Miami PD. He told her about his first weeks with the SFPD and his take on the people she knew in his department. Then there was that moment when he stopped talking in midsentence to say, "You're really somethin' special, Yuki."

She had told him about her Italian-American father and Japanese mom, whose voice she could sometimes still hear. He hadn't laughed at that. The conversation rolled on and the chemistry between them was immediate.

Now, as they followed the hostess past the cascading copper waterfall through the near-empty restaurant, Yuki hoped that something good would come from hijacking her husband, hoped that they would feel that connection that had bonded them the night they met.

CHAPTER 30

WHEN YUKI AND Brady were seated in "their" booth, their drink orders in, Yuki put her hand on her husband's arm.

"Brady," she said. "Full disclosure. My birthday is *next* week. I called an emergency dinner."

"You're kiddin' me. What, hon? What's wrong?"

She looked down at the table, her rehearsed speech feeling thick and stupid and stuck in her throat. She remembered what Claire had said: *That man loves you to death.*

Maybe Brady didn't realize the width of the gap that was opening between them.

She felt the weight of the angel skin coral beads around her neck, Brady's wedding gift to her before their honeymoon cruise. People had died on that ship. Brady had saved lives. He'd saved *her* life. She'd loved him then and had come to love him even more. What was *he* feeling?

"Yuki? What is it?"

"I miss you, Brady. We never talk anymore," she said. "We need to talk."

Brady smiled, grabbed her hand, and said, "Aw.

Thanks for the sneaky heads-up on your birthday. I'll be sure to send flowers next week."

Yuki thought, *He doesn't get it. Or he doesn't feel the same way. Or he doesn't want to open up.* All of that was possible. All of that was painful.

Their waitress materialized with a blood orange margarita for her, sparkling water with a slice of lemon for Brady. Yuki downed half her drink right away. She had told Claire that neither she nor Brady liked to talk about squishy feelings, but hell, an uncomfortable talk was not just necessary, it was overdue.

Bolstered by tequila, Yuki took the plunge—again.

"It feels like we're losing each other," she said.

"I'm right here," said Brady. "Scooch over."

She slid toward him, and Brady reached over and dragged her close, wrapping both of his arms around her, resting his chin on the top of her head and saying, "What brought this on? Oh, I get it."

He pulled back to look into her face.

"This *is* about your birthday. And now you're thinking about having a *baby*?"

Yuki leaned against Brady's chest, slipped her fingers between his shirt buttons.

"No," she said, "no, this isn't about a baby. Not now."

"Okay, good. What is it, then?" her husband asked.

"Don't you feel it?" she said. "That we're kind of drifting apart?"

There was some silence before Brady said, "I see. I see. I'm neglecting you."

He disengaged from their embrace, seemed flustered or as if he was looking for the right words. He sipped his water before saying, "Jacobi unloaded a pile of administrative work on me. He just can't handle it all anymore. On top of that and every other dog biting my butt, I'm primary on that attempted murder and suicide."

Yuki had heard about the case. A woman had left divorce court and driven her car onto a sidewalk and into her husband, his girlfriend, and the husband's lawyer. Then she had sped to the Golden Gate Bridge, climbed over the railing, and jumped to her death.

Brady said, "The husband and girlfriend are okay, but the lawyer is in ICU. If he dies, it's got to be processed as a homicide, even though the killer already self-inflicted the death penalty."

Yuki said, "See, I miss talking like this. Even about work. Hearing what you're thinking about."

He tipped up her chin and pecked her lips. When dinner came, Yuki turned down another drink. Brady ate like he hadn't eaten in the last twenty-four hours. After he had put down his knife and fork, he asked her to bring him up to speed on her woman-on-man rape case.

While she was telling him, he glanced at his phone a couple or three times, saying "Hang on" and "'Scuse me," returning texts before shutting the phone off.

"Sorry," he said. "Work. My phone is always open."

He couldn't turn off his phone for an hour? That clinging sadness she'd been carrying around had finally lightened, and now it was weighing her down again.

They skipped dessert and coffee. Later that night when they were both in bed, and rain clouds veiled, then revealed, the full moon outside their bedroom window, Yuki lay wide awake.

Had Brady been telling her the truth when he said he was just overly busy? Or was he keeping something from her?

What in the world was wrong?

CHAPTER 31

YUKI DROPPED OFF to sleep sometime after two and slept through the alarm that went off at half past seven. Later, when she started awake, Brady's side of the bed was empty.

She would just get to work on time if she pulled herself together fast—and somehow she did it, walking smartly through the doorway to the DA's suite of offices at nine fifteen. Apart from the fact that her hair was still damp, she was good to go.

The DA's office was organized with small windowed rooms at the perimeter, surrounding a maze of cubicles at the center. The cubes were fully occupied with paralegals and assistants on the phones, making casework hum.

As Yuki passed Len's corner office, his assistant, Toni Reynolds, who manned the desk outside his door, waved her down.

"Yuki, Len needs to see you and Arthur. *Right away.*"

"Now?"

"As soon as his meeting breaks up," Toni said. "Oh. Good. Here's Arthur. Both of you, please sit down. He'll be right with you."

Yuki was surprised at this summons to Len's office. "Right away"? What had happened?

Yuki and Arthur had hardly settled into chairs in the hallway when Len Parisi's office door blew open.

Len's assistant said to Yuki, "I hope you don't mind, but I had to coordinate a lot of schedules. Judge Rathburn wants to see all concerned at ten."

Yuki didn't know why the judge wanted to see them, and she didn't get a chance to ask. Parisi appeared in his doorway looking exasperated and told Yuki and Art to come in.

They took the love seat and watched the big man edge behind his cluttered mahogany desk and sink heavily into his chair.

He moved stacks of papers around on his desk, lined up his pens, then got into the business at hand.

"Giftos filed a motion to suppress the sex video," he said. "That video is all we've got. I've never felt at peace with that. Rathburn is reasonable," he said. "He listens and he can be reached. Don't let Giftos intimidate you, Yuki. And he will try."

Yuki said, "People underestimating me is my secret weapon."

Parisi cracked a smile, then said, "Toni set the meeting for ten. It's nine thirty. Don't be late."

She and Arthur sprang from the sofa and out the door. At the elevator bank Yuki watched the indicator lights track the car down from the jail on the seventh floor. The elevator was old. Creaky. Slow. Like everything in the Hall of Justice, outmoded.

"Stairs," Art said.

"Done."

They took the fire exit, and as they jogged down to the second floor, Arthur said, "I had a dream. We were in court and a pack of dogs came rushing through the door. They were on the scent of something big, and they were determined."

"How'd you know that?"

"I don't know. I woke up."

Yuki laughed. "That's it? The whole dream?"

"The lead dog had red fur."

She smiled at her new deputy. "Well, Arthur, we're about to face off against the man who set Len's hair on fire."

As they walked along the hallway, Yuki turned her mind back to this complication that could kneecap the case against Briana Hill.

Without the video, it was Marc Christopher's word against Briana Hill's, a coin toss that left plenty of room for a jury to find reasonable doubt.

Yuki didn't know Judge Rathburn, but she knew James Giftos.

He was the type of defense lawyer who was sometimes called a bomb.

Would Rathburn allow the video into evidence? Or would James Giftos, a man twenty years older than she, with twice as much trial experience, blow up her case before she ever presented it to the jury?

CHAPTER 32

MY HEAD WAS still swimming with images from the Pier 45 murder scene when I arrived at my desk the morning after.

I envisioned the sparse crowd on the pier; the deceased, Laura Russell, in her blood; her crying teenage daughter. I thought about the sketchy secondhand report that the shooter was white, and had worn a nice coat. And of course, I was still stuck on the rude dismissal by Sergeant Garth Stevens.

Conklin hadn't yet punched in, so I headed for the break room and found that Sergeant Paul Chi and his partner, Cappy McNeil, had appropriated the table. I've worked with these two homicide pros since back in the far-distant day, when Jacobi and I were partners.

Chi is precise, diligent, a man Jacobi refers to as "human ground-penetrating radar." I remember Jacobi toasting Chi when he was promoted to sergeant, saying, "Chi can see around corners and beyond time."

Cappy is a different kind of cop—a career detective who, in twenty years on the force, has solved case after case without ever getting ruffled or into a jam.

I thought Chi and McNeil could give me some advice about the murder of Laura Russell. They made room for me at the table, and we sat together with a box of pastries between us. When I had laid it all out, including the intel from my confidential informant and my personal experience with Stevens and Moran, I asked, "Do either of you know these guys?"

"I know Stevens," Cappy said, tucking into a honey bun. "What do you want to know?"

"Whatcha got?"

He chewed slowly, swallowed, and finally said, "This is just between you, me, Chi, and Honey Bun, and I'm about to take Ms. Bun down."

"Agreed," I said.

Between bites the wise Cappy McNeil told me that Stevens was a dedicated drinker—no surprise, since he and my father had been fellow barflies. Cappy added that Moran had been violent with two different girlfriends, or so he'd been told.

"He didn't introduce his gun into the fights, but he knocked those women around pretty bad. If he was a pro ballplayer, he'da been suspended for at least a year."

I pushed for more.

"Any known misbehavior on the job?"

Chi said, "This is all gossip, you understand, Boxer?"

"I understand. What's the gossip?"

"When Stevens was in Narcotics, there was talk that he may have gotten payoffs from a big-time dealer. Well, I only heard about it after some evidence against that guy went missing."

"Come *on*. He's that dirty?"

"The talk never became an investigation," said Cappy. "Stevens's boss, Lieutenant Chris Levant, liked him then and likes him to this day. Their wives are friends. So Stevens was moved to Central Station's investigative team and later partnered up with Moran. The two of them became the hub of Levant's Homicide detail."

Cappy continued, "They did close out that case of a teenage girl who went missing in Polk Gulch. Found her body in a storage locker, and they collared the perp, who was then convicted. So whatever else, they do a good job."

I told Chi and McNeil what my CI had said: that a string of homeless people had been shot, with no arrests.

"She said about three, and that was before the last two."

"You sure about that? You checked out the database?" Chi asked me.

"I did. But I don't have names. I'm not even sure if the victims had IDs. If the cases weren't worked up, they could have easily been filed as 'identity unknown,' case to be solved after the Second Coming."

The bull pen was starting to get noisy. The night shift was checking out, and the day shift was drifting into the break room, calling back and forth, laughing, filling up their mugs and grabbing sugared breakfast treats.

Chi hunched over the table and said, "Say there's something to this, Boxer. What would be the point of Stevens lying down on the job?"

I shrugged. "I hoped you'd tell me."

"Careful," said Cappy. "Like I said, Levant is Stevens's godfather. He has weight with the mayor."

I mimed zipping my lip.

Chi grabbed hold of my arm.

"Trust your gut."

"Okay. Thank you."

I was rinsing out my mug when Conklin came through the doorway. He pulled a cup off the drain board and joked around with Chi and Cappy about not getting any sleep last night.

"Your girlfriend pretty glad to see you, sonny?" said Cappy.

I rolled my eyes and left them to the boy talk.

At my desk I booted up my computer and started going through my e-mail. I was thinking of telling Brady that I was disturbed about how poorly the murder scene had been handled. But I vividly remembered that he'd told me to step back. He was the boss, and he wasn't subtle. I knew I should listen to him.

All I had to go on was Millie Cushing's bug in my ear and a strong feeling that Stevens and Moran, key players in Lieutenant Levant's obsolete Homicide fiefdom, weren't right.

Hunches are valuable in this line of work. As Paul Chi had said, I had to trust my gut.

CHAPTER 33

JUDGE RATHBURN WAS on the phone when Yuki and Art arrived, but waved them into his chambers and offered them chairs in the seating area at the far end of the room.

The judge was in his fifties, bearded, and wearing glasses, suit pants, a white shirt with the sleeves rolled up, and a gold-and-green-striped tie. His office walls were hung with family photos and framed quotes from famous people, ranging from Ronald Reagan and John Wayne to Theodore Roosevelt and Mother Teresa. A sculpture of the scales of justice took up a corner of his desk, and he had a pretty good view of the traffic on Bryant Street under an overcast sky.

Rathburn was saying, "Margot, I said no. And if that doesn't work for you, talk to your grandmother. I'm hanging up."

Which he did.

He shouted out the open door to his assistant, "Beverly, no calls unless it's James Giftos or my mother."

Scowling, Rathburn came over to the seating area and took the ergonomic recliner, lowering the back a few degrees.

He said, "My back. Sciatica. Sorry about that call. My daughter backed out of the driveway into my mother's car. Everyone's okay. My daughter asked me to open an Uber account for her. Hah."

Beverly stuck her head in the doorway.

"Mr. Giftos is on the way up. And your mother's on line two."

"Excuse me again," the judge said to Yuki and Art. "I'll be right back."

He left the room and closed the door behind him.

Yuki walked over to the wall with the quotes from two presidents, a great actor, and a saint. There was also one from Vince Lombardi, the Green Bay Packers' legendary coach: "We would accomplish many more things if we did not think of them as impossible."

Yuki rejoined Art, who quipped, "Seems like the judge is in a pretty good mood. Am I right?"

"I'm feeling lucky," she said.

The door opened and Judge Rathburn came in, with James Giftos right behind him. Giftos nodded at Yuki as he and the judge settled in, all the parties facing one another across a coffee table.

Rathburn said, "Everyone know each other? Good."

He reached under the coffee table to the shelf beneath it, pulled out a sparkly stick about two feet long, and shook it a couple of times.

"This is my magic wand. I use it to solve those problems that can't get fixed any other way. Don't make me use it. All right?"

He dropped the wand onto the coffee table.

"All right, then," said Judge Rathburn. "Let's get to it."

CHAPTER 34

THE ESTIMABLE JUDGE Kevin Rathburn and opposing counsel in the case against Briana Hill were sitting around the coffee table in the judge's chambers, ready to discuss the critical issue.

Rathburn said, "James, you filed a motion to exclude the video of the alleged rape. Talk about that."

Giftos said, "The prosecution claims that my client, Ms. Hill, raped Mr. Christopher. The alleged victim recorded this sex act. We contend that this so-called sexual abuse was a game designed by the so-called victim himself. Mr. Christopher's pregame setup is not in the video, and therefore it does not accurately reflect what happened that night."

"I see," said Rathburn. "Ms. Castellano? You say what?"

"Judge, Mr. Christopher is a victim, no 'so-called' about it. Ms. Hill had aimed her gun at his head. He most definitely did *not* design a game to be raped. As shown in the recording, he protested throughout the sex act, which was clearly *not* consensual. And that's why Mr. Giftos wants this evidence excluded."

Rathburn leaned back in his recliner and stared at a place above the bookcases on the opposite wall. After a minute he righted his chair.

"I'm going to allow the video. James, you're free to attack its accuracy during the trial."

Yuki exhaled, but Giftos leaned forward and said, "Your Honor, I move for a change of venue."

Yuki had been afraid of this, had worried about it. Change of venue meant that the case would leave San Francisco, and if Marc Christopher still wished to press charges, she would be reading about the trial like every other person in the world. She really wanted to try this case.

Rathburn said, "Really, James? And why would I grant that motion?"

"Because the press has been all over this, Your Honor."

Giftos opened his briefcase, took out a folder, and put it down on the coffee table. Then the shark criminal defense attorney fanned out the papers.

"I've collected some of the articles and blog posts about Ms. Hill, who has already been painted as the villain," Giftos said. "The public has her tied to the stake and is ready to light her up. We will not be able to find an unbiased jury."

Rathburn said, "Ms. Castellano?"

Yuki said, "Your Honor, if Ms. Hill can't get a fair trial in San Francisco, where *can* she get a fair trial? As Mr. Giftos knows full well, if the story is out, it's out. The internet isn't restricted to this city, and pretrial noise is just fake news. Ms. Hill is sometimes painted as the villain. And sometimes Mr. Christopher is the baddie. It's even steven."

Rathburn looked impatient and somewhat distracted. Would he decide to send the case else-where? Or, like most judges, would he want to preside over what was looking to be a high-profile case, with all of the valuable publicity that would accrue to him?

He adjusted his chair, placed his feet firmly on the floor, and said, "Okay, here it is. The case stays in this jurisdiction. The two of you, with my help, will pick a jury untainted by gossip and chatter. We're all capable of doing that.

"Anything else?"

There was silence for the next five or six seconds.

"No? Good," said the judge. "See you in court."

Yuki, Art, and James Giftos left the judge's office together and when they reached the stairs, Giftos leaned down to speak into Yuki's ear.

"I've only just begun, young lady. I'm going to crush you. Do you hear me?"

Yuki stepped away from him and said, "Do your best and your worst, James. Our case is solid. Do *you* hear *me*?"

"Wonderful," he said. "Game on."

CHAPTER 35

AT ABOUT NINE o'clock on a drizzly Sunday night, Michael walked south along the four-lane-wide section of Columbus Avenue that cuts through the North Beach neighborhood.

The asphalt was slick with rain. The mist haloed headlights and reflected the brilliant neon signage on both sides of the busy roadway.

Michael was restless, and his temper was simmering. He had eaten his microwaved lasagna dinner over the kitchen sink. After that he'd gone to his closet full of work clothes and reached for the newest coat.

The coat was hip length, charcoal gray, with a zip-in lining, and had been purchased at one of the many vintage clothing and secondhand thrift shops around town. He opened a drawer, took out the well-used leather gloves, scissors, his knit cap, and his gun.

He cut the tags off the coat, put the gun into his right-hand pocket, pulled on the cap and gloves, shut the drawer. He looked at himself in the mirror. He looked completely unremarkable.

Leaving the house on Russian Hill, Michael

grabbed the still-wet umbrella from the doorstep, crossed the street, and dropped his alimony check into the mailbox on the corner.

He could have wired the money, but the check was better. She would have to open it. She would have to read the word *bitch* he'd put in the memo line. She'd have to cash that check, and the bank teller would see that someone hated her.

From his end, writing her name and filling in the blanks by hand forced him to recall the way his marriage had dropped dead, ending against his will. And he thought about what had led to the loss of his wife, and his prospects for a happy life ever after. His life interrupted.

As always, all roads led to HER. She was to blame for his failed relationships. But he would deal with her sins. He put up his umbrella, patted his gun through the pocket of his coat, and walked toward Columbus Avenue.

It was a busy night, the sidewalks and street spilling over with pedestrian and vehicular traffic. Michael stayed on Greenwich and headed toward downtown. At Mason he waited for the Powell–Mason cable car to pass, rattling its way downhill to the waterfront. Then he took a right onto Columbus toward the heart of North Beach.

He pressed on, passing the Condor and then Tosca Cafe on his left and the City Lights bookstore on his right, all the shops and clubs and bars brightly lit. Inside, customers were socializing, enjoying their tiny little plans.

Stupid people. Aliens. He told himself that he wasn't bothered by their pointless cheerfulness. He thought about the ways he was different from other people as he fixed his eyes on the Transamerica Pyramid up ahead. It was like a beacon urging him to focus.

Humming his own take on a popular tune, Michael veered right onto Kearny at Cafe Zoetrope—and that's when he saw HER. She was only thirty feet up ahead of him, no doubt heading toward the Tenderloin, where the vermin liked to congregate.

The woman was bundled up, carrying a heavy shopping bag in each hand, wearing a pink, translucent poncho, her head lowered against the fine, unrelenting rain.

God, he hated her.

And finally the odds of doing something about that were on his side.

CHAPTER 36

IT ALMOST SEEMED to Michael that he could kill that woman by just drilling through her back with his eyes.

Bam. Bam.

He was keeping her in sight, walking at a comfortable pace. He was starting to wonder where her trek would end, where she'd hunker down for the night, when she picked up her pace and awkwardly trotted across Clay just before the light turned red.

Damn it. God*damn*it.

He was stranded on the sidewalk as traffic swept along between himself and her. The sidewalk across the street was opaque with a moving wall of pedestrians shuffling along beneath their umbrellas.

And then he lost sight of her.

He was sure that he could catch up with her—if he could still *see* her.

Michael wiped rainwater away from his eyes with his sleeve. He was so *close*. He might not be this close again anytime soon.

Kearny was one-way, but he looked right and

left, his usual overabundance of caution, then dashed off the curb into the street, shooting the gap between two vehicles. He narrowly missed getting clipped by a red sports car, whose driver leaned on the horn, letting him know exactly how close he'd come to buying the farm and everything around it.

But the risk had paid off. He was on the opposite curb unharmed.

But where was *she*?

He jogged ahead, cutting between couples, turning right onto Geary, weaving around a boisterous gang of drunkards leaving Hawthorn, a club teeming with customers.

And then there was a clearing in the field of umbrellas. Michael peered through the opening and saw her leaning against the 77 Geary building, adjusting the hood of her plastic poncho, setting her bags down at her feet.

A memory came to him. College graduation day. She hadn't shown up. When he went to dinner with a few friends, there she was—rooting through the trash outside. He was humiliated.

His heartbeat was in overdrive. This was it.

He walked toward her, and when he was close enough to read the name *Peking Bazaar* on one of her shopping bags, he called out to her.

"Hey, hey. Imagine meeting you here."

The woman looked up.

She gave him a gappy smile and the dizzy look of a person who couldn't quite see straight.

She said, "Hi, good-looking. Got some change? I haven't eaten today."

His disappointment was fierce and sudden. The loopy female leaning against the wall of the historic office building wasn't HER, wasn't even close. Michael cried out, "Oh, *shit*."

The woman's ditzy look changed to concern.

She said, "Are you all right?"

"Fine," he snapped.

He stood in that glistening clearing of sidewalk that would soon close around him.

"I'm just fine," he said. "I do have something for you."

Holding his umbrella with his left hand, he pulled his gun with his right. He was standing so close to the woman in the many-layered clothing under the shiny plastic wrapper he could almost count the beads of water on her eyelashes.

He fired into her chest.

She gasped, "What?"

"I fucking *hate* you," he said.

He fired the second round, and as she sagged against the wall, he scooped up the casings and started walking.

He didn't look back.

That dirty old lump of dump. No one would even know she was dead until morning. Michael crossed Geary, his umbrella obscuring his face, but he saw a man running through the rain, coming toward the dead woman with a phone to his ear.

He was shouting into the phone, "Send an ambulance to Geary and Grant. *Hurry*."

CHAPTER 37

MICHAEL STOOD OUTSIDE the POLICE LINE
DO NOT CROSS tape, a gray man within a gray crowd
under a heavy night sky, the flashing red and blue
lights from the squad cars beaming and slashing
through the mist.

He thought of himself as a cool, professional-
grade assassin, but he couldn't quell the heart
palpitations and sweat beading up at his hairline,
running out from under his cap and mixing with
the rain streaming down his face.

He rarely had this feeling. This was fear. Extreme fear bordering on panic.

He knew that he had screwed up. But he didn't
know how badly. Had the woman lived? Could
she identify him? What about the man with the
phone?

After firing on the woman, he'd crossed the
street, skirted traffic, passed through alleys, and
circumnavigated Union Square. He walked
among other pedestrians, returning to the wide avenue, and stopped on the sidewalk to put his hands
on his knees and take calming breaths.

Then Michael resumed walking. He made a

wide loop around the scene of the shooting, taking a route from one end of Post Street to Kearny, then to Market and back up Grant, finally drawn back to Geary Street and what he'd done there.

He had a grip on himself now.

A crowd of curiosity seekers had assembled across the street from the office building behind the police tape that held them back from the scene of the shooting.

Michael merged into the dull gray crowd, taking a place at the end of a row three people deep. He asked the man in front of him, "What happened over there?"

"Don't know. Someone must have died."

Michael hoped.

His view of the dead woman was blocked by two squad cars parked up against the curb. He saw cops talking to one another, heard radios squawking and finally a shrill, whooping siren of an ambulance screaming up the street, braking hard only yards from where Michael stood.

Ambulance doors flew open. Paramedics jumped down from the back with a stretcher and moved quickly toward where Michael had last seen that woman.

Did the presence of an ambulance mean that she was still showing signs of life?

Even in the crowd and under his umbrella he felt exposed and transparent. He wanted to slip away. Go home. Go online. Look for news. He should do that, but instead he stood. More people had joined the crowd, and some of the cops had broken away from their cars to hold back the swelling mob.

"Go on home, everyone. This isn't the circus."

Michael looked beyond the cop and saw another car pull up, a gray Chevy sedan. Two people got out. The driver was a tall woman with a blond ponytail who was wearing a vest marked *SFPD* over her jacket. The man with her was the same height and was wearing a matching vest.

He'd seen cops at the scenes of his other crimes, but he'd never seen these two before.

The woman cop seemed to be in charge. She walked past the line of cruisers, and for a split second a sight line opened up. Michael saw paramedics standing near the body, not lifting it onto a stretcher, not doing anything.

Because the lump of dump was dead.

Relief flooded through his body, lifting his heart like a lifeboat on a swelling sea.

He watched the female cop pull her phone from her pocket. He thought that she was going to take pictures of the body before it was taken away.

But no, the cop crossed the street toward the people standing, jammed together, behind the yellow tape. She turned the phone so that it was facing his end of the crowd, and fanning it from left to right, she snapped off several flash shots with her phone.

Michael felt as though she had actually shot him. His lifeboat of a heart deflated and sank. The cop held up her badge and said to the gathering of bystanders, "I'm Sergeant Lindsay Boxer of the SFPD. Did anyone see what happened?"

Michael pivoted on his heel and headed away from the crowd, the feeling of exposure making him reel.

Damn her to *hell*. That bitch cop who'd just snapped his picture had caught him off guard and pinned him in perpetuity to the crowd standing thirty feet away from the body.

All women were trouble, and this one, especially this one, looked like she had mastered the art of female bitchery. When she snapped those pictures, he took the mental image of *her*. Sergeant Lindsay Boxer. He would remember that.

PART TWO

CHAPTER 38

IN CINDY THOMAS'S view, the gossip, rumors, and overheated cross talk about the alleged rape of Marc Christopher had electrified and divided the people of San Francisco before the trial had even begun.

But in just over an hour the curtain would go up on *The People* v. *Hill,* and actual testimony and evidence would deny or feed the internet speculation. With luck, Cindy thought, she would score one of the few available press seats in Judge Rathburn's courtroom.

Cindy parked her car in the All-Day lot on Bryant, grabbed her computer bag, and, as she got out of her car, was smacked with a gust of chilly morning breeze. She buttoned her coat, got her ticket from the attendant, and hurried toward the corner, where she waited for the light to change.

As traffic sped past her, Cindy took note of the media satellite vans jammed tightly at the curb and the press setups on the sidewalk in front of the Hall of Justice. The excessive media coverage of a local event underscored what she'd been feeling for weeks. A cultural belief was being challenged, and this story was going surprisingly large and wide.

The case against Briana Hill wasn't Cindy's first media storm, but it was the first that didn't involve a kidnapping or loss of life. The rape of a full-grown and athletic man in his late twenties by an attractive young advertising executive weighing in at about 110 pounds had neatly split the followers on her crime blog.

Half of the commenters fiercely maintained that a man couldn't be raped by a woman. The other half insisted that, yes, a man could be raped by a woman and the determining factor was consent.

Consent was legally correct.

But could Yuki prove her case?

The light changed, and as Cindy crossed the four-lane street and approached the wide front staircase, she tugged on the chain around her neck, freeing her press pass so that security could see it.

She worked her way through the gathering of people at the base of the Hall of Justice steps. She guessed that most of them were hoping to glimpse one of the major players in the trial: Marc Christopher, Briana Hill, either of the attorneys who would be trying the case, or Judge Rathburn, who was known to make colorful, off-the-cuff remarks.

The courtroom itself held only fifty people in the gallery, and as the senior crime reporter for the *Chronicle,* Cindy generally got a seat. Today, with a trial attracting so much media attention, those precious seats would go fast on a first-come, first-served basis.

Breathless, Cindy joined the line, which went from the steps into the courthouse, and slowly climbed toward the security station just inside the doors. When she got to the walk-through metal detector, she placed her computer bag on the table, showed the guard her pass. He ran the wand alongside her body, and when her bag appeared at the end of the conveyor belt, she slung it over her shoulder and sprinted to catch an elevator.

It was only eight fifteen. Court wouldn't convene until nine. She would be standing outside the courtroom door when it opened.

Right now, getting a seat in Judge Rathburn's courtroom was the most important appointment of her day.

CHAPTER 39

COURTROOM 23 WAS a no-frills wood-paneled room with two flags flanking the California state seal on the wall behind the bench, two counsel tables facing it, and eight rows of upholstered, metal-frame seats behind the bar that were divided by the center aisle.

At eight forty-five Yuki and Arthur Baron were at the prosecution's counsel table, and Yuki was nerved up. She felt like an athlete coming into the stadium before the big game against the current champions. Or like a BASE jumper pushing off the cliff into the wide-open air, wearing only a wingsuit. Would the wingsuit support her flight? Or would a stiff breeze dash her into the rocks?

As the hands on the clock over the side door notched ever closer to 9 a.m., Yuki thought about her preparation for this trial.

Since Briana Hill's arraignment, she and Arthur had dug into relevant case histories of rape trials in California. They had prepped their witnesses and they had fine-tuned their arguments. Yuki had rehearsed her opening statement with Arthur until she could hit every beat without consulting her notes, but not sound mechanical when it really counted.

Last week had been devoted to voir dire.

Judge Rathburn had made good on his promise to help counsel select unbiased jurors, and up to a point, both attorneys were satisfied. As always in picking jurors, attorneys were making calculated guesses but could often be surprised by the decisions the jurors made.

No one knew what a jury was going to do, as Yuki had first learned by watching the film of the O. J. Simpson trial when she was in law school. She would never forget the stunned look on criminal defense attorney Robert Kardashian's face when his client was found not guilty. His team had won. Their client had been found not guilty—but Kardashian was blindsided.

This morning Yuki had been awake before Brady. She had dressed in her fighting red suit and awoken her husband for a good-luck kiss.

"Today's the day," she said.

"I wish I could be there," he said. "You look hot."

Yuki hadn't really expected Brady to show up for her first day of trial, but she would have loved it if he had. She hid the pang of disappointment, kissed him, and minutes later drove to the Hall of Justice.

Art had been waiting for her inside courtroom 23. As Yuki settled into her seat at the prosecution table, she shot a quick look across the aisle.

Giftos was at the defense table with Madison Benson, his second chair. He was speaking softly to Briana Hill, no doubt assuring her that everything would go well.

Until her world had come crashing down, Hill had been on the success track in advertising. She was dressed today as though she weren't out on bail and unemployed but rather still on the executive payroll at the Ad Shop. Her patterned gray-and-white skirt suit was smart, and her wavy chestnut hair hung to her shoulders, adding to her already very young, even innocent, appearance.

Behind the bar, at Yuki's back, the gallery filled with spectators, who conversed and laughed as they found their seats. Unlike with murder trials, there was no sense of solemnity or tragedy. Instead Yuki picked up the daytime-talk-show giddiness in the air. The audience was titillated, as if they were hoping there would be goody bags under the seats.

When she last scanned the gallery, Yuki had picked out Marc Christopher's parents, Lily and Fred Christopher, sitting two rows back from the rail.

Yuki had also spotted Cindy in the last row, with Lindsay right beside her. Yuki felt a rush of gratitude toward her friends for being here.

Just then Arthur nudged her with his elbow, and Yuki turned around as the bailiff took a stance in front of the bench and intoned, "All rise."

The spectators, the attorneys, the victim, and the defendant all got to their feet as Judge Rathburn came through the door behind the bench and took his chair.

The bailiff called court into session.

CHAPTER 40

YUKI WATCHED THE judge swivel in his chair, getting comfortable. He poked at his laptop, spoke a few words to his clerk, then greeted the jury.

After saying how important jury duty was to the justice system and thanking the jurors for their service, the judge began to explain the case that would be presented to them.

"In California the rape statute broadly defines rape as nonconsensual sexual intercourse accomplished by means of threats, force, or fraud.

"It's common to think of rape as a sex act committed by means of physical force. But other situations can also lead to rape charges in our state.

"A woman is passed out, drunk. A man has sex with her. That's rape. A doctor or a psychologist tells a patient that having sex with him or her will cure an illness. That's rape."

Rathburn went on to explain clearly and forcefully to a rapt audience that if a cop pulled over a motorist and told the driver there would be no ticket if said motorist agreed to have sex with him, that was rape, too.

"Now, it is commonly believed that only men

can commit rape. That's not true," said Rathburn. "The defendant in this case is a woman, and she is charged with forcing a man to penetrate her without his consent."

Rathburn cleared his throat before telling the jury that he had a duty to instruct them on the elements defining penetration, which he would read to them from the California penal code.

The judge pulled his laptop close and read, "*Sexual penetration,* however slight, of the genital or anal opening of the other person or causing the other person to penetrate the other party's genital or anal opening—"

The language of the statute was more than one man in the gallery could handle. He laughed sharply, igniting titters from the back of the room. Even one of the jurors grinned before clapping her hands over her mouth.

Rathburn's face darkened. He slammed down his gavel, the cracks sounding like gunfire and having a similar effect.

"Enough," Rathburn barked. "Will the court officers show the man in the red tie to the door?"

The man with the red tie and matching complexion sputtered an apology, but Rathburn ignored him. When the disrupter had been marched out and the doors had been closed, the judge addressed the spectators.

"Anyone who cannot sit quietly in this courtroom, who cannot control their emotions, please leave now. Likewise, any members of the jury who are having second thoughts about serving in a case about rape, let me know now."

Rathburn waited.

The spectators were mute and motionless. The jurors as a body seemed to have stopped breathing.

There was no question in Yuki's mind that His Honor, Kevin Rathburn, had laid down the law in his court.

CHAPTER 41

JUDGE RATHBURN WAITED out the dense silence, cleared his throat, and, after putting down his gavel, directed his attention back to the jurors and alternates in the jury box.

He said, "Here's the crux of the matter. In order to prove that the defendant is guilty of rape, the People must show that Ms. Hill caused Marc Christopher to sexually penetrate her, however slightly, and that Mr. Christopher *did not consent* to this sexual act. Specifically, the People must show that Ms. Hill accomplished this sexual act by force or violence, duress, or menace."

Yuki exhaled as Rathburn resumed his explanation of the charges and the responsibilities of the jury. This time no one in courtroom 23 sniggered or even twitched.

"I'm going to define some terms," Rathburn said.

The judge listed and defined the terms. "If the victim was reasonably afraid that he would be harmed, his consent was not freely given.

"Furthermore," he said, "if Ms. Hill and Mr. Christopher were intimate previously, that in and of itself does not constitute consent.

"So what exactly is consent?"

"Consent means that the person acted freely and voluntarily and understood the nature of the act. The People must prove *beyond a reasonable doubt* that Ms. Hill did *not* reasonably believe that Mr. Christopher had consented to this sexual act.

"If the People have *not* met this burden, the jury must find the defendant not guilty."

Yuki shot a look at James Giftos. In a word, he looked pleased.

Rathburn told the spectators again about proper decorum and then swiveled his seat so that he was directly facing Yuki.

He leaned back in his chair. Springs squeaked, and when he said, "Ms. Castellano. Are the People ready to make their opening statement?," Yuki felt an adrenaline rush—and she liked it.

"Yes, Your Honor," she said, "the People are ready."

CHAPTER 42

YUKI PUSHED BACK her chair and walked around the counsel table to the podium that stood at the midpoint of the well, facing the jury box.

She adjusted the mike attached to the stand, greeted the jurors, and introduced herself and her second chair, Arthur.

Feeling the wind beneath her wingsuit, Yuki took a breath and launched the prosecution's version of the events that had brought the defendant to trial.

"The defendant, Briana Hill, committed rape," Yuki said. "She may not look like a rapist, a criminal, but that is *exactly* what she is.

"The defendant and Marc Christopher both worked at an advertising agency called the Ad Shop. Ms. Hill was head of the TV production department, and Mr. Christopher reported to her. They started dating, going out to dinner once a week for a couple of months and often spending the night together."

Yuki continued, "On the night of October eleventh the defendant and Mr. Christopher had dinner at a restaurant called Panacea, and afterward they hung out in the bar, talking and drinking. According to the bar tab, which has been preadmitted into evidence, the defendant had three shots of Jameson and Mr. Christopher drank five beers.

"Mr. Christopher will tell you that at about midnight they went back to his apartment, where, if things had progressed according to their habit, they would have had sex and fallen asleep. In the morning the defendant would have gone home to change her clothes, and separately they would have gone to work.

"Now, here's the critical piece of this incident. The defendant customarily carried a registered Smith and Wesson .38 revolver in her purse for protection. You will see and hear evidence," Yuki said, "that the defendant had that gun in her possession on the night in question."

At this point in the trial the jurors were uncommitted to the outcome because they had not heard the story. Yuki had to engage them, inform them, and leave them with an indelible vision of how Marc Christopher had been victimized by the defendant.

Putting a gun on Briana Hill's person had set the hook.

From here on Yuki would lay out the scene so that the jurors would not just hear but visualize, even *feel,* what the defendant had done to the victim—how Briana Hill had derailed the trajectory of his life.

CHAPTER 43

YUKI CASTELLANO WAS five foot two in heels, but she commanded the room in her fire-engine-red suit as she left the podium and took a position ten feet away from the jurors. Then she began to lead them directly into the heart of her case.

Yuki said, "On October eleventh, after their evening out, Marc Christopher opens his apartment door and the defendant follows him inside. He strips off his clothing in the living room, and after using the bathroom, feeling the effects of dinner and much beer, he goes into the bedroom and falls facedown on his bed.

"He wakes up because the defendant is sharply calling his name. He turns over and sees the defendant is holding a gun pointed right at his face and saying that she wants to have sex. At that moment Mr. Christopher thinks she's just kidding around.

"He tells the defendant that he is *wasted*. Can't. Doesn't want to. Needs to sleep. So what does the defendant do? She opens Mr. Christopher's closet and brings out a handful of his neckties. She demands that he tie his feet to the footboard *or she will shoot him.*"

Yuki continued, walking slowly in front of the jury box, taking the time to look at each of the jurors.

She went on.

"Mr. Christopher says, 'You're being *ridiculous,* Briana. Come to bed.' But that's not what happens. The defendant taunts Mr. Christopher, tells him that she is going to do whatever she wants with him. Again Mr. Christopher asks her to 'knock it off.' He says, 'Briana, stop.'

"But she doesn't stop. She waves her gun in his direction and again orders him to tie his ankles to the footboard. Mr. Christopher knows that the defendant is drunk and maybe she's *crazy,* too. He figures that the gun is loaded and might even go off by *accident.*

"The defendant is not slurring her words, but she is acting totally unhinged, and now Mr. Christopher has gone from stupefied to irritated to *terrified.* This crazy woman may actually fire the gun. *That,* ladies and gentlemen, goes directly to the victim's state of mind.

"Mr. Christopher will tell you that he tries to convince himself not to panic; rather, he tries to mollify her. He says, 'Jesus, Briana, what's gotten into you? Are you okay? You're freaking me out! Please put the gun down.'

"That's when the defendant screams at him, *'Do what I tell you, you little bitch.'*"

Yuki paused and saw that the jurors looked stunned.

Then she went on.

"Mr. Christopher gets it. The defendant is not joking. He is shaking, and as he ties up his ankles, the defendant makes her next demand. She tells him to tie up his left wrist to the headboard.

"Thinking he may be in his last moments on earth, Mr. Christopher reaches over to his night-stand"—Yuki acted it out—"and surreptitiously presses the Record button on his clock, which is in fact a disguised spy cam. He will tell you that he's thinking if the defendant murders him, at least the police will be able to find who killed him.

"And the terror does not stop. Now that Mr. Christopher's left hand is tied to the headboard, the defendant secures his right hand, leaving Mr. Christopher lying naked, spread-eagle, faceup on the bed.

"He's staring down the barrel of a gun.

"I urge you to imagine how that must have felt."

CHAPTER 44

YUKI HAD NOT taken her eyes off the jury since she began her opening statement, and she didn't do it now. Nor had the jurors taken their eyes away from *her*.

She wanted to keep it that way.

She said, "At this point the defendant puts down the gun and undresses. Then, naked, she advances on Mr. Christopher, who is trussed to the bed and utterly helpless. The defendant takes her victim's genitals into her hands and mouth and manipulates him until he is erect. But she's not done. Not yet.

"Even though Mr. Christopher begs her to stop before she does something she will regret, the defendant mounts him and succeeds in having him penetrate her. She has sexual intercourse with him without his consent."

Yuki paused to let her narrative sink in. Then she asked rhetorically, "So what happens after that?

"Just before the video recorder runs out of space, we see that both parties are asleep. Mr. Christopher will tell you that in the morning, when he wakes up, the defendant is gone and his wrists are untied. He releases his ankles, and although still shaken to his core, he goes to work—where both parties avoid each other. Like the legendary plague."

Yuki said, "What is the defendant thinking? We will probably never know, but the victim will wonder for the rest of his life.

"For his part, Mr. Christopher will testify that he feels mortified and he's worried—what if the defendant is now pregnant? Is he responsible? What will happen to him at his job? Who is he now that he has been violated by a woman that he cared about, when it is clear to him by her actions that she didn't care for him at all?

"Days go by and Mr. Christopher is having nightmares and is in a crushing depression. He neglects his job. He stops socializing with friends. It takes a couple of weeks for him to fully understand and get angry about what was done to him.

"He understands now that he has been raped," Yuki told the jurors, "sexually assaulted, and he is ashamed. He blames himself for not knowing the woman he was dating at all. And as rape victims often experience, the pain doesn't fade in the passing days. In fact, it gets worse.

"Two weeks after the assault Mr. Christopher goes to the police. Over the next few days Briana Hill is interviewed, arrested, and charged with rape."

Yuki let the word *rape* resonate in the silent courtroom. Then she told the jury about the witnesses who would testify for the prosecution: the police officer; the video technician; the psychologist specializing in human sexuality; and Paul Yates, another man who had gone out with the defendant.

And then she began to wind her opening statement to a close.

"We will also introduce to you the unedited recording that Mr. Christopher made of this assault, and you will see for yourself what happened to him on the night of October eleventh.

"Now, some might say, 'So she made him have sex at gunpoint. Big deal. They'd had sex before.'

"But it *is* a big deal.

"Marc Christopher said no. As Judge Rathburn told you," Yuki said, "forcing someone, menacing that person, causing that person to be reasonably afraid that he would be harmed, to have sex with someone *without his consent* is a felony. You will see that Mr. Christopher did not consent and that Ms. Hill clearly knew that he did not.

"She took what she wanted for her own gratification, without any regard for Mr. Christopher at all.

"After our witnesses have testified and you have seen the evidence, the People will ask you to find the defendant, Briana Hill, guilty of rape and punish her for that crime."

CHAPTER 45

YUKI STEPPED AWAY from the jury box filled with a tremendous soaring feeling. She had delivered the best opening statement of her life. No regrets. No wish for a redo. She'd done good.

As soon as she was reseated at her counsel table, Judge Rathburn said, "Mr. Giftos. Is the defense ready to make their opening statement?"

James Giftos stood up, looking as straight and sharp as a knife. He responded to the judge, saying, "No, Your Honor. We reserve the right to make our statement at a later time."

"Okay, then," said Rathburn. "Ms. Castellano, please introduce your first witness."

Yuki was surprised by Giftos's decision. He was leaving her version of Marc Christopher's night-from-hell story uncontested in the jury's mind until he put on his case. Normally, that would be a risky, even reckless, move. But Giftos wasn't reckless. He had a plan. What was it?

"Ms. Castellano," the judge said.

"Yes, Your Honor. The People call Officer Phyllis Chase."

The bailiff opened the heavy wooden door at

the front of the room, and Officer Chase, wearing khaki pants and a blue blazer, sporting a choppy blond haircut, entered the room and strode up the aisle. She was sworn in at the witness stand, and after she'd taken her seat, Yuki approached her.

Yuki had had a good feeling about this Sex Crimes cop from the first time she met her. She was absolutely professional and confident. She was a perfect witness.

Yuki elicited preliminary information from Chase—where she worked and when she'd received Marc Christopher's call saying that he had been sexually assaulted.

"Please go on," Yuki said.

"My partner, Officer Al Martinez, and I invited Mr. Christopher down to the station and took his statement."

Yuki asked the officer a series of questions about the interview, and Chase answered that she had observed fading bruises on Mr. Christopher's wrists and ankles that appeared to be ligature marks. Photos had been taken, and after that Chase and Martinez had accompanied Mr. Christopher to his apartment, where he showed them the clock that was also a low-tech recording device.

Yuki guided Officer Chase through her testimony that the recorder and the video had been reviewed by the techs at the SFPD, that Ms. Hill had been brought in for questioning.

Chase said, "She denied that a rape had taken place. She said the sex was consensual. We showed the recording to the DA's office, and then we arrested Ms. Hill and logged in her S&W .38 handgun."

Briana Hill put her folded arms down on the defense table, lowered her head, and began sobbing softly.

Yuki showed the photographs of Marc Christopher's faded bruises to Chase, who said, "Yep, I took those photos."

Yuki passed the photos to the jury foreman, and then, after entering them into evidence, she thanked Officer Chase for her testimony.

"Your witness," Yuki said to James Giftos.

Giftos had his arm around his client's shaking shoulders, and he spoke from his seat. "No questions," he said.

Of course Giftos had no questions. Chase was unimpeachable. Yuki was thinking ahead to her next witness when Rathburn called for a recess.

"We will resume at two. Don't be late," he said.

CHAPTER 46

JAMES CIFTOS'S ARM was still wrapped around Briana Hill's shoulders as they left the courtroom together.

Yuki, walking not far behind them with Arthur, thought that Briana Hill looked pitiable, like her heart was breaking, and Yuki didn't doubt that it was. When she decided to rape Marc Christopher, maybe on impulse, she couldn't have imagined that it was going to lead to this—a trial where she would be exposed in every sense of the word, with a possibility of going to prison for as long as eight years.

Yuki shook her head as she walked with Art along the marble-lined hallway.

Arthur said, "What's wrong?"

"I was feeling sorry for Briana. Don't tell anyone."

"Trust me. I won't. And with all due respect, she doesn't deserve it. Yuki, you're giving voice to sexual crimes against men. Personally, I appreciate it."

"Thanks, Art."

Art said that he was going to head for the men's room and would meet her in the lobby. Yuki pulled out her phone to call Parisi, when James Giftos was suddenly right in her face.

"Yuki."

"James."

"Your opening statement was a little wooden but not terrible."

"Actually, the jury looked quite moved," she said.

"Don't get your hopes up," he said. "I've watched you blow up several cases God knows you should have won. Alfred Brinkley. Mass murderer. Not guilty. Junie Moon. Killer. Not fucking guilty. Then, of course, more recently, another mass murderer, this one world class and acting as his own attorney. Hey, I was there. I saw him take your case apart like he was playing pickup sticks. He wasn't even a lawyer. You know, most people would have gone into a different line of work after a disaster like that."

Yuki snapped, "Don't you get tired of yourself, James? Don't you want to run home and take a shower? Because you really stink."

She was ten yards from the elevator bank and on the move, having to weave through and around clumps of attorneys and court workers clogging the hallway, while trying to fend off James's jujitsu attacks on her morale. Meanwhile, he tagged right along with her.

"I'll be honest with you, Yuki," Giftos said.

"I'm sure of that," she said.

"You have a real weakness when it comes to running the sword through. You just roll over and show your own underbelly."

Shit. How could he see through her like that?

"Say what you like. Think what you will," she said, attempting to push past the aggressive jerk. He stuck with her all the way to the elevator.

"What more can I say? I think you're a nice girl, but you're a loser."

Briana Hill came out of the ladies' room into the corridor. She called out to Giftos and he called back, "I'm coming." To Yuki he said, "You should really go back to that pro bono law firm. What is it called? The Defense League?"

Yuki stopped walking and Giftos stopped, too. He towered above her.

She stared up at him and said, "Sounds to me like my opening really freaked you out, James. You're showing your own underbelly, you know. And I *will* run the sword through."

"Sure you will. Be careful not to cut yourself."

James Giftos was laughing as he turned and walked back to his client.

CHAPTER 47

ARTHUR BARON QUESTIONED the prosecution's next witness, Frank Pilotte, the SFPD's IT specialist who testified that the video recording had not been altered.

James Giftos had no questions for Pilotte, and he also had no challenges for the prosecution's next witness, a seasoned psychologist and author who had well-established credentials in the emotional effects of rape on the victim.

And then Yuki called Paul Yates to the stand. From the first moment Yates twitched, sweat, and was pretty much a steaming-hot mess.

Responding to Yuki's questions, Yates replied that he worked at the Ad Shop as a copywriter, that when his creative group shot a commercial, Briana Hill, as head of production, was in charge.

Yuki asked, "Did you ever have a social relationship with the defendant?"

"I wouldn't call it a relationship. We went out once."

"Please tell the court about that date, Mr. Yates."

He sighed, then said, "I took Briana to a Chinese restaurant after work. It wasn't a fancy place. She seemed to like me. We weren't far from my apartment. I asked her, 'Do you want to come back to my place and hang out for a while?' I thought she'd say, 'No way.' She said, 'Sure.'"

"Please go on."

Yates said, "We started making out on my couch, but I felt like it was all happening too fast. I didn't know her very well. I started thinking what it would mean to have sex with her and how I would handle that at the office. I was in my head too much. I didn't think I could do it if I tried. So I kind of patted her back and told her, 'Sorry, no offense or anything, I have an early-morning meeting.'"

"How did she take that?"

"She got mad. She leapt off the couch in a huff, and when I looked up, she had pulled her gun out of her purse. She dropped her purse and showed me her other hand. It was clenched, like this."

Giftos shouted, "Sidebar, Your Honor."

"Approach," said Rathburn, waving them in toward the bench.

When both legal teams were standing before him, Giftos said in a voice thrumming with barely controlled anger, "Judge *Rathburn*. Evidence of an uncharged crime is prejudicial and should not be allowed."

"Ms. Castellano?"

"Your Honor, Mr. Yates didn't go to the police out of fear of retribution by the defendant. But his testimony about the gun shows her pattern of abuse. The jurors have a right to hear what the witness has to say."

Rathburn asked, "You deposed the witness, Mr. Giftos?"

"He wasn't forthcoming."

"Well, I think this is a question of weight versus admissibility. I'm going to allow the testimony, Mr. Giftos. It's admissible and you can cross-examine as to its weight."

When James Giftos returned to his counsel table, his face was stormy.

Yuki remained standing near the witness box, keeping her elation under wraps. She'd won the very valuable point, the admission of Paul Yates's testimony. But she'd also seen that Yates was high strung. Even now he looked ready to bolt for the exit. She asked him if he needed to take a short break.

"No. I'm okay."

Yuki nodded and asked, "Do you remember what you were feeling when the defendant pointed her gun at you?"

"Terror," said Yates. "Stark terror. It was the most frightening thing I've ever experienced. I froze. I could hardly hear what she was saying. My mind was jumping all over the place. The phone. The door. Pop her in the face with my fist. Was she jerking my chain or was she totally psycho? Fuck. I didn't know what to do. She told me to take off my pants. At the moment that seemed like the best thing to do."

"Did you take off your pants, Mr. Yates?"

"I dropped them to the floor."

"What did the defendant say to you, Mr. Yates?"

"She said something like 'We're going to, you know, fuck.' And then she opened her hand and showed me the two blue pills. It was Viagra. She told me to take the pills. I said, 'Sure,' and as she held them out, I took a chance and batted her gun away. When she went after it, I pulled up my pants and ran out the door."

"And what happened after that?" Yuki asked.

"I went down to the basement, where I stayed until I thought it was safe to come out."

"Paul. Is the woman who assaulted you in this courtroom?"

"Yes," he said.

"Please point her out for the jury."

For the first time since he'd taken the stand, Paul Yates looked at the defense table. He pointed to Briana Hill.

Yuki said, "Let the record show that the witness has indicated the defendant."

The judge said, "The record will so reflect."

"Thank you, Mr. Yates. Your witness," Yuki said to James Giftos.

CHAPTER 48

GIFTOS STOOD, BUTTONING his jacket. He kept his eyes on Paul Yates as he crossed the courtroom's polished wood floor. Giftos greeted him, then launched into preliminary questions about his work as an advertising copywriter.

Yates described his job. "I write ads and campaigns. Print and TV commercials, et cetera."

"Do you do other kinds of writing other than advertising?"

"You mean for myself?"

"That's right," said Giftos. "Do you write poetry? You know, creative writing."

"I've written some screenplays," Yates said tentatively.

"So, fiction. You'd call yourself—in fact, many people would call you—a creative person, isn't that right?"

"I haven't sold any of my scripts."

"Well. Maybe your luck will change, Mr. Yates. The events you just described taking place in your apartment. You said that you and Ms. Hill were making out and you stopped the action."

"That's right."

Giftos stood close to the witness without blocking the jurors' view. He said, "And your testimony is that she pulled a gun. You were terrified. Is that correct?"

Yates straightened his posture and answered, "Yes."

"Did that really happen, Mr. Yates, or did you make this all up once you heard the fantastic story Mr. Christopher spread around?"

"No, sir. Not at all."

Giftos said, "Is this one of your creative ideas? Trying it out for your next script?"

Yuki jumped to her feet. "Objection. Counsel is badgering the witness."

Rathburn said, "Sustained. Don't do that, Mr. Giftos. Do you understand me?"

Unruffled, Giftos said, "Sorry, Your Honor. I'll rephrase. Mr. Yates, is it true that Ms. Hill pulled a gun on you?"

"Absolutely."

Giftos walked back to his table. Ms. Benson, his second chair, handed him a manila envelope, and Giftos brought it back with him to the witness stand.

He said, "You said you were really scared of that gun, Mr. Yates. Is that right?"

"Yes."

"You must have been staring at it the whole time it was pointed at you," said Giftos. "I'll bet you'd say it was etched in your memory, right?"

"I guess it was," Yates said.

Giftos asked, "What kind of gun was it, Mr. Yates?"

"A .38-caliber Smith and Wesson."

"Very good. It's common knowledge that's the type of gun Ms. Hill carried, right?"

"I guess."

Giftos said, "Mr. Yates, what I'm going to do is show you pictures of various handguns. Please point out the .38 Smith and Wesson, the type of gun that you've testified Ms. Hill used to terrify you."

Giftos started slapping eight-by-ten photos down on the arm of the witness stand, one after the other, and asking, "Like this one? How about this one, Mr. Yates? Was it like this one? This?"

Yuki watched as Giftos worried Yates like he was a dog with a bone. "Is it this? This? This?"

Paul Yates shook his head, saying, "I don't know. Maybe. I don't think so. No."

Giftos picked up the last photo of a handgun that Yates had dismissed and turned it over.

"Will you please read the notation on the back of this photograph?"

Yates said, "This isn't fair."

"Your Honor?" Giftos said to the judge.

"The witness will read the caption."

Yates glanced down, then turned his eyes back to James Giftos, saying, "It says that it's a Smith and Wesson .38-caliber handgun."

Giftos gathered the photos together, handed them to Yuki, and said, "Let the record show that the witness failed to identify the gun of the type he testified was used in his *terrifying* encounter with the defendant."

Yuki glanced through the photos, then handed them back to Giftos, and he entered them into evidence. Just when Yuki thought Giftos was going to say that he had no more questions, he turned back to Yates and said, "One more thing, Mr. Yates. When you decided to come forward with this story, did you check out the statutes? Do you understand that perjury is a crime?"

Yuki objected. Paul Yates looked like he'd been punched.

Rathburn said, "Sustained, and I want that stricken from the record."

"Withdrawn. I'm done with this witness," Giftos said, turning his back, again returning to the counsel table. Once seated, he took the defendant's hand.

Judge Rathburn said, "Mr. Yates. You are excused."

CHAPTER 49

TWELVE HOURS HAD passed since an un-armed middle-aged woman was shot dead on Geary Street for no apparent reason.

Conklin and I were thinking about the victim as we faced each other across our desks that morning, trying to get a handle on the *why* in the hope that it would lead to a *who*.

Why? She hadn't been robbed. She hadn't put up a fight. She'd simply been shot to death at close range.

Who did it?

We had no witnesses, no forensics, no motive, no videotape, and it wasn't our case. But we did have our CI, Millie Cushing, the most productive confidential informant with whom I'd ever had the pleasure of working.

Millie had called me last night within minutes of the murder, and it was her call that had sent me and my partner out into the night.

"It's the same pattern, Lindsay," Millie had said. "It's another execution. Lou was homeless. She fre-quented Union Square. Someone is trying to rub us out," Millie said before her voice melted into sobs.

"Millie? Does Lou have a last name?"

"I don't know it."

And then she hung up.

Dressed for work with a gun, a weatherproof jacket, and sturdy shoes, I kissed my family good-bye. Conklin was waiting for me outside his apartment in the rain and the dark, and we sped off to 77 Geary with lights and sirens.

The first units on the scene had taped off a small perimeter, and Conklin and I took charge of it as we waited for the red carpet to be rolled out for Moran and Stevens—or anyone in Central's Homicide Unit.

When my patience ran out, I radioed Central dispatch to report, "No investigators are on the scene. It's raining. CSI has to get here fast."

We waited a total of two hours and fifteen minutes, and because I had called it in, the ME's van and CSI mobile arrived.

It's basic crime scene procedure that homicide investigators have to see the scene before the body is moved, so we all waited. When they finally showed, I greeted Garth Stevens at the door to his vehicle.

I said, "I took crowd photos and called CSI."

He said, "I guess you're going to win the Wonder Woman of the Year award."

"What's wrong with you?" I asked him.

He opened his car door, and I stepped away and watched him and Moran mosey over to the dead body. No rush. The shooter was long gone and so were the witnesses. Stevens had all the time in the world.

I was raging as I drove Conklin home and then

lay awake most of the night, aggravated to obsession because of those two freakin' cops from Central. When I woke up this morning, I was still obsessing and I had a throbbing headache. I left Joe asleep in bed, and I took care of the best baby girl in the whole wide world until Joe was on his feet.

Then I gulped aspirin with unadulterated caffeine and flew out the front door like Wonder Woman.

So I was in a state of high anxiety as I sat across from Conklin at our ancient gray desks. I downloaded the photos from my phone and spun my monitor around so Conklin could see my nighttime panorama of the crowd, banked three deep opposite the Geary Street crime scene.

The next shots on my chip were of the dead woman, ID'd by Millie as Lou, currently known as Lou Doe. She was slumped against a brick wall, two bullet holes punched through her poncho, glistening in the rain.

I switched back to the crowd shots.

"Maybe someone saw something and will say something," I said, looking at the spectators' faces.

"Push in on the faces," Conklin said.

I zoomed in on the onlookers, whose faces had been caught in midexpression by my flash. Many of their eyes were shaded by their umbrellas or raincoat hoods. I'd sent this bleak lineup to CSI last night. Maybe facial recognition software would hit on a known criminal.

Wouldn't that be amazing?

World peace would also be amazing, but I had no control over that.

I said to my partner, "I'm going to take this to Brady. Again."

"Look," he said. "In case there's any doubt in your mind, I want you to go after Stevens and Moran. I'm with you all the way."

"I didn't doubt that for a second," I said.

CHAPTER 50

I LOOKED ACROSS the squad room, over the heads of Homicide cops at their desks, to Brady's glass-walled corner office. A visitor sat across from him with his back to me.

"Who's he with?" I asked Conklin. "Wait. It's Jacobi. That's even better."

"Wait until he's gone, why don't you?"

"I'm walking the plank," I said. "I can't help myself."

"I'll come, too," said Conklin.

I said, "You should probably stay here and man the lifeboat."

"Watch yourself," said Conklin.

I knew full well that if Brady got involved in Central's string of unsolved homicides, there could be an interdepartmental squabble that would be unpleasant for him.

I hated to put pressure on Brady, but I had to do *something* about a very bad situation that was getting worse. I'd already crossed Central's line in the sand and had dragged my partner over it, too. With good reason.

A spree killer was executing people unimpeded,

and no one seemed eager, willing, or able to stop him from killing again.

How did an interdepartmental squabble stack up to *that*?

I walked down the bull pen's center aisle and knocked on Brady's glass door. I didn't wait for an invitation. Jacobi stood up when I entered the small office, saying, "Hey, Boxer. How ya doing? I'm just leaving."

"Please stay," I said. "I want to talk with you both."

Jacobi sat back down. I was washed over with love for him, for all the years on stakeouts together, the night when we'd both almost died of gunshot wounds in an alley, the days when he'd reported to me and we'd exchanged offices and I'd reported to him. I remembered a perfectly beachy day when he'd stood in for my father and given me away to Joe.

My feelings for Brady were also strong. We'd stood shoulder to shoulder under fire, and I'd witnessed his remarkable bravery and strong leadership many times. When we weren't on duty, he was Yuki's husband and my good friend.

But in this situation that I'd created there was a chain of command. And between the three of us, I was the lowest link.

I took the chair closest to the door and said, "Sorry to crash your meeting, but there was another homeless killing last night."

"That woman on Geary," said Jacobi. "What do you know about it?"

Brady sighed, leaned back in his chair.

"Go ahead, Boxer. Tell him."

I said, "Let me back up a little ways, Jacobi. Chief."

I started with Millie Cushing, the woman who had tagged me outside the Hall a few weeks ago to tell me about the murder of a homeless man near Walton Square. I followed that up with a brief rundown of the shooting of another vagrant on Pier 45.

"It took Central's investigators, Stevens and Moran, nearly two hours to arrive. During that time the scene was corrupted by passersby and witnesses evaporated. I've checked. There are no suspects on either the Walton Square or the Pier 45 killing. My CI believes that there is a serial killer putting down the homeless. I agree with her."

Jacobi said, "She's homeless, too?"

I said, "That's right," and went on.

"Conklin and I went to the Geary Street scene, and as before we had to take charge.

"It's a pattern, Chief. This is the third homeless killing that we know about, and my CI says there are more. She says that cops stroll in after the scene degrades, and witnesses and suspects have taken off without a trace. I say it looks like this killer is on a roll."

I took a breath. Jacobi was looking at me fondly, but Brady was annoyed and he showed it.

"Boxer. Are you done?"

"That was the short version," I said.

"I'm not going to Lieutenant Levant to complain that it took his guys two hours to arrive at a crime scene," Brady said. "No good will come of it, I promise you that."

Jacobi said, "Is that what you want to do, Boxer,

go to Levant? How about if Levant complains to Brady that you're interfering in his crime scenes? How would that play out?"

"We have to do *something*," I said, louder than I intended.

Brady said, "Jesus Christ."

"Drop it, Lindsay," Jacobi said. "I know that that's not what you want to hear, but listen to yourself. Levant is going to call this politics, and it will sure look like it."

"Are you kidding, Jacobi? You think *I'm* political? Me?"

"No. I said how it's going to *look*."

I couldn't stop myself now. "So you're saying I should drop this and mind my own business?"

Jacobi said, "I'm sorry to come down on you like this, but we're your *friends*. Think what Levant is going to say and do."

Then he stood up and said to Brady, "This is Lindsay when she gets her stubborn on." He turned to me. "Not to pile on, Boxer, but you look pale. Are you okay?"

I glared at him. "I feel fucking wonderful. Can't you tell?" I took a deep breath. "I'm going to file a report with Internal Affairs."

Brenda Fregosi, our squad's assistant, was outside Brady's door, either to see what the hell was going on or to bring news to Brady. Either way I was blocking Jacobi's exit. I left the office. Nobody tried to stop me.

CHAPTER 51

HOURS AFTER MY dustup with Brady and Jacobi, Conklin and I huddled with Millie Cushing inside Interview 2. She was our only key to the murders of three people. Conklin was meeting her for the first time, and he made the right impression. He found a blueberry donut in the break room, fixed her coffee the way she liked it, and adjusted the thermostat to her preferred temperature.

Millie beamed at him, enjoying the attention, then she answered his questions.

"I have two grown-up kids. My life didn't turn out exactly as planned, but I have no complaints. I help out at some of the shelters, and they help me out, too. I met Lou at the Columbus Avenue shelter."

Millie looked good. Her blondish-grayish hair was fluffed, and her turtleneck and sweater and trousers all looked laundered.

I told our CI that this meeting was being taped for the record, and that Conklin and I were fighting to insert ourselves into a case that was out of our jurisdiction.

Conklin said, "It would help if we knew more

about Lou, like what her movements were just before she was killed. First thing we've got to know is if someone had a beef against her or if she witnessed a crime."

"You know I want to help. But if I start asking too many questions…"

She didn't have to finish the sentence.

"Got it," said Conklin. "We don't want you to put yourself in danger."

I was thinking that if this were our case, we would take Lou's picture to homeless shelters, ask around, do the job of detective work.

I bit down on a sigh, then said, "Millie, I took pictures of the crowd of onlookers on Geary last night. They're pretty grainy, and the light was terrible. But will you take a look at the printouts and see if anyone seems familiar?"

I put the envelope on the table. Millie dug into her bag and pulled out her reading glasses. Then she moved the photos to her and began a close examination of the crowd. While she was absorbed, I scrutinized my informant.

I had searched her name on the internet and our own databases and had found nothing on her, not a driver's license or an address or a warrant for her arrest. I supposed that without a computer or a car or a house or a criminal history, there was little record of a life. She'd told Richie that she had grown kids, but not where they lived. Cushing wasn't a common name, but it wasn't one of a kind, either.

It was possible that Millie Cushing wasn't even her name.

"I don't recognize anyone in this photo," she

said, shuffling it to the bottom of the stack. I watched her look over the second photo, and it seemed to me that her eyes snagged on one of the faces in the crowd.

"You know someone in that picture?" I asked.

"No. I thought I did for a second, but no."

"You're sure?"

"Yep. Sure as can be."

Millie looked through the remainder of the enlargements and returned them to me, saying, "I don't see many street people in that crowd. Everyone's wearing nice clothes, umbrellas, hats. They look like solid citizens. Every one of them."

We thanked Millie, and while Rich was walking her out, I pulled out the second photo from the group, the one that had caused Millie to give it a second look. This section of onlookers was standing behind the tape, three rows deep. I counted fourteen men, six women in the shot. All were wearing hats or hoods, or holding up umbrellas.

I peered at each face, looking for what? A guilty expression? A crazed grin? Or maybe one of those faces would jog my memory. I'd seen all of those people in real life. Had one of them said or done anything that I could have noticed at the time and forgotten?

And then something kicked in.

One of the men did stand out in the crowd. He was in the back row, at the end of the line, wearing a black knit cap. He looked angry.

He could have been justifiably pissed off that there had been a shooting. Or maybe he hadn't liked my phone flashing in his face. Or, hell, could be that the umbrella beside him was dripping water down his neck. Or something else. Like maybe that there were cops at his murder scene.

I memorized his face and the nineteen others in that photo, while waiting for forensics to run the whole batch of maybe sixty people through facial recognition.

Drilling in on faces. That was something I could do.

CHAPTER 52

BACK AT MY desk, I got Charlie Clapper on the line.

Clapper is head of our forensics lab, a former LAPD homicide cop, and a real law enforcement treasure.

No pleasantries were exchanged or required.

"I got back the DNA on the coat Conklin found in the trash near Pier 45."

"Good. And?"

"There was DNA on it, all right. It's been fondled, worn, or slept in by innumerable people, making the tests useless. Like a bedspread from a thirty-dollar-a-night motel."

"Yahoo," I said.

"On to the next," said Clapper. "Facial recognition didn't give us a hit on any of the faces in your crowd shots, Boxer. But it was a good try."

"Thanks for pricking my balloon," I said. "What about the ballistics?"

"That's more interesting," Clapper said. "The rounds in Laura Russell matched those in Jimmy Dolan, the deceased from the Sydney G. Walton area four weeks ago."

"So. Same shooter," I said.

"Same gun was used," he said. "But it's a cold hit."

A cold hit. Bullets matched each other but didn't match any gun on record. I thanked Clapper, told him that there was a new body at the ME's office, a Jane Doe, and likely another couple of rounds would be coming to the lab today.

I just had to make it happen.

Conklin was on the phone with the Columbus Avenue shelter. I signaled to him that I was going down to the ME's office, then I split. I took the fire stairs to the lobby, ditched out the back door, trotted down the breezeway to the office, and pulled open the glass doors.

The receptionist was Gregory, the latest in a long list of people who averaged about three months behind Claire's reception desk before the grimness and tedium of the job drove them to greener pastures.

After the face-off Greg and I had on his first day, we'd reached an understanding. Claire was never too busy to see me, and Greg no longer went bureaucratic when I showed up.

I said, "Greg, I have to see Claire."

About eleven people sitting in the reception area—cops, ADAs, family of the deceased—gave me the evil eye.

Honestly, I couldn't blame them.

Greg said, "Dr. Washburn is on the phone."

"I'll just be a minute," I said. "Or less."

Greg pressed the buzzer to the inner sanctum.

I pulled on the handle, walked down the short gray corridor, and found Claire in her office, on the phone. She gestured for me to sit down and I did.

After a minute she hung up and pulled a file out of a desk drawer.

"I'm going to take a wild guess you're here about the Geary Street victim—even though your name isn't on the case file."

"Never mind. Let's hear it," I said.

"As you know, there was no ID on the victim's body, and so far there have been no inquiries about a victim who looks like her. It's early yet. Someone could miss her in another couple of days, and I have room to keep her for a little longer."

Claire opened the folder and read to me from her findings.

"Manner of death: homicide. Cause of death: two 9mm rounds, one to the heart, the other to the left lung, only a few inches away from the first. The shooter came in close. Gunpowder on her rain slicker shows that he or she was no more than two feet away."

"I'm wondering. Did he know her?" I mused out loud.

"The post showed that she was in poor health. Arterial plaque, fatty liver, diabetes, lungs full of tar. I reckon she was in her late forties, but her organs tell a story of neglect and bad habits. Anyway. She was killed by lead to her heart."

"What was in her shopping bags?" I asked.

"Soda cans. A soiled blanket. Dirty clothes."

"Clapper is waiting for the rounds. If someone comes looking for her, call me, okay?"

"Will do. You okay, Linds?"

"Never better," I said. I leaned across her desk and kissed my best friend good-bye.

CHAPTER 53

I WAS EARLY for my four thirty meeting with Internal Affairs' Lieutenant Johnny Hon, upstairs on the fifth floor. I knew of Hon, but we'd never met. IAD was opaque, the most secretive department in the SFPD.

Neither Brady nor Jacobi had tried to stop me, and now I was flying blind on my own.

I sat in the reception area and flipped through a left-behind copy of the *Chronicle* while getting my fractured thoughts in order. I had a realization. Ever since Jacobi had told me that I looked like crap, I'd been feeling that way, too. According to my loose waistband, I'd lost weight; my holster was at the tightest setting and still felt uncomfortably loose. And the headache I'd had this morning was back and had brought its younger brother.

Was I putting myself under too much pressure? Was I becoming a nervous wreck?

Before I could follow this thought, a gray-haired man of about fifty entered the room and spoke my name.

I stood up, saying, "That's me."

"I'm Johnny Hon," he said.

We shook hands. I followed the IAD lieutenant to his office and sat in the chair across from his desk. The room was devoid of personality: white walls, plain wooden desk, some framed certificates on the wall. No photos or personal items.

The lieutenant was all business.

He said, "I got a call from Chief Jacobi. He speaks very highly of you, Sergeant."

"We've been through the wars together."

"So he said. He was vague about why you wanted to see IAD. Why don't you lay out the issue for me?"

I told him that I had come to register a complaint about two homicide investigators from Central Station, giving an almost verbatim recitation of what I'd told Jacobi and Brady that morning. A tipster had called my attention to killings of homeless people that had not been solved by Central Station's Sergeant Stevens and Inspector Moran, who appeared to be working the cases with an utter lack of urgency.

I told Hon what I knew about the dead poet at Walton Square, and about my own experience with Stevens and Moran at the Pier 45 and Geary Street murder scenes.

I said, "I accessed whatever information I could find, Lieutenant. I have Stevens's report on the three crimes, all in progress. And I've also gathered up the reports I filed and an autopsy report on Laura Russell, the Pier 45 victim, from the ME."

I reached across the desk and handed him a folder.

"So, what are you saying exactly, Sergeant? You think Stevens and Moran are goldbricking?"

"Something like that. Maybe they're padding their overtime. I don't know. But I do know that they don't seem too eager to nail a serial killer who may be executing vagrants and planning to continue his spree."

Hon nodded, said, "Do you have any evidence that Stevens and Moran are dragging their feet or scamming the system or committing a crime?"

"Lieutenant, what could be a legitimate motive for letting these homicides slide?"

"So, what I'm hearing is that you have nothing but unsubstantiated theory. They could be working feverishly behind the scenes and may even be following a suspect or a lead, and you wouldn't know that, would you?"

I said, "They keep telling me to bug off. Why? I may have seen something. I may have a theory."

"Could they suspect a political motive? That 850 Bryant is trying to put Central out of the homicide business?"

"Maybe," I said. "But they'd be wrong. I care about the unworked homicides. I care about a killer who hasn't been caught."

"Okay. I'll accept that. And how would you have reacted if Stevens and Moran had shown up at your crime scene?"

I thought about that. I didn't like the image.

Hon said, "Sergeant Boxer, you're taking this case to heart. I know a little about you, and what I know tells me that you're a very good cop. So let's just keep this quiet. Let it play out a little longer. I'll keep my ear to the ground. If I decide to launch an investigation, I'll let your lieutenant know. If you learn something I should know, call me.

"Now I have another meeting," he said, getting to his feet. "I'll show you out."

Feeling awkwardly dismissed, again, I thanked Hon, shook his hand, and took the fire stairs down to Homicide.

Conklin had left for the day.

I left, too, got into my car, and drove home.

I was still obsessing, having conversations in my head with Hon, Jacobi, and Brady, all at once and one at a time.

As in real life, the talking was getting me no-where.

CHAPTER 54

YUKI HADNT SPOKEN with Marc Christopher since Giftos's scathing cross-examination of Paul Yates, and she was worried. How would Marc stand up under Giftos's scorched-earth style?

She had called Marc and suggested that they meet once more before his upcoming testimony. He'd said, "Let me take you out to dinner. You deserve it, and I would rather have this chat over osso buco."

Now she was waiting for him at Mancini's, a popular after-work Italian restaurant in the Financial District. She hadn't been here before and now took in the pleasant ambiance of the place, with its clean lines, brick walls, and cove lighting.

Marc had called to say that he was running late because of traffic. Yuki sipped ice water and answered e-mail, and when she looked up, the maître d' was leading Marc to the table. He apologized for his lateness, bent to kiss her cheek, and sat down beside her.

Marc had always appeared boyish, but he looked younger still this evening. He wore a baby-blue sweater under his blazer. His hair had recently been cut, and his long lashes and dimples completed the look of youthful innocence.

Over drinks and fritto misto Marc said, "I can't quite believe this trial is for real. It's like I'm watching a movie about someone else's life. Online, on TV, everywhere, people are talking about me, what happened, what I said and did. This very personal thing that happened to me is both virtual and hyperreal."

Yuki understood Marc's inside and outside perspective. His future turned on a verdict by strangers. He would be vindicated. Or, if the jury went with the defense, Marc would be branded a liar for the rest of his life.

She said to Marc, "You read the transcript. What are your thoughts on Paul's testimony and Giftos's cross?"

"I found Paul completely credible," Marc said. "I could see exactly how it happened. He was scared. He ran. I commend him for slapping the gun out of Briana's hand. If I'd done that…"

"What about Giftos's cross-examination?"

"Well, as I read it, it was pure hell for Paul. His testimony was honest, but when it came to the gun identification, he choked. I don't know if I could identify her gun, either."

Yuki said, "It was a smooth move by the defense. Not probative, and yet Giftos got it in."

Marc shook his head. Then he said defiantly, "Giftos can't shake me. I know what happened."

It was brave talk. Did he mean it? Or was he talking tough to himself? Yuki had never seen him looking so vulnerable. She felt for him, and she wondered again what was wrong with Briana. Was she a predator who had never been called out before? Or had she, like untold numbers of men in top jobs, taken her executive position at the agency as license to be sexually abusive?

After a long pause Marc asked, "Do you think Briana is going to testify?"

Yuki said, "It's generally not a good idea to put the defendant on the stand. But in this case I think she has to speak to the jury. If she does, I'll be ready for her."

There was no point telling Marc what she was thinking: After Marc gave his testimony, Giftos was going to do his damnedest to gut him.

CHAPTER 55

MARC WENT SILENT and stared at his wine-glass.

Yuki wondered if he was worried about what Briana would say on the stand. More likely, he was worried about his own performance. He looked scared.

She reached over and patted his hand.

"You did a perfect job when you testified to the grand jury. You can do this," she said.

Marc's trance was broken and he gave her a direct, confident gaze.

"I know. *We* can do this."

She was glad that she had persuaded Red Dog to let her try this case. If she won, Marc would be vindicated. Men who'd been sexually assaulted would be more free to say so and to pursue justice in the courts.

Dinner arrived and it was delicious. She had duck breast; he had braised short ribs. She and Marc went off topic and for the first time didn't strategize about the trial.

Yuki told him about the break she had taken from the DA's office and what it was like to come back.

"Exhilarating," she said with a smile.

He confided that he was in line for Briana Hill's job.

"I've been told off the record that it's mine if I want it," Marc said. "I don't think that would look or feel good. I'll probably go to another agency when this is over. Maybe I'll relocate—to another country."

They each had a second glass of wine, but when the waiter came to take a dessert and coffee order, Yuki said, "No, thanks."

Marc asked for the check, and Yuki said, "Are you sure, Marc? I can expense this."

But he handed his card to the waiter and said to Yuki, "I'll give you a ride home, okay?"

"I drove," she said.

"Then I'll walk you to your car."

Yuki's Acura was parked on California. Marc kept to the street side of the sidewalk, and when the car was in sight, he reached across her shoulders to straighten the collar of her coat.

Yuki looked up at him, and then his arm was around her and pulling her close to him.

"You have no idea how much I like you," he said.

Yuki demurred, but Marc lowered his face and came in for a kiss. She was shocked and offended, and she pushed him away, saying, "Hey, Marc, no."

He released his hold and tried to laugh it off. "I'm sorry. I'm just nothing but wide-open feelings right now. I have no defenses at all."

"That's not good," she said.

"I'm really sorry. I didn't plan that. It was an impulse."

She said, "I have to get home. We'll talk tomorrow."

Yuki walked on ahead, unlocked her car, and, after buckling in, gunned her engine. She drove up California without looking into her rearview mirror and turned north onto the straightaway of Sansome.

Those last minutes with Marc had really thrown her and changed her feelings and her perspective on him. She was thinking now that his invitation to go out for dinner rather than meet in her office had been calculated. That, in fact, he had planned this or something like it.

Marc's boyishness, the charm, this was his stock-in-trade. It was easy to imagine him as a flirt or as a rape victim. She thought back on the recording she'd seen so many times, which showed him being violated by Briana Hill. James Giftos had said that the recording started while the sex was already in progress. His theory of the case, Briana's version, was that Marc had staged a rape game.

Was that true? Did Giftos know something that she didn't know? Was that why he had put off his opening statement until she'd presented her case?

Yuki's phone rang. It was resting in the cup holder in the console beside her.

She picked up.

Marc said, "Yuki, please forgive me, okay? I was inappropriate and I'm embarrassed. I won't do that again."

"Okay, Marc. All is forgiven. Good night."

She clicked off and dropped the phone back into the cup holder. For the first time since she'd met Marc Christopher, Yuki had a sense of foreboding, like she had entered a tunnel and a bright light filled her vision.

Like a train wreck was looming, directly ahead.

CHAPTER 56

MICHAEL WAS LOITERING with purpose on the Embarcadero near the Ferry Building when he spotted her almost by chance.

Was it her?

He'd been wrong before.

His eyes locked on her features and he felt a contraction, a tightness that started in his groin and shot up the center of his body to his throat. It was as if he were zipped up.

The older woman was accompanied by an animated, stoop-shouldered younger man, who gestured expansively as he talked. He had the look of a junkie transported by the rush of a meth high.

The woman laughed. She was enjoying his company. She was dressed appropriately for a walk through the fog on a chilly night. Her coat was old but looked sturdy. She had a canvas carryall slung over her shoulder, and on her head she wore a knit cloche hat in several shades of green.

The pair of weirdos was on the move, taking a leisurely stroll. Michael fixated on her familiar rolling gait as she and her piece-of-shit companion continued past him.

He waited until they'd covered twenty-five

paces, about two car lengths, then followed the couple as they cleared the smattering of pedestrians around the Ferry Building, crossed the street, and turned onto Mission, one of the main arteries through the South of Market neighborhood.

The traffic was sparse after 9 p.m. A wind blew through the canyon of office buildings, what Michael thought of as Wall Street by the Bay. He jammed his hands into his new well-used thrift-shop coat and gripped the gun butt with his gloved hand. It felt good. Like a handshake with a friend.

Up ahead the woman and her companion stopped under a streetlight and embraced, before the round-shouldered man crossed the street and the woman continued walking along Mission, crossing Spear. Michael kept his eyes on her while humming a made-up tune to the cadence of her unhurried walk.

And then, almost as if he had willed it, she stopped and reached into her bag, poked around inside it, and pulled out a wrapped sandwich. She was busy, intent on removing the clinging wrapper, her body limned in the glow of the streetlights. And not another soul was on that sidewalk. They were alone.

Michael closed the gap between them and called out her name. She looked up, watched him pull the gun from his pocket and point it at her.

She looked into his face and almost smiled. No fear. That pissed him off.

"I thought it was you," she said, holding her sandwich.

"Well," Michael said. "For once you're right. Any last words?"

"God help you," she said.

CHAPTER 57

MICHAEL FELT THAT his gun was an extension of his arm.

He squeezed the trigger.

The gun cracked, the bullet thudded into her chest, and his arm thrummed with the shock. He was electrified with a thrill that was monumentally more satisfying than what he'd felt the other times he'd fired his gun.

He watched all of it, committed every minute move to memory. She screamed, dropped the sandwich, and clapped her chest with her hand. She sucked in her breath and stared into his eyes. He read her expression.

Disappointment.

That was good. It was how he'd felt his whole life.

"Have some more," he said.

He fired again and she dropped, falling sideways, disillusionment frozen on her face. She was the picture of eternal sadness. But she was still alive.

She wheezed and looked up at him.

She tried to speak, but nothing could be more

irrelevant to him than her words. She'd told him so many times, *It's not what you say that counts. It's what you* do.

He pumped three more rounds into her, watching her jerk and twitch with each shot until he put the final bullet in her head. At last she lay still on the sidewalk. She was dead. DEAD.

He wanted to take a moment to do a war dance, to scream out his relief and pleasure, to revel in the pure ecstasy of the best moment of his life.

But he'd promised himself that night while he was standing in the rain on Geary, as the police cars screamed up to the body, that he would make no more mistakes.

He knew what to do. He scooped up the shell casings, chasing one into the gutter, then clutching them in his fist, he walked quickly two blocks southwest to the intersection at Beale. There a small paved plaza filled a niche between two office buildings. It was an arty little space, organized with a grid of small trees standing in concrete planters.

Two people were in the plaza. A man sat on the edge of a planter, his head bent as he spoke into his phone. A woman leaned against a building wall, smoking a cigarette, maybe waiting for someone or just deep in thought.

Michael spotted the trash can between two planters and walked nonchalantly toward it. It took only seconds to stuff the coat and gloves into the black plastic bag lining the can, and to transfer the gun and spent shells to the pocket of the black jacket that he wore under the coat.

He left the plaza, disappearing into the fog and shadow on Mission.

What a wonderful night.

What a wonderful fucking night.

If he missed her at all, it was because now he had to find another target. And he had an idea who that would be.

That bitch who'd taken his picture on Geary.

Sergeant Lindsay Boxer. He remembered.

She was like his mother. Shaming him for drinking milk from the carton. For taking a few bills from her purse. For his magazines. Shaming him, in front of his sister, their neighbors, his own friends.

And Sergeant Boxer had done the same with the flash of her camera. Exposing him, nailing him there on the street.

She would have to pay for that.

CHAPTER 58

WHILE THE DISHWASHER hummed and sloshed, Joe and I folded laundry at the kitchen table.

I was on autopilot. My hands turned the jumble of shirts and towels into warm cotton packets, but I was thinking of other things. Among them was my mother's Limoges vase, which Julie had pulled off a table, smashing it into ungluable shards. I also kept rerunning my cringeworthy meeting with IAD's Hon, and the cherry on top was that I was weak and headachy, a little bit queasy. It was an overall sick feeling that was becoming harder to ignore.

Joe said, "That's it? No woo-hoo?"

"Aw, geez, Joe, sorry. Say it again. Please?"

He said, "I got a call from the new head of antiterrorism at the Port of San Francisco."

"Wow. About a job?"

Joe said, "Yep. There's a new guy, Benjamin Rollins. Ex-marine. He's looking for a hands-on risk assessment pro, freelance or on staff, to be decided. He's known to be kind of a dick, but I think I'd like him."

I said, "He's 'kind of a dick' but otherwise fantastic?"

"Correct," said Joe. "This isn't about love. It's about money."

"Three cheers for money."

Joe cheered. I laughed and we went back to folding.

Actually, this breaking news *was* fantastic. Joe was healing well from his injuries. It wouldn't be long before Julie would be going to preschool, and Joe needed a job. Even though my thoughts were scattered, I could focus on that.

I said, "So, what's the next step?"

Joe was telling me about the interview with Security Director Rollins next week when, of course, the phone rang.

It was a weeknight, and to me that meant I was still on duty. I took the phone out of my jeans pocket and glanced at the caller ID. Joe watched me and shook his head no.

"Brady," I said into the phone. "What's wrong?"

He jumped right into it.

"A homeless woman was shot dead on Mission near Spear. Same MO as the others. Point-blank range. No witnesses. But here's something a little different. She was shot on our street."

"Say that again?"

"She was shot on the *south* side of Mission. Our beat. Take it away, Lindsay. You're lead investigator. Call Conklin. And you might want to compare notes with Stevens."

"When did this happen?"

"Bystander called it into dispatch thirty minutes ago. Dispatch bounced it to me. Stay in touch."

"Brady, wait. I need all units, every cop with a pulse."

"You got it," he said.

With Brady, I considered it done.

CHAPTER 59

THE FRESH HOMICIDE on Mission Street required a Code 3 high-speed-with-lights-and-sirens response.

I switched on all of that, and while driving through the fog, I worked myself up into a fine lather.

This was *it*.

I was finally going to have a shot at taking a bite out of the killer's spree. This shooting was going to get a first-class investigation, which I hoped would end with the doer in an orange jumpsuit, looking at life without parole.

Twenty-two minutes after Brady's call, I pulled up to a crime scene that was eerily lit by the mist-rimmed flashers and headlights of a dozen cruisers lined up at the curb. Unis had set up a perimeter, closing off Mission in both directions for two blocks down to Beale, with barricades at the cross streets.

This was more like it. *Thank you, Brady.*

I parked, ducked under the tape, and asked a uniformed cop to point me to the first officer.

"That would be Sergeant Nardone. Over there. With the body."

I knew Bob Nardone. He was meticulous and irreverent, and I was glad he was on the scene. I called out to him and he lifted his hand. I pushed through the loose grouping of units to where he was standing by the victim.

As first responding officer, he was responsible for cordoning off the street, sequestering witnesses, keeping bystanders from trashing the area, and briefing investigators.

Nardone said, "Sergeant Boxer? What brings you out on a night like this?"

"It's my turn to howl at the moon. What've we got?"

"Elderly woman, looks to me like she was down on her luck, and that was before someone pumped about six rounds into her."

"ID?"

"See the strap? Her bag is under her body. Officer Anthony is talking to the guy who called it in. Tourist in the right place at the wrong time. He saw the body from his car."

Headlights sent shafts of light across the body. I turned on my flashlight and Nardone guided me in.

I stepped around the pool of blood outlining the victim, who had fallen onto her side. I snapped photos with my phone, which would do until CSI came in with halogen lights and German lenses.

I heard Conklin calling my name and turned to see him materialize out of the gloom.

I told him what Nardone had told me. He bent to the body and peeled the dead woman's green hat away from her face.

He said, "Awwww, shit."

I looked over his shoulder. What I saw was like a hard punch to my heart.

"Oh, no, Rich. *No fucking way.*"

He said, "Proof that no good deed goes unpunished."

This was just wrong. How could Millie Cushing, a kind and gentle soul, be dead?

I had to come in for a closer look. Her face and hair were soaked with blood. She'd taken one shot to her forehead and innumerable slugs to her body. The killer had stood close. He'd looked into her face and she'd looked into his. And he'd shot and shot and shot some more, until he was sure she was dead.

This execution was overkill. Overkill meant rage or that the murder was personal—or both.

Millie had come to me because of a wave of murders that had gone largely unnoticed. I'd encouraged her. I'd asked for her help. Standing over her body, I felt literally sick with sorrow and guilt. Had Millie been killed because she was working with me?

"Is this my fault?" I asked Conklin.

Conklin said, "Come on. No. Lindsay, here's CSI. Let's give them some room."

I heard a van door slide open and looked up to see Charlie Clapper step out onto the street. I was so glad that our forensics chief, my good friend, was on the job.

Clapper said to me, "How is it we're both pulling night shift?"

"I know the victim, Charlie. Millie Cushing. She was my CI. Maybe the killer found out."

"Or he was looking for a victim," said Conklin, "and she just happened to cross his path."

I said, "Sure. Could have happened like that."

But I was unconvinced.

I crouched down next to Millie's body. I don't normally talk to dead people, but this was an exception, and I didn't care who heard me.

"I'm sorry, Millie. So sorry this happened to you."

CHAPTER 60

YUKI WAS ENSCONCED in the snug green lady chair in front of the TV.

It was after nine. Two hours ago Brady had said he'd be bringing home Thai food for dinner. So where was he? He hadn't called. He hadn't answered his phone. Was he under some kind of siege? Had he fallen into the sack with a lady friend? Or had he just forgotten about her?

She was hungry and she was getting mad. It was becoming increasingly impossible to see him as the man "who loved her to death."

Yuki went to the kitchen and threw together a mayo and Kraft Singles sandwich. She ate it over the sink, then returned to the living room and re-took her chair. She stretched out her legs on the footstool, then logged back in to her ThinkPad, glancing at her other necessary work tools—pens, sticky pad, coffee, pretzel sticks, clicker, phone—arrayed on the lamp table to her left.

She was watching cable news out of the corner of her eye, while emptying her mailbox, when her phone vibrated. She shot her hand out to grab it and knocked over her mug. Milky coffee spread quickly across the table, over the edge, and onto her mother's ancient carpet.

Yuki shouted, *"Nanda,"* Japanese for "What the hell?" and grabbed the phone. She barked into it, "Brady?" as she ran to the kitchen for a dish towel.

The voice said, "It's Marc. I've been shot."

She could hardly hear him.

"*What*? Marc? Where are you?"

"Uh. In an ambulance."

She mopped up coffee while shouting over the wail of sirens in her ear, "Where were you shot? What's your condition?"

"Two blocks from my apartment. I was crossing the street to the dry cleaner when I, like, fell down. I didn't even hear anything."

His voice faded out.

"Marc. Marc. Can you hear me?"

"I really *hurt*."

"Where on your body were you shot?" Yuki asked.

"Right thigh. Paramedic said that the bullet went in and out the other side," Marc said. "That's what you call good fricking luck."

"It sure is. Thank God you're okay."

He said, "It was dark, Yuki. If that bullet had hit my femoral artery, I would be dead now." He laughed. "Maybe I should buy a lottery ticket."

Marc sounded hysterical. Yuki took her own voice down a couple of notches and said, "Where are they taking you?"

"Metro, right?"

She heard a woman's voice saying, "We're two minutes out."

"My parents are going to meet me there," Marc said.

"Okay," she said. "Okay, that's excellent. Marc, who *did* this?"

"I don't know. I didn't see anyone. My arms were full of laundry. Oh, shit. My laundry..."

"Marc? Keep your head down," Yuki said. "You have to talk to the police."

"You know what?" Marc said. "Now I'm scared."

"Cops will meet up with you at the hospital. Tell them what you know and what you think and have them call me, okay? Marc? Do you hear me?"

"They're telling me to put my phone away. Uh. Bye."

The phone went dead.

Yuki stood in the doorway between the kitchen and living room, holding her phone, thinking through what Marc had just told her. Who wanted to shoot Marc? Had Briana Hill stalked him, fired on him? Was Briana that crazy?

Yuki had Sex Crimes officer Phyllis Chase on speed dial. She punched the button and waited impatiently for Chase to pick up.

"Phyllis, it's Yuki. Marc Christopher was just shot....No, it's not fatal. He's on the way to Metro. Have someone take his statement, and pick up Briana Hill. I'll meet you at the Hall."

CHAPTER 61

YUKI STOOD IN the observation room with her arms tightly crossed, intently watching Briana Hill's interrogation through the two-way mirror.

The interview room on the other side of the glass was closet size, furnished with a table pushed up against a grimy wall and three straight-backed aluminum chairs that were all occupied.

Inspectors Phyllis Chase and Al Martinez from Sex Crimes sat catercorner to each other. Briana Hill faced them and the mirrored window. The camera in the corner of the ceiling recorded it all.

Hill looked wrung out. Yuki knew that she had been arrested at her apartment after returning from the gym. She was wearing gray sweatpants, her hair bunched up in an off-center knot at the top of her head, and she was red faced from crying.

Chase, who had confiscated a pistol from Hill's gym bag, was saying, "You know you can't have a gun, Briana. So right away you're in trouble here. What's going on?"

"I'm getting hate mail and vicious phone calls," Briana said angrily. "I'm getting death threats. I think I'm being followed. What am I supposed to do?"

"Stay home. Keep your door locked," Chase said.

"I have to eat," she shouted. "I went to the deli on Duboce and Sanchez for soup and a sandwich sometime around lunch. Then the gym tonight at around eight, and I was there for an hour. There's got to be cameras all over that place. You can see for yourself."

Martinez said, "So from eight to nine you were at the gym? That's your story?"

"Yes. Something like that."

Chase asked her, "And before you went to the gym?"

"I was at home. The doorman can say when I left."

"Okay, Briana," said Martinez. "We'll check your alibi. Or you can save us a lot of trouble. I know this Christopher guy is a miserable pain in your butt, so look, you didn't kill him. If you did shoot him, now's the time to say so. I guarantee if you speak up, it will all go better for you."

"I did *not* shoot him. Send my gun to your…your lab or just smell it. It hasn't been fired in two years."

"This here," said Martinez, digging a plastic bag out of his shirt pocket, "is a gunpowder residue test. I'm going to apply some goop to your hands. It's not going to hurt."

"I don't have to agree to that. Do I?" Hill asked incredulously. "I want my lawyer and I want to call him now."

"In a minute," said Martinez. "But first show me your hands, palms up."

"And if I refuse?"

"You can chill in a holding cell with fourteen or fifteen pissed-off prostitutes until we get a court order."

"Briana," interjected the motherly Phyllis Chase. "Saying no to a GSR test makes it kind of look like you've got something to hide. If you didn't fire a gun, this will clear you. You want that."

Yuki knew it wouldn't clear Briana absolutely. She could have worn and discarded gloves. She could have washed her hands before Chase and Martinez picked her up.

The gun would tell the truth.

Hill said, "Fine. Be my guest." She held out her hands.

Martinez put on latex gloves and applied the test. Then he exited the room, leaving Chase alone with the distraught Briana Hill.

Chase was saying, "You'll get to make your phone call in a little while, Briana. First we have to process you."

"I didn't shoot him!"

"You have a gun, dear, and it was loaded. You violated your bond."

"Oh, my God, no. Please. Don't send me back to jail!"

The door to the interview room opened and two cops came in.

Chase said, "Stand up, Briana. Put your hands behind your back."

Yuki watched the cops cuff the woman, who had not long ago had an extremely promising future. No more.

Hill was crying as she was led out. She turned her head to look at Chase.

"Why is this happening to me? No, let me tell you. He's setting me up. He set me up *again*."

Martinez came into the observation room and said to Yuki, "Ms. Castellano, the GSR test was negative. We'll send the gun and her clothes to the lab for testing."

"Thanks, Martinez. What do you think?"

He shrugged. "She's a sad case. I like her, but I don't trust her."

"Check the security tapes in her apartment building and at the gym. See if her alibi holds up."

Yuki called Brady. It was after midnight. He picked up, sounding disoriented.

Yuki asked, "Are you sleeping?"

"Was," he said. "Where are you?"

"Do you mind heating up the noodles?"

"Noodles? Oh, shit. I forgot."

"You're a bum, Brady. You know that?"

Yuki made a detour to the vending machine on the second floor and spent four bucks on sugar and carbs before going downstairs to her car. She slammed her car into gear, and by the time she got home, she was steaming.

CHAPTER 62

CONKLIN AND I crowded into Brady's office without invitation the morning after Millie Cushing's murder.

My sadness and sense of responsibility had no place in this meeting, so I gave my account while keeping personal thoughts to myself. I wrapped up our report by saying, "We're canvassing homeless shelters today to get as much info as we can on Millie, her friends, enemies, habits. And we'll be looking into her family and so forth.

"We need help," I said. "We could use Nardone and Anthony, also Chi and McNeil and any volunteers. I put in a call to Stevens. As you suggested."

Brady okayed my request for help, then said, "Conklin, I need a moment with Boxer."

When we were alone, he said, "I got a call from Hon."

"Oh?" I felt a pang of dread. *What now?* I gripped the arms of my chair.

"Stevens filed a complaint against you."

"Against *me*? What was the complaint, exactly?"

"Interfering with his crime scene. Wrecking the

chain of command. You're going to hear about this in person."

I said, "How so?"

"Hon is holding a hearing to consider Stevens's complaint against you and vice versa. After that he and the panel will send their recommendation to the chief."

"When is this supposed to happen?"

"Thursday morning. IAD offices at nine."

"You mean tomorrow?" I asked.

"I'm afraid so."

I'd never even heard of a face-to-face IAD hearing before. I didn't know what to expect. But this I knew: I'd stood up to Stevens before. I'd do it again.

Brady said, "Jacobi will determine disciplinary action, if any. So dismissal of charges is possible. Desk duty is possible. Suspension is possible. If Stevens is found to be bending the law, that's something else again. Either way...this'll get cleared up."

He shook his head.

I knew what he was thinking: *I told you so.* I was wishing I had listened to him.

"Levant will be there," Brady said, referring to Central's renowned Homicide lieutenant. "I'll be there, too. You're entitled to representation, so if you want a lawyer or union rep, get on the phone and make your calls."

I had estimated a full week of work ahead of me on Millie Cushing's murder. It would have been basic door-to-door detective work, starting at the beginning. I didn't even know if my informant's name was Mildred or Millicent, or if Millie Cushing was a made-up name entirely.

And now digging into this case was going to be roadblocked by the IAD hearing.

I asked, "If IAD finds against me, what happens to the Cushing case?"

"It's up to the chief. Now please leave me with all this...stuff." He looked down at the multiple tall stacks of papers on his desk and threw up his hands.

I got out.

CHAPTER 63

IT WAS EARLY morning chez Molinari, and a shaft of sunlight was piercing the south-facing windows.

I had to present my case to a panel of Internal Affairs Division honchos in an hour. I was still in pj's. Unbeknownst to Joe, I had thrown up that morning. While standing in the shower, I did some fourth-grade math in the condensation on the tiles, adding up days and weeks since Joe and I had made love in a danger zone.

My math was sketchy.

I might have forgotten a half-asleep morning tumble or miscalculated my cycle. It was pretty clear that somehow I'd screwed up and that I was an idiot. Correction. A pregnant idiot.

I draped Joe's robe over my pajamas and went to the kitchen table, where he had set out a plate of buttered toast, a jar of blackberry jam, and a cup of tea.

Joe said to me, "Sit, Lindsay. How many eggs?"

"None. Thanks, though. I'm a little edgy about the hearing."

I sipped tea. I nibbled a corner of the toast. I

wondered if there would be time today to go to CVS and pick up a pregnancy kit.

Joe saw that my mind was far, far away.

"Talk to me," he said.

"Martha needs a senior checkup," I said.

"I'll call the vet. What's worrying you about the IAD meeting?"

"I'm nervous, Joe. Let's face it. Stevens is going to try to ruin me. But I know what I saw. My intentions are damned good, and if that's not enough, well, what else can I do?"

Julie ran out of her bedroom, entering the large living room, waving her arms and making sputtering, airplanelike noises. Joe tensed, ready to jump into action if she took a fall.

"Joooo-leee," he called out. "Come to Daddy."

She dipped her wings and course-corrected. The curly-haired single-engine aircraft flew to her daddy's knees.

After she'd climbed into Joe's lap, I said to him, "If the panel finds that I was out of line, the punishment phase is up to Jacobi. I saved his life once, don't forget."

"I know," said Joe. He grabbed my hand and squeezed. "You'll do fine. I'm sure of it. Call me as soon as it's over."

"I will."

I got up, kissed him, then bent to kiss my daughter, wondering how she'd adjust to the intrusion of another little attention-getter in the house. And what about Joe and me? How would a new child impact Joe's hoped-for job, and what would it do to my own? Assuming I still had one.

I left the kitchen–living room–dining room and

went to the bedroom closet. I hit the light switch and stared at my wardrobe. Next to my long red cocktail dress hung a raft of mostly white button-down shirts and a dozen pairs of blue, black, and khaki trousers. I had three blue blazers and one gray one in a dry cleaner's bag, along with a pair of dark-gray slacks.

I went with the gray.

I put on makeup with an overly careful, possibly shaky hand, then drove to 850 Bryant, arriving at eight forty. I parked across the street, dodged traffic against the light, entered the Hall, and passed through security without a hitch.

The elevator whisked me to the fifth floor, and I didn't run into anyone I knew. That was good. I wasn't in a chatty mood.

I had rehearsed my complaint in my head, but when the elevator doors slid open on five, my mind blanked.

I no longer remembered even my opening line.

CHAPTER 64

THE DOUBLE DOORS to the IAD hearing room were wide open to the hallway.

I crossed the threshold and quickly got my bearings.

The white-painted room was no-frills. The overhead strip lighting was fluorescent. The California state flag and the Stars and Stripes flanked the long wooden table for the panel at the front of the room.

Hon was speaking to a man I didn't know.

There were two front-facing tables at midpoint for the complainants, and a stenographer sat off to the side with her console. Neither Stevens nor my union rep nor Brady were there.

A row of folding chairs had been set up at the back of the room. Given the renowned secrecy of IAD, I wasn't surprised that there was no gallery for press, curiosity seekers, or interested parties.

My phone buzzed.

I reached into my blazer pocket and checked the caller ID before answering. It was Carol Hannah, my union rep. I'd sent her an e-mail and left her a couple of messages but hadn't heard back. Carol was a solid and feisty defender. It would be good to have her sitting next to me even if she didn't say a word.

I took my phone to the rear of the room and faced the corner. In the privacy of my imaginary phone booth, I said, "Carol? Where are you?"

"On a steamer about ten miles off the coast of Norway. Since you asked."

"What? No. Really?"

"Really. I want to see reindeer before they're extinct. It's still night here, though."

"Aw, no. I mean, good for you."

But it was bad for me. My hopeful expectations were dashed, against Norway's frigid shoreline.

Carol's voice was staticky. "You didn't murder anyone, right, Lindsay?"

"Right. I committed no crimes. Well, except for stepping over the thin blue line hard onto Sergeant Stevens's toes."

"From your e-mail, I say you did the right thing, and this is why we have IAD. Just remember who you are, a *great* police officer with a dozen commendations. Tell the whole truth. And don't cry."

I laughed. "Okay. No tears. Love to Rudolph and Blitzen and the rest of them."

I was disappointed that Carol wouldn't be here with me, but I was less afraid of crying than of tossing my breakfast. We said our good-byes and clicked off. I turned around just as Stevens came into the room with his advocate.

This sleazy former pal of my very dodgy father was dressed in friendly earth tones. Even with a middle-aged beer gut and a comb-over, he looked clean cut. And damn it. He had an honest face.

I, on the other hand, was wearing scuffed shoes. I needed a haircut. I was nauseous.

I sat down at the right-hand complainant's table and folded my hands in front of me. Stevens and his advocate sat at the table across the aisle. The IAD brass took their seats up front. Hon sat in the middle seat between two men wearing severe expressions, jackets, and ties.

Brady came through the doorway in his usual denim everything, but he was wearing a tie. He nodded to me and took one of the folding chairs behind me. Central Homicide's Chris Levant did the same.

A hush came over the hearing room and Hon spoke, saying that investigators from two homicide squads had filed complaints against each other. He said that each complainant would speak, the panel would ask questions if needed, and after the hearing they would come to a recommendation that would be sent up to Chief Jacobi.

My heart was galloping now. My impromptu meeting with Brady and Jacobi three days ago had been rough—but safe. Hon had been kind, bordering on condescending, in our one-on-one, but this speech was clinical. There was no wiggle room, no backing out, no place to hide.

I called my rehearsed speech to mind, and thank God, I remembered the first line. I hoped that once I got rolling, the story of unsolved murders would unfold without a hitch.

My mouth was dry. Bright spots sparkled in front of my eyes. I felt the presence of a stone-faced Brady behind me.

He had told me that the worst-case scenario was

desk duty or a thirty-day suspension. But he was wrong. The worst-case scenario was the waterfall of humiliation and disrespect that would spring from bringing a charge against another cop—and losing.

CHAPTER 65

HON SPOKE FROM his seat at the front of the room.

"Sergeant Boxer. If you're ready, you may proceed."

I said, "Thank you, Lieutenant. I'm here today—"

Hon interrupted, saying, "Please stand, Sergeant."

I did it, the legs of my chair scraping loudly against the floor. The room faded around me. I steadied myself against the table and focused my tunnel vision on the gray-haired IAD lieutenant. And I reminded myself of Carol Hannah's words. *You're a great cop. This is why we have IAD. Don't cry.*

I took in a breath and started my speech again.

"About a month ago a homeless woman named Millie Cushing sought me out to tell me that a man she knew had been shot dead on the street. His name was Jimmy Dolan. He was a poet and a friend, and she told me that other homeless people had been shot to death near places where they often congregated. Millie told me that the police were not taking these crimes seriously, that no one had been arrested or even questioned. She was afraid for her friends, for her community of street people, and she begged me to help.

"I didn't know her, but she seemed sincere and mentally competent. I promised I'd look into these homicides. I didn't expect that I would become involved in them, and I didn't imagine that only weeks after Millie Cushing grabbed my arm on the front steps of this building, she herself would become a victim."

Hon nodded. I was in a good groove, so I kept talking.

I told the panel about the shooting of Laura Russell at Pier 45 and the similar execution-style shooting of the still-unidentified Jane Doe on Geary Street. I sketched in the corrupted crime scenes, the way I had become the de facto primary on these cases while waiting hours for Sergeant Stevens and his partner to arrive. I mentioned that although I had introduced myself to Stevens, he had not wanted my help.

"Each time he told me not to worry. It was under control.

"I've filed my report. And I've looked into the progress of these homicides. As far as I can tell, there are no suspects, no arrests, and because my CI was murdered around thirty-six hours ago on the south side of Mission near Spear, I'm officially the primary on her case."

Hon said, "In a sentence or two, what is your complaint against Sergeant Stevens?"

"He didn't work these cases with urgency. Perhaps if these victims hadn't been homeless, if there were family members making inquiries, the cases would have received more attention. Perhaps, then, a woman who was doing her civic duty by coming to the police would be alive—and a spree killer would be awaiting trial."

I said, "Thank you," and sat down.

I heard Hon call Stevens, asking him to speak.

I had no idea what to expect, but I was sure he wouldn't be blowing kisses at me from across the aisle.

CHAPTER 66

SERGEANT GARTH STEVENS stood up, put his hands in his pockets, and smiled.

He looked cool, composed, and confident. There was no murder too heinous, no charge against him too dire, to disturb his good mood. Noooo problems at all.

"Lieutenant Hon," he said. "Gentlemen. I can make this real short. My partner, Evan Moran, and I work graveyard shift for Central Station, Homicide. Over the last six months a number of people have been shot in areas, as Sergeant Boxer put it, where homeless people congregate. We have worked seven of these cases.

"While being called to those street crimes, we have also been called to gang killings, domestic homicides, liquor store shootings, and hit-and-runs. Same day as the Geary Street murder, we were called to a home where a five-year-old boy had drowned his baby sister.

"In short, we've been busy and have closed 70 percent of our cases, which is a high-water mark for the entire SFPD. We have not made similar progress in these homeless murders, but it's not because we were sleeping in our cars. Our squad is small and sometimes shorthanded. We get to our crime scenes as fast as we can, and we work the scenes in a professional manner.

"I have filed my report as well as the reports of the first-responding officers, CSI, and the medical examiner. Lieutenant Levant has been kept up to speed on all of my cases, and he has not found me or my partner negligent in any of them.

"If I may, I wish to put forth a theory as to why this series of possibly related crimes has gotten Sergeant Boxer into such a twist."

"Go ahead," said Hon.

"Okay," said Stevens. "I was a psychology major back when I went to Fordham. Skipping ahead, I became a police officer for the SFPD. Back in those early days I was friends with Sergeant Boxer's father, Marty. I even knew Lindsay, here, when she was a child."

"Can we move it along, Stevens?"

"Yes, sir. Sergeant Boxer didn't get along with her father. This isn't gossip. It's common knowledge, and maybe she has valid reasons. Regardless, I think she has transferred her anger at Marty Boxer to me. I think she sees me, she sees him. And she sees red."

As Stevens had said, I saw red. Blood red. I was flooded with rage.

"Okay," said Hon. "Thank you, Stevens."

"One more thing," said Stevens. "I'm requesting that the Cushing case be transferred to Central. My partner and I are conversant with this string of shootings and therefore have a better chance of closing the lot of them if we have all of the information."

Hon said, "Duly noted."

Stevens sat down.

Somehow the hearing ended and I left the room under my own power. I took the stairs down to the squad room.

Conklin was there.

"How'd it go?"

"I don't have any idea," I said. "I don't have a clue in the world."

CHAPTER 67

WHEN I PULLED open the door to MacBain's, a wave of lunchtime chatter washed over me.

Most days the laughter and exuberant din recalled the good times I'd spent there. But not today.

Today I needed to see Claire.

I looked for her, hoping she'd nailed down the small table near the window, then Syd tapped me on the shoulder and pointed. I followed her finger with my eyes. Claire was at a table in the back, half hidden by the bar.

I parted the crowd with my hip and shoulder and made my way toward my best friend.

"I'm starving," she shouted when she saw me.

Food wasn't on my top twenty list of concerns, but I said, "Let's order. What're we waiting for?"

Claire grinned, waved Syd down, and placed our order in the fewest possible words, "The usual." Meaning deluxe burgers and a double order of fries.

"The fish tacos rock," said Syd.

"Maybe some other time," Claire said.

She put her elbows on the table and I did the

same, both of us leaning in so we could talk without shouting.

Claire said, "So, what's the verdict?"

She was asking about the IAD decision. She knew what was at stake. Had I been suspended for a month—or worse? Had Sergeant Stevens been sidelined? Who was going to track down the person killing homeless people in our city?

And now I knew the answers to all of the above. I told Claire, "Brady says that the panel recommended no action."

"None? That's great, right?" she asked.

"Yes and no. Stevens wasn't disciplined and neither was I. So that makes me feel like I blew this whole thing up, and for what? 'No action recommended'?"

"Okay," Claire said. "I get it. But you weren't wrong. This is how it turned out. So work the Cushing case as best you can."

The best I could do was under a lot of pressure. Time had been lost. The killer was a ghost, of a lethal variety. Serial killers have distinct MOs. Some have a preferred victim type or method of killing or a favorite location. Some have unique signatures: markings left on the bodies or methods of disposal or even letters to the press.

This killer's MO was to shoot a defenseless vagrant at close range in the dark, and in a location without a surveillance camera. And then, *poof*. Gone with the wind.

That this psycho had gotten so close to his victims told me that they weren't afraid of him. None had screamed, run, put up a fight. Maybe he knew them. Maybe he was one of them.

One crummy lead.

We needed one crummy lead: a video, a finger-print, a bullet linked to a gun in our database, a witness statement, even an anonymous tip. Some-one had to know *something*.

I didn't know how I'd catch this ghost, but I had to. Millie's killer mustn't win.

CHAPTER 68

"HEY, HEY," SAID Claire, snapping my attention back to the present.

Syd put platters down in front of us, saying, "Two daily specials with all the extras. Anything else I can get you ladies?"

"Thanks, we're good," Claire said, grabbing the ketchup bottle.

I stared down at my burger and fries. They had all the appeal of a wriggling pile of alien life-forms.

Claire noticed my revulsion and said, "Okay, Lindsay. What's up? You're usually a girl with an appetite, and seems to me you've dropped some pounds. What are you now? A size four?"

"I have to talk to you about this," I said. I reached for my handbag and extracted a white paper bag. I handed it to Claire.

"What is this?" she asked. She peered into the bag. "Oh, my. Really, Linds?"

"I need you to be with me."

"Right here?"

"There's no place I'd rather be, Butterfly. No one I'd rather be with."

Claire grinned and said, "I love you, too."

I told Claire to go ahead and eat, and I nibbled. When our plates had been cleared and the check had been paid, Claire and I headed back past the cigarette machine and the old wall phone to the ladies' room.

I took the home pregnancy test into a stall. My hands shook and the instruction sheet rattled, but I performed the procedure and a moment later brought the little stick out to where Claire was waiting for me.

Claire said, "What are we hoping for? Positive or no?"

"*Que será será,*" I said.

The refrain to an old song my mom used to sing to me. I imagined that millions of moms sang it to their daughters who wanted to know their futures. It meant, "What will be will be."

Claire and I waited thirty seconds, and together we stared at the stick.

"Look it. There's only one bar," Claire said, examining the tester. "That would be a no."

I must've been holding my breath, because I exhaled deeply.

"You okay, Linds?"

I leaned against a sink and said, "I'm not ready to be pregnant right now, Claire. But *something* is wrong. I feel…fatigued. Depressed. Nauseated."

"How long has this been going on?"

"The last few weeks."

She placed her hand on my forehead.

"You don't feel warm to me. When are you seeing your doctor?"

"It's just exhaustion," I said. "I've been working like a donkey."

"Call your doctor, Lindsay. I mean it."

"Okay."

"And call in sick right now. I say so. I'm a doctor."

I called the squad room and left messages for Conklin and Brady. Then I went home and got under the bedcovers at two in the afternoon. Joe, Julie, and Martha made a fuss over me while I reassured them and tried to empty my mind.

Tomorrow. I would call the doctor tomorrow.

And then I slept.

CHAPTER 69

TWO AND A half days had passed since Marc Christopher was shot, and Judge Rathburn granted a continuance.

Ten minutes from now court was due to reconvene.

Yuki and her second chair, Arthur, sat together on a bench outside the courtroom, waiting for their star witness to arrive.

When Yuki spoke with Marc last night, he had said, "I'm good to go." But his tone had been shaky, and she had been obligated to tell him that she couldn't stall the proceedings any longer. If he didn't show up, she'd have to run the video for the jury without him, which would dramatically diminish its impact.

Yuki said to Arthur, "I don't like that he doesn't answer his phone."

He said, "Let me make sure I've got this right. He was shot in the thigh? One shot only?"

"Yep. One shot. Through and through."

"The slug wasn't recovered?"

"Not so far," she said.

"So the shot could have been accidental. Like a random shot from two streets away."

"Yep. That's possible."

"Or maybe the shooter had a motive," Art said, inserting a long pause before adding, "Like an eight-hundred-pound gorilla wearing a designer suit."

Yuki said, "The gorilla has an alibi. There's no evidence that she shot him. In fact, her gun wasn't recently fired. Video supports her whereabouts. Giftos got Rathburn to reinstate her bail, and she's been released."

"Maybe she hired someone to freak him out."

"So that he wouldn't testify?"

"I wouldn't put it past her."

"Good theory, Art. That had not occurred to me."

The bailiff swung open the courtroom doors.

"Let's go," said Arthur. "I want to get a good seat."

Yuki smiled. Art was funny, but he was also very sharp. Committing a sex crime and hiring a hitter were two entirely different kinds of crimes, but they weren't mutually exclusive. Had Briana paid a shooter to intimidate Marc? Had Marc in fact been intimidated? What kind of testimony would he give today?

Yuki and Art joined the throng entering the courtroom and had just taken their seats at their table when James Giftos strode up the center aisle.

He stopped beside Yuki's seat.

"Neat trick, Counselor," he said. "I'm already writing up my appeal."

Of course Giftos was mad that Briana had been arrested and held overnight. It had weakened and depressed her, and that could make her a poor witness for herself.

Yuki was torn between saying "Dude, she had a

loaded gun" and "Knock yourself out, Counselor," but Giftos was already on the move. He crossed the well and opened the side door that led to the interior stairwell used by court personnel.

Giftos's second chair came through the doorway with Briana Hill, who was wearing a plain gray skirt and sweater, with a silver cross.

Her polished look was gone.

Hill had just taken her seat between her two attorneys when the jurors entered the courtroom and filled the seats in the jury box. Behind Yuki, the gallery was loud with the sounds of spectators talking, settling into their seats, putting down their computer bags. Yuki looked for Marc but didn't see him or his parents.

This was very worrisome. It was five to nine.

Judge Rathburn came through his private entrance, and the whispers stopped cold. Right then Yuki heard a ruckus behind her.

She turned in her seat to see the bailiff trying to close the door and heard a man's voice pleading, "We got here as fast as we could. He has a right to be here."

The bailiff relented and opened the door, and with the help of his parents, Marc Christopher hobbled into the courtroom on crutches. An elderly man on the aisle got up to give Marc his seat. Marc glanced in Yuki's direction, and she nodded at him as he awkwardly took a seat in the gallery.

Like Briana Hill, Marc had lost his look of dewy youthfulness.

And now, after he'd been injured and traumatized, the curtain was about to go up on the drama of his life.

CHAPTER 70

JUDGE RATHBURN WAS at the bench.

He took an unsmiling visual tour of his court-room, popped a couple of Tums, and tapped on his laptop. After exchanging words with his clerk, the judge said, "Ms. Castellano. Please call your witness."

Yuki was ready—but what about Marc? Would he push through the pain and nervousness and do a good job of testifying on his own behalf? Or would he fold on the stand?

It could go either way.

She watched Marc pull himself to his feet, then limp and hop through the gate like a long-legged waterbird with a broken wing. He crossed the well in this awkward manner, drawing the attention of every soul in the courtroom.

Maybe he'd draw their pity, too.

The bailiff held the Bible and, after Marc swore to tell the whole truth, so help him God, gave Marc a hand up to the witness box. Marc said, "Thanks," then fumbled his crutch. It spun out of his grasp and bounced down the step to the floor, the clatter sounding through the room, which was otherwise silent.

The bailiff retrieved the crutch and asked Marc if he was okay.

"Good enough," he said.

It was a dramatic and, she hoped, sympathetic introduction to the jury, who had heard much about Marc but had not actually seen him.

Yuki looked at Marc as if she were a juror seeing him for the first time. He still looked like a college kid, but one who had gotten knocked around on the football field. Along with the leg injury, Marc's cheek was scraped from jaw to hairline, and he had dark smudges under his eyes.

When his leg went out from under him on the street, he must've taken a pretty good fall.

Yuki flashed on the sex video she had seen many times. Within the next hour she would be showing it to the jury while Marc sat in the box, pinned under the lights by the appraising eyes of the jurors. Thinking of what Marc had endured, Yuki felt sorry for him. Her doubts about his sincerity since he'd tried to kiss her dropped away.

Marc had been raped and shot, and now he was going to have to tell a roomful of strangers that he had been tied to his bed and assaulted by a woman who weighed 110 pounds.

Yuki left her seat, walked to a spot about ten feet from the stand, and smiled at her witness.

She said, "Mr. Christopher, how are you feeling?"

He made the universal flip-flop hand sign for fifty-fifty, managed a weak smile, and said, "I'm good."

"Glad to hear it, Marc. Is it all right with you if I call you Marc?"

"Sure."

"Okay. Marc, if you can tell us, what is the nature of your injury?"

"I was shot in the thigh," Marc said.

"Do you know who shot you?"

"I didn't see anyone. It was dark."

He switched his eyes to the defense table, where Briana Hill sat silently and steadily looking back at him. Whether indicating Briana with his eyes was calculated or reflexive, Marc had made a subtle yet powerful point. Briana Hill had raped him. Had she also shot him?

Yuki asked, "Marc, tell us about the night of October eleventh."

"Where should I start?"

Yuki asked him a series of questions that they had run through before. He answered, beginning with leaving work that day with Briana and going to a restaurant near his apartment where they'd had dinner before. During and after the meal both of them had had a lot to drink.

"And what happened then?" she asked.

Marc cleared his throat, and when he spoke again, he sounded deflated. He said, "This is very hard. Actually, this is the most embarrassing thing that has ever happened to me. It's beyond humiliating. Then I had to tell the police. I had to tell you. I had to tell Mr. Giftos. I've had trouble telling this to a *psychologist*."

He shook his head and grabbed at his crutch. Yuki thought maybe he was going to take it and go.

Yuki was getting that oncoming-train-wreck feeling again. What could she do? Should she ask for a time-out? Or should she call an end to Marc's testimony and say, "I'm done here"?

She said, "Do you need a moment, Marc?"

"Thanks, but I'd rather just get it over with," he said.

CHAPTER 71

MARC WAS VISIBLY upset, but he stayed in the witness stand and had given Yuki his okay to continue his testimony.

She pushed on.

"Okay, Marc. Let's go back to the moment when you and the defendant were drinking in the restaurant and bar. Tell us what happened."

Marc cleared his throat, then said, "Briana was very clingy, and over dinner I made up my mind. I told her that I thought we should stop seeing each other socially. She threw a fit."

Yuki couldn't show it, but she was thinking, *Nanda*. What the hell was this? Marc hadn't told her that he had tried to break up with Briana. In fact, Briana had sworn in her deposition that she was thinking of breaking up with *him*.

Why was he embellishing the story?

Yuki continued on as if she hadn't just gotten hot breaking news from her witness. She said, "Please continue, Marc."

"Well, I tried to reason with her, calm her down, but she was crying hysterically. I said that it was late, and I started to call an Uber for her, but she insisted that she didn't want to go home alone. She said we could discuss this in the morning, but she really needed to crash at my place, since it was close and she was so wasted."

Marc said, "I felt bad. I hadn't warned her that I wanted to stop seeing her, and I couldn't just walk out on her like that. So I said okay. We went to my apartment, a couple of blocks up the hill. I stopped thinking about her. I stripped down and fell into bed. Next thing I know, Briana's calling my name. I look up and she's got a gun pointed at me and she's threatening to shoot me if I don't give her, excuse my language, the best fuck of her life."

Yuki had gone over Marc's story three, if not four, times, and he had never mentioned that Briana had been hysterical. Nor had he quoted any demands she'd made inside the bar. Why the hell not?

Was he telling the truth now?

Yuki had no choice but to ask Marc to continue, and he did, saying, "Briana was drunk, but she had a firm hand on the gun. I told her to knock it off, but I was scared. She's a very determined and powerful woman, and now she was acting crazy, saying, 'If you want to live, you'd better get your limp dick into the mood....'"

Marc shook his head. Tears flew off his cheeks. Judge Rathburn handed him a box of tissues.

As he dabbed his eyes, Yuki was thinking, *What the fuck?* Maybe Marc was trying to help their case, but he had added too many new and damning details to his story. James Giftos had deposed him and would blow big, gaping holes in these inconsistencies on cross.

Marc answered Yuki's questions, filling in details about the neckties, his protests, his terror, and the fact that he'd taken a chance in recording the rape.

"Briana had sex with me against my will," he said. "She kept the gun on me until I was tied up. Then she did things to make me get hard."

He stopped talking, shot a panicky look at Yuki, and said, "Then she did it. She raped me."

Yuki said, "Thank you, Mr. Christopher. Please remain seated."

She turned to the judge and said, "Your Honor, we're ready to show the recording."

"Go ahead, Ms. Castellano. Will someone please get the lights?"

CHAPTER 72

ARTHUR BARON HAD cued up the video, positioned the laptop at the edge of the table, and set up the screen so that it faced the jury. But before Yuki got a chance to say "Roll it," James Giftos got to his feet and said angrily, "Your Honor. May we approach?"

Rathburn signaled to the attorneys to come to the bench.

He said, "Mr. Giftos, I've already ruled. The video is in."

"Judge Rathburn, with all due respect, I've seen this recording and you have not."

The judge said, "Let's take this into my chambers."

Counsel for both sides followed the judge through his private doorway out of the courtroom and into his office. He took his desk chair and the four attorneys grouped at the front of his desk.

Giftos said, "Judge Rathburn, I feel strongly that by showing this recording, the prosecution is going to perpetrate a miscarriage of justice."

Rathburn said, "As I said before, James, and will say again, you will have your chance to rebut the video and cross-examine the witness. What don't I understand?"

Giftos was red faced and the cords in his neck were standing out. He said, "Your Honor, I don't think you understand that this recording is hard-core porn. There is full-on nudity and full-on sex, or more accurately, bondage.

"As I have said from the beginning, this video is a setup. Marc Christopher recorded it in such a way—"

"Using the same argument isn't going to change my ruling."

"Putting our argument aside," Giftos said, "watching the stark visualization of this sex act is inflammatory and prejudicial in the extreme.

"Once the jury sees it, it cannot be unseen. The spectators and the press will also see it, and even though Briana is entirely innocent of this charge, she will be convicted in the court of public opinion, and that verdict will cling to her for the rest of her life."

Yuki thought Giftos was making a strong case for excluding the video, and that was very worrying. Without it, her case would hang entirely on Marc's testimony—and Giftos hadn't yet set out to discredit him.

Giftos went on.

"Once again I move that the video be excluded. It's prejudicial, defamatory, and the basis for a whopper of a civil suit against the People of San Francisco."

Rathburn said, "All right, Mr. Giftos, you've made your point. Ms. Castellano?"

Yuki said firmly, "Your Honor, the video is a

recording of Ms. Hill threatening violence, brandishing a gun, and raping Mr. Christopher. It's irrefutable evidence. The jury has to see it or they won't have the full facts of the crime."

Rathburn leaned back, considered the remarks, and then returned his seat to its upright position.

"James, here's what I'm willing to do. I'll clear the courtroom. The spectators, including the press, will not see the tape, just the jurors. Fair enough?"

Giftos snorted, huffed, and, after a walk over to the windows, returned to the grouping around Judge Rathburn's desk.

"All right," said Giftos. "Jurors and no spectators."

Said Rathburn, "If Ms. Castellano agrees."

Yuki was ready with her answer. "That works for me, Judge."

Giftos said, "If it's okay with you, Your Honor, Ms. Benson can sit with Ms. Hill outside your chambers while Ms. Castellano runs the video."

Yuki said, "Mr. Christopher can wait in the hallway."

"Another hurdle cleared," said Judge Rathburn. "The recording is in."

CHAPTER 73

THE COURTROOM HAD been cleared of spectators and press.

Sixteen men and women sat in the jury box staring at Yuki as she told Arthur to play the recording.

Lights were dimmed, but it was bright enough for Yuki to see the resolute faces of the jurors. During voir dire they had been told that evidence would include a sexually explicit video, and they were asked if they were willing and able to see such a recording and remain impartial. The twelve plus four had all said yes.

Truth was, it was still hard for Yuki to watch. The screen faced away from her, but she'd seen the ten-minute-long video so many times, she could see the action in her mind.

In the first moments the view of the bed was partially blocked by Marc's body as he faced the hidden camera and struggled to tie his left hand to the headboard with his right.

Briana's voice was heard clearly.

Briana: That knot isn't tight enough, damn it. Fix that, Marc, you stupid little bitch.

Marc: I'm doing it. I'm *doing* it. Put the gun down, okay? Please, Briana. That thing could go off.

Yuki knew that Marc tightened the knot and then rolled flat onto his back.

Briana: Grip the other bedpost with your right hand. Do what I tell you, Marc, or I *will* shoot you and walk the hell out of here.

Yuki saw alarm on the jurors' faces. Mrs. Moloney, for instance, a mother of three and a bank executive, was frowning. At the other end of the row Mr. Koenig, a twentysomething high school math teacher, had drawn back in his seat and was covering his mouth with both hands.

On-screen, even in the darkened room, Marc could be seen nude and spread-eagle on the sheets. Briana Hill, fully dressed, was standing at the foot of the bed, holding a gun with both hands, the muzzle aimed at Marc.

Yuki knew that it was at this point that Briana put the gun down on a chair and cinched a necktie around Marc's wrist, lashing it to the headboard.

Briana: There. There we go. Got you now.

On the tape Marc was breathing loudly. Could be from panic.

Marc: You're going too far, Briana. I'm not into this. I don't even know you right now.

Briana checked each of the ties, then slowly undressed, folding her jacket, sweater, slacks, stacking them on the chair. She peeled off her panties and passed them over Marc's face, then hung her bra over the footboard.

Marc strained at the ties and could be heard saying, "This is crazy. This is wrong. This isn't going to work, Briana."

"We'll see about that," she said.

When she was naked, she got onto the bed and, kneeling between Marc's spread legs, manipulated his genitals with her hands and her mouth before she mounted him.

Two women jurors partially covered their eyes, but there was no way to shut out the sounds of both parties breathing hard, moaning, Briana saying, "Say it, Marc. You like this. This is what you want."

Briana's rising, falling, grinding motions would continue for another five minutes and some seconds.

Yuki had an impulse to grab the remote and hit Fast-Forward. Arthur shot her a questioning look, and she shook her head no. Eventually the sounds stopped.

Yuki knew that Briana had rolled off Marc's body, pulled up the blankets around her shoulders, and fallen asleep without untying him or speaking again.

Yuki said, "Your Honor. Both parties slept until the camera's memory card was full and had stopped recording."

The judge muttered, "Thank God."

Art shut down the laptop, crossed to the front of the room, and brought up the lights.

Yuki felt blasted as the dim light gave way to

brightness in the courtroom. She looked at the jurors. She had never seen a jury look so shattered.

Even the judge looked disturbed. He grabbed at the tissue box and blew his nose.

Yuki said, "The People enter this recording into evidence, Your Honor."

"Done. And this would be a good time to take a half-hour recess. Back here at eleven sharp."

He brought down the gavel and left the courtroom.

CHAPTER 74

DURING THE HALF-HOUR recess Art helped Marc to the men's room, sat with him in the corridor, and told him that he had done a great job on the stand. He said casually, "I must have missed the part where Briana said she wanted the best bonk of her life."

Marc answered, "I'd forgotten. It just came back to me."

Yuki used the time to think through every last word that Marc had spoken. She questioned much of it. She got a bottle of water from the vending machine and, keeping an eye on the time, got back to the prosecution table as Art was helping Marc up to the witness stand.

Arthur joined her at their table and updated her on his brief chat with Marc. "He said he'd had a sudden recurrence of memory," said Art. "It was like a miracle."

A moment later Briana Hill and Madison Benson returned to the defense table. Briana was nodding as if Madison had given her an affectionate buck-up speech.

The spectators filled the gallery, no doubt wondering what the hell had happened that had caused the judge to throw them out. Then the jury came in and took their places in the box. Some of them still looked as though a bomb had gone off in front of their faces.

At eleven sharp the judge took the bench, and a moment before the doors were closed, James Giftos sat down at his counsel table. Yuki guessed that he had used the recess to sharpen his knives and prepare himself to give the cross-examination of his career.

Red Dog Parisi had once told Yuki that litigation was a storytelling contest and the best story won. James Giftos had a mighty big job ahead of him if he hoped to undermine the prosecution's story. Yuki had provided something light-years more effective than a secondhand narrative.

She'd *shown* Briana Hill threatening and then raping the victim. She had presented proof.

She expected that Giftos would tell the jurors that the video was open to interpretation. But was it? The jury had been exposed to the rape as if they had been inside Marc's actual bedroom, staring down the barrel of Briana Hill's actual gun.

The judge said, "Mr. Christopher, you're still under oath. Understand?"

Marc nodded.

The judge said, "Court reporter has to hear you. Is that a yes?"

"Yes, I understand that I'm under oath."

Rathburn said, "Mr. Giftos, are you ready to cross-examine the witness?"

Giftos stood, smoothed his tie, and said, "Sidebar, Your Honor."

Judge Rathburn couldn't keep the irritation off his face.

"Approach," he said.

Yuki and Art got up from their seats and met Giftos and Benson at the bench.

Judge Rathburn put his hand over the mike and said to James Giftos, "Make it good, Counselor."

"We've just uncovered some new evidence."

"During the recess?"

"We found voice-mail messages from Mr. Christopher to Ms. Hill after the so-called rape."

Judge Rathburn growled, "In my chambers."

CHAPTER 75

THE FOUR ATTORNEYS and the judge trooped out and convened in Rathburn's office. This time the judge didn't sit.

He said, "How did these messages come to light at just this moment, James? Convince me."

"Can do, Your Honor. After the incident in question Mr. Christopher started dogging my client. He wanted to go out with her. She brushed him off. Then he started calling and e-mailing with threats to blackmail her."

"Judge Rathburn, this is the first I've heard about blackmail threats," said Yuki.

Giftos didn't look at her. He said, "Until now they were unsubstantiated. Briana avoided Christopher and stopped answering his calls and e-mail. When he went to the police, management at the Ad Shop put Briana on unpaid leave. She never cleared messages from her office phone."

"Until *now*?" the judge said.

"We grilled her during the recess," said Giftos, looking very much like the proverbial cat after consuming the canary. "We asked if there was anything at all we could use to refute Mr. Christopher's bullshit. Pardon me. His lies. She remembered that there were unanswered calls on her office phone. It was a Hail Mary."

Yuki's heart thudded almost audibly. The judge was listening in earnest.

"Keep talking," he said.

Giftos went on.

"We called her office number and accessed the voice-mail system. It still retained her un-deleted new messages. There were three messages from Mr. Christopher, none longer than six seconds. The first two messages were essentially, 'Call me or else.' The last one was another coded threat.

"I've transcribed these messages by hand," said James Giftos. "We also recorded the time-stamped audio. Of course, we preserved the original messages on her voice mail at the agency."

Giftos handed his pen-and-ink transcript of the three phone messages and a pocket tape recorder to Judge Rathburn.

Judge Rathburn passed the transcript to Yuki and asked Giftos to play the recorder.

He did it.

As Giftos had said, the calls had all been made within a week of the incident. And the technical quality was good.

Yuki said, "Your Honor, these calls are vague and ambiguous."

"I'm allowing them in," said Rathburn.

Yuki felt a vortex opening under her feet, but she steadied herself, dragged herself back from the terrible sinking feeling. She wouldn't go down. She couldn't go down.

She followed Judge Rathburn back to the court-room.

Back at their table, Art said so quietly only she could hear him, "Don't worry. Don't worry. You've got this."

If only she could be sure. There were two opposing stories. Only one of them was true. Which one? And whom would the jury believe?

CHAPTER 76

MARC CHRISTOPHER WAS fidgeting in the witness box, staring out over the heads of the court officers, looking to where his parents sat in the gallery.

Judge Rathburn pulled his chair up to the bench, appearing to Yuki as if he'd crossed his maximum irritation threshold. Even the jurors looked like they were ready to scream *Come on, already.*

As for James Giftos, Yuki knew that he was on his mark, all set, and good to go.

Giftos stood and, holding notes and sheets of paper in his hand, walked across the floor and addressed the witness.

He said, "Mr. Christopher, I have here a transcript of your deposition with my associates and myself. Could you please read the highlighted section aloud?"

Giftos handed the paper to Marc, who skimmed the transcript and then began to read:

"'J. Giftos: What did you and Briana talk about in the restaurant bar before going back to your apartment?' I answered, 'I don't really remember.

I was getting pretty drunk. I just wanted to go to sleep.'"

Giftos thanked Marc and took back the paper.

"Mr. Christopher, you just testified to something very different from what you swore to in your deposition. You told this court that you broke off your relationship with Ms. Hill during dinner. That she was clingy and hysterical, and that she insisted on spending the night so you could revisit the issue in the morning.

"Is that still your testimony?"

"That's what happened. I mean, yes."

"How so, Mr. Christopher? You've made two opposing sworn statements; one in my office and one in this courtroom, isn't that right?"

Marc said, "You do realize that this is a complicated issue, Mr. Giftos. I was raped by a woman I had feelings for. This is not a linear situation. I'm still trying to understand how she got over on me. I could work on this in therapy for the rest of my life...."

"You made two opposing sworn statements, yes or no?"

"This isn't a yes-or-no kind of thing, I'm telling you."

Giftos said, "Your Honor, permission to treat the witness as hostile."

"Go ahead," said Rathburn. "Mr. Christopher, answer the questions. Don't hypothesize. Don't rationalize. Don't make excuses. Get me?"

"Yes, sir. Your Honor."

The judge said to defense counsel, "Mr. Giftos, please proceed."

CHAPTER 77

JAMES GIFTOS STUCK his hands in his pockets and said, "Mr. Christopher, do you need me to repeat the question?"

Marc looked more annoyed than chastened. "Yes," he said. "Good idea."

Giftos said, "You've made two opposing sworn statements about what transpired between you and Ms. Hill in the restaurant, yes or no?"

Christopher said, "Both are true. We made small talk *and* she got hysterical when I tried to break up with her."

Giftos said, "In fact, *neither* story is true, is it? While you were drinking together in that bar, you told Ms. Hill that you'd like to experiment with a sex game, didn't you?"

"No," said Marc. "I did not."

"Isn't it true that you told her that you'd like her to act out a rape scene in which she threatened you with a gun and you pretended to be the victim?"

"No. Definitely not."

Giftos said, "Isn't it a fact, Mr. Christopher, that you suggested this sexual role-playing with a plan in mind to *entrap* Ms. Hill?"

"No. No way. I did not. That's totally crazy," said Marc.

"Let me ask you this. Did you know that it is illegal to record a person in a sex act without his or her knowledge?"

"I thought she was going to *kill* me."

"Really? Mr. Christopher, did you know that Ms. Hill had just come into a sizable inheritance?"

"I guess so. Yes."

"Mr. Christopher," Giftos said pleasantly, "we've uncovered some voice mails from you to Ms. Hill that were left on her office phone. Could you tell us if this is your voice?"

"You're saying I made the calls?"

Yuki tried to beam a thought to Marc: *Answer the questions in as few words as possible. Do not give Giftos any shit. Do not.*

"I'm going to play them now," said Giftos.

He held the small recording device and pressed a button. As each message played, the mechanical voice of the phone system announced the date and time.

First message: "Briana, for the last time. Call me. I'm serious."

Second message: "It's Marc. You shouldn't screw with me, Briana. Call me."

Third message: "Briana, I've had enough. Either you pay up or there're going to be some traffic problems in San Francisco."

Giftos stopped the recorder and said to Marc, "Is this your voice?"

"Yes. Sounds like me."

"When you said to Ms. Hill, 'Either you pay up or there're going to be traffic problems,' what did you mean?"

"That was a saying. Like from Fort Lee, New Jersey."

"I understand the reference. But what did you mean, 'pay up'?"

"I don't even know. I just said it. I was trying to get hold of her so I could get closure on what she did to me."

Giftos said, "So once again I ask you, when you phoned Ms. Hill in the week following your overnight date and left this message, 'You pay up or it's time for some traffic problems in San Francisco,' you were reinforcing your blackmail attempt on Ms. Hill, weren't you? 'You pay up or I'll go public with the video'?"

Yuki said, "I object, Your Honor. There is no evidence of a blackmail threat."

Rathburn said, "Overruled. It's relevant and I want to hear this. Mr. Giftos, ask your question again."

"Mr. Christopher, were you blackmailing Ms. Hill?"

"Not at all," Marc said. "Far from it. All I wanted was to talk to her. I needed to talk to her. She did this to me. Raped me and left me lying there like roadkill. I needed an explanation. She needed to apologize. I needed something from her. And you *bastard,*" he said to Giftos. "You should be disbarred for even suggesting this crap."

Judge Rathburn said, "Mr. Christopher, I'm warning you. Any more outbursts and I will find you in contempt. I will fine you, too. Jurors, you will disregard Mr. Christopher's personal remarks to Mr. Giftos, and the clerk will strike those remarks from the record."

Giftos said, "Thank you, Your Honor."

To the witness he said, "I guess we'll let the jury decide what you meant when you left a message for this wealthy young woman—whom you had recorded in a compromising act that *you* orchestrated—'Pay up or else.'"

Yuki was on her feet. "Argumentative, Your Honor."

"Sustained."

Giftos said, "Your Honor, I have nothing more for this witness at this time, but I reserve the right to question him again."

The judge asked Yuki, "Redirect, Ms. Castellano?"

"Yes, Your Honor."

Yuki approached the witness and said, "Marc, please tell the jury what you have to gain by accusing the defendant of rape."

Christopher wiped his eyes with the back of his hand and said, "I don't want or need her money and never have. I'm here to get justice and peace of mind. She shouldn't get away with what she did to me."

"Thanks, Marc. I have no further questions."

Rathburn told Marc Christopher that he could step down. With much bumping and limping, Yuki's star witness left the courtroom.

When the doors had closed behind him, Yuki said to the court, "The People rest their case."

Judge Rathburn said, "Okay. Mr. Giftos, you're up with your opening statement."

CHAPTER 78

JAMES GIFTOS HAD delayed making his opening statement until after the prosecution had concluded its case.

Yuki knew that it was risky to let the jury steep in the prosecution's theory for four days. But James was smart, a trial-tested veteran with an impressive record of wins. He surely had a plan and it was about to be revealed.

In the next few minutes he would begin to present his defense, in which he would do everything possible to blow up the prosecution's case and win the jury over to Briana Hill's side.

She watched Giftos walk back to his table, return the notes and transcripts to a file folder, exchange looks with his client, and respond to a note from his second chair.

Yuki was glad that Art was here to witness what could well be a master class in how to deliver an opening statement.

Giftos walked into the well, faced the jurors, and began, "Briana Hill is the victim here.

"Marc Christopher is a liar, and his accusations are damned lies. Even the video the prosecution produced is a lie, and in fact was a planned setup by Mr. Christopher. He designed the scene, directed it, and edited it by turning on the recording device after the discussion of the role-playing had been agreed upon. This way, the viewer would see only a staged sex game. Without the prologue, it's understandable that this entirely orchestrated drama would seem real.

"As you have heard, Marc and Briana were coworkers. They dated and had sex. And when the flames cooled for Ms. Hill and she let Marc know that she wanted to see other men, Mr. Christopher became angry. And he came up with a scheme to hurt Ms. Hill. Why? Because my client had lost interest in him and he was in love with her—an attractive, wealthy, powerful young woman who was rejecting him.

"Mr. Christopher wasn't just angry, he was determined to hurt her financially, destroy her reputation, and even send her to jail."

Giftos paused for effect, and when he was sure that the jury was dying for him to begin again, he did.

Giftos said, "On the night in question, when they were in the restaurant bar, Mr. Christopher told Ms. Hill, and she will tell you, that he wanted to act out a rape scene with himself in the role of victim."

Giftos proceeded to summarize the defense's version of the crime for the jury. Ms. Hill thought she knew Mr. Christopher and was intrigued by his proposition. She had never role-played before. He told her what to do, and as agreed, he would pretend to protest as she tied him up and made demands.

"The morning after this overnight date," said Giftos, "Ms. Hill went to the office, feeling that she'd betrayed herself by going along with Mr. Christopher's game; but she had no idea that she'd been played and was about to be victimized by his extortion scheme.

"Mr. Christopher asked her to go out with him again several times, and when she refused, he went to her office and told her that he had recorded their sex play. He wanted a payout of $250,000, or he would post the video on the web.

"Ms. Hill told him to get lost, and that's when Mr. Christopher took the video recording to the police.

"Ms. Hill was arrested and charged with a felony that she did not commit. Mr. Christopher's premeditated extortion scheme cost my client her job and her reputation, and now she is forced to defend herself against the false testimony of this vicious and vengeful man.

"Please. Don't let him get away with it."

CHAPTER 79

BRIANA HILL, WEARING dark-gray jersey down to her boots, looked as vulnerable as a soaked kitten as she took the witness stand.

Giftos took her through the events of October 11, and she responded with her version of the conversation in the bar in which Marc introduced the idea of the rape sex game and beyond.

"What were your thoughts the day after?" he asked.

"I felt…disgusted with myself. I hadn't enjoyed the role-playing. And Marc still reported to me. We had work to do. I asked him to meet with the creative team about a Chronos commercial that had been approved. He said, 'You bet. Right away.' He had worked on other Chronos commercials. It's a plum account. But this time he didn't follow up. I asked him a second time, and again he said, 'Okay,' and blew it off. I had to assign another producer."

"How did Marc react to your executive decision?"

"He didn't respond at all to losing the Chronos spot, but he called me on my cell three days after what happened in his apartment. He asked me out again. I told him no, that we were through. I told him that if he didn't snap out of it and do his job, I was going to have to report him to management."

"What did he say to that?"

"He laughed at me. He told me I didn't know what trouble was."

"Did you ask him to explain what he meant by that?"

"Yes. I remember. Marc came to my office after work. He was sitting on the couch, talking to me from across the room. He said, 'You're a star, you know.' I said, 'What are you talking about, Marc?' I was waiting for a client to call. Marc said, 'I watched that video of you raping me, and wow, you are something else.' He grabbed his...crotch."

Her last words came out cracked into pieces.

Giftos said, "Do you need a moment, Briana?"

"No." She cleared her throat and said, "So he told me that he had recorded our sex and that he wanted me to deposit $250,000 into his brokerage account. Otherwise he would post the video to YouTube, Facebook, and internet porn sites."

Briana pulled back, showing indignation, and at the same time her eyes were screwed up and her face was crumpled. She reached for a tissue from the judge's box and covered her eyes.

When James Giftos spoke again, his client looked startled and dazed.

"And how did you respond, Briana? To this extortion attempt?"

"I dismissed the demand for money at first. How could he be serious about that? But it was easy for Marc to set up a hidden camera. He's a professional film producer. I was scared to death. I told him that he was crazy. And I mean, I saw for the first time that he was actually *crazy,* for real."

"Did you call the police?"

"No. I still hadn't wrapped my mind around the extortion. I was furious about the video—I didn't know if he was even telling the truth.

"Then the call from my client came in. I asked him to hold on. I put my hand over the receiver and said something like, 'No more threats, Marc. Let me know if you still want to work in production.'

"Marc left, and I thought of how much crap would rain down on me if I fired him for insubordination. I mean, that was true. He just stopped doing his job, but he could call it sexual harassment. How could I prove otherwise?"

"Did you tell anyone about Marc's extortion threat?"

"Finally. I told my sister Angela. She's a lawyer. Estates and trusts. She said, 'He'll never do it. Extortion is a felony.'"

Giftos said, "What happened after that?"

"Stories started circulating around the agency that I had threatened Marc with a loaded gun, that I had raped him and that he could prove it. I denied it, of course, and set up a meeting with our CEO, Mr. Keely, to report Marc. But before I saw Mr. Keely, Marc took the video to the police, and they arrested me for something he dreamed up in the depths of his very sick mind."

CHAPTER 80

YUKI FOUND BRIANA'S testimony credible and very compelling. She tried to shut down her sympathy for the young woman and thought about how to get the jury to do the same.

She approached the witness.

"Ms. Hill, have you ever heard the expression *buyer's remorse*?"

"Yes."

"It means after a purchase the buyer has regrets. Would you go along with me on that definition?"

"Okay."

"Is that what happened to you? You decided to rape Marc and afterward realized you'd made a bad mistake?"

"I regretted going along with him. That's all."

Yuki had an idea for a line of questioning that she might get away with up to a point. It was worth a try, even if Judge Rathburn smacked her down.

She said, "Ms. Hill, after the police arrested you for raping Mr. Christopher, you were released on bond, weren't you?"

"Yes."

"But you were arrested again, weren't you? Why?"

Giftos was on his feet, yelling, "Objection! Relevance."

Yuki knew that Briana's return to jail had nothing to do with the rape, but it would raise questions in the jurors' minds. *Why was she back in jail? Did she shoot Marc Christopher?*

Yuki said, "Withdrawn, Your Honor."

Rathburn said, "You know, you're walking a fine line, Ms. Castellano."

She said, "Sorry, Your Honor," thinking she'd made a good decision. Desperate times called for desperate measures. She turned back to the witness.

"Ms. Hill, would you say that it's risky to date someone who reports to you?"

"I do now."

Yuki asked, "Are you telling us that you've had other interoffice relationships?"

"Objection," Giftos shouted.

"Sustained."

"I want to answer," said the witness.

The judge said to her, "You understand that the question does not apply to the action against you. As your attorney was about to say at the top of his lungs, anything that does not pertain to this case is irrelevant."

"I understand. I want to set the record straight."

"Then, go ahead."

Briana said, "Interoffice dating is no big deal in advertising. I have dated people I've worked with, but I've never done anything like what I did with Marc that night. I should never have done it. He sold me on it, saying it would be fun. It wasn't fun. And it wasn't a crime. It was regrettable."

And with that, Briana started to cry and couldn't seem to stop. The judge spoke her name. Her lawyer stood up and said, "Your Honor, can you give the witness a few moments?"

Yuki found Hill's sobs heartrending—but would the jury find her convincing? If Yuki pushed her any further, she risked coming off as a bully.

"Thank you, Ms. Hill. I have no further questions," she said.

Rathburn told the defendant that she could step down, and called the court into recess.

Out in the hallway Yuki told Arthur, "I didn't have a hook to hang my hat on."

He said, "Didn't hurt, could've helped. She doesn't seem stable."

Yuki checked her phone and saw that she had a dozen missed calls. One of them was from Red Dog.

She called him back.

"Talk to me," he said.

"Giftos has got three character witnesses on deck," she said. "Briana's sister, her boss at the agency, and her ex-boyfriend of about a year prior to her relationship with Marc. They're all going to say she's a fantastic person."

"You still like our chances?"

"What I think is that she's naïve. He's calculating. Whether this rape was her idea or his, she was never an even match for him. As things stand right now, there's enough reasonable doubt to fill a freight train.

"My gut," Yuki said, "tells me that this jury is going to hang."

Parisi said, "My gut says make time to go over your closing argument with me."

"Will do," said Yuki. She welcomed input from Parisi. Because she believed Briana's story, and that worried her.

CHAPTER 81

CONKLIN AND I were at our desks Monday morning when he said to me, "Want to go for a ride?"

I said, "When I say that to Martha, she goes nuts."

Conklin cracked up, then held up some keys.

"Get your leash. We're going on a mystery road trip. I've checked out a squad car."

I'd just returned after a weekend of bed rest that I had truly needed. A hundred e-mails were waiting in my in-box, and I had a million questions for Conklin about our ongoing homicide case. My first cup of java sat untouched and chilling on my desk.

I really needed to work.

I tried to get my partner to tell me what he wanted me to see, but I couldn't budge him. He wouldn't even give me a hint. I finally gave up.

"How long is this going to take?" I asked.

"Trust me. You'll like this. Get up, Boxer."

I threw a big sigh, gulped down half my coffee, pulled on my jacket, and said, "What're we waiting for?"

We took the stairs down to the lobby, left by the

rear door, and speed-walked along the breezeway to Harriet Street, where a standard gray Chevy squad car was parked under the overpass. Conklin took the wheel, and we headed out toward the Mission District.

Over the crackle of the police radio, my partner started to fill me in.

"I spent Friday afternoon at Millie's favorite homeless shelter."

"I take it you learned something useful?" I turned up the heat, turned down the radio.

"I did," Conklin said. "Millie's maiden name was Renee Millicent Cushing. Thirty years ago she married an accountant by the name of Ronald Dunn."

"She's married?" I said. "Jeez. Did anyone notify her husband?"

"He died fifteen years ago of a heart attack. She told us that she has two adult kids—we didn't ask their names. But I have an address."

"For?"

"You shall see," he told me.

We cruised through the gritty commercial section of the Mission, which broke out into the residential community of Eureka Valley. This is an upscale area, lined with the lovely Victorian homes our town is known for.

I was sightseeing as we drove up hilly Collingwood Street, when Conklin pulled the car up to a gray wood-frame house. It was nice, plain, well kept, and it looked like it had been built in the mid-sixties. There was a green Kia in the driveway with a Berkeley sticker in the rear window.

I said, "Who lives here?"

"Used to be Millie Cushing Dunn's house. Yeah. I know what you're going to say. 'She owned a *house*?'"

"And it's a nice house, too."

"Her husband left it to her with a bunch of money, amount unspecified, but enough that she had plenty to spare," said Conklin.

I was impressed. "Nice work, partner."

"Here's the rest of it. According to the administrator at the shelter, Millie was a social worker. She often posed as a homeless person to gain trust, lived on the street three or four days a week, then stepped it up to 24/7."

"Odd way to go about gaining trust, huh?"

"I'd say. Ready, Boxer?"

We got out of the car and walked up to the front door. Conklin rang the bell.

CHAPTER 82

A WOMAN IN her midtwenties opened the door about a foot, enough for us to see that she was barefoot, wearing yoga pants and a loose top. I thought that she looked a little like Millie.

"May I help you?" she asked.

Conklin badged her, introduced us, and asked, "Do you know Millie Cushing?"

The woman said, "I'm her daughter. Sophie Dunn. What's wrong? What happened to my mother?"

Conklin said, "I'm sorry to tell you, but she was shot last week on Mission Street, and unfortunately, she died. It took us this long to find her address. We're very sorry."

"She's *dead*?"

Sophie Dunn spun away from the doorway and cried out, "No, no, no. That can't be right. She can't be dead. She can't be."

The door swung open, and we walked Millie's distraught daughter through the entranceway to a sitting room with a brick fireplace, wall-to-wall bookshelves, and a large window onto a high city view.

She circled the room, still crying out denials.

"This isn't right. I don't believe this. How did this happen?" Then she stopped circling and, with tears streaming down her cheeks, said directly to me, "I always hoped that one day I would have my mother back. Do you understand?"

And then, wiping her face with her sleeve, Sophie Dunn collapsed into a chair.

When we were seated across from her, I told her again how sorry we were, that we had known Millie and why.

I said, "Ms. Dunn, I'm confused as to why your mother was living as though she was homeless."

Sophie got up, paced some more, and eventually got her thoughts and words together enough to confirm what Conklin had learned at the shelter. Millie's street life had begun after her husband's death. By the time Sophie was in her teens, Millie was on the street more than she was home.

"I haven't seen her in over a year," Millie's daughter told us, "but when we last spoke, she seemed *happy*. She liked the people. She would give anyone her last nickel. I can't even imagine who could have anything against her. But as I'm sure you know, a lot of street people have mental illnesses. My mother included."

She went over to the bookshelf and came back to her chair with a framed photo taken in front of this fireplace.

I got a glimpse of a family of four: mom, dad, two kids. Normal as could be.

Conklin asked, "Sophie, did your brother stay in touch with your mom?"

"Michael? He hardly stays in touch with me.

After he moved out, he got married, got divorced, and kind of lives a small, quiet life. Mom wasn't at the wedding. He never mentions her."

"We'll need to speak to him," Rich said.

Sophie began crying again. She apologized, left the room, and returned a minute later with tissues and a Post-it note.

She said, "Here's his number. Good luck getting anywhere with him, though. Michael is a professional introvert."

Sophie asked when she could see her mother. I gave her the information as well as my card, and we said our good-byes.

Conklin called Michael Dunn from the car and got him on the first try.

He agreed to meet us at the Hall.

CHAPTER 83

THREE HOURS AFTER leaving Sophie Dunn, Conklin and I were sitting at a small table in Interview 1 with her older brother, Michael.

Conklin took the lead, and I used the opportunity to look Michael over.

Dunn was about thirty, of medium height and build, with dark hair, a five-o'clock shadow, and his mother's kind hazel eyes. He was wearing office-job attire: a dark-gray sports coat, blue button-down shirt, standard striped tie, gray slacks, and, notably, a wedding band. I wondered about that. Sophie Dunn had said her brother was divorced.

Conklin was telling Dunn where the shooting had taken place and the results of the autopsy. I looked at Millie's son for signs of grief or shock, but Michael was showing very little emotion.

"She put herself in danger," he said, "but why would someone kill her? She was harmless and not confrontational."

"When was the last time you spoke with your mother?" I asked.

"Three years ago maybe? I don't exactly remember. She doesn't carry a phone—or maybe she didn't give me the number. I stopped by the house a few times, but I never caught her at home."

He shook his head.

"She wasn't right in the head after my dad died. She left school, moved back home, but she detached from me, Sophie, the house. For her it was all about being with the homeless."

I said, "That must've felt pretty bad."

He shrugged and then said, "I don't see how I can help you."

I changed my tack. I said, "Your wedding band. Sophie said you were divorced?"

There it was, at last, a flickering, barely there hint of sadness on his face.

He said, "My ex called her 'thoroughly nutty Millie.' Anyway, there's no reason to take the ring off. I like it. I don't like change."

And yet his life had been disrupted by his father's death, his mother's absence, and then a divorce that Michael apparently hadn't accepted as final.

I felt a flash of pity for Michael, and I bought Sophie's view that he was an introvert. But it was odd that he had no curiosity about his mother's death. And the few times he made eye contact, I thought he was trying to get a fix on *me.*

I said, "Mr. Dunn, we're totally in the dark here. Anything you can add, even a guess, would be appreciated. I liked your mother, and I really want to catch her killer."

Dunn twisted the band on his ring finger, calling

my attention to it again. It was pretty nice, white gold with rims of yellow gold.

He said to me, "As I've told you, I don't know her friends, her habits, or anything about what happened to her. I can't even guess." Then he looked away.

I said, "I have to ask, Mr. Dunn, where were you the night your mother was shot?"

"Me? What night was that again? No, it doesn't matter," said Michael Dunn wearily. "I have the same routine every day and every night. I get to work at nine. I do research for the three lawyers at Peavey and Smith Financial Management. I eat lunch at my desk. I leave work at six, come home, nuke dinner, watch TV for a few hours, and then I go to bed after the news. That's my *Groundhog Day* life. It's what I want. No stress. Quiet. Predictable."

And he had a predictable alibi, too. I didn't like that. Something was going on with Michael Dunn that he hadn't told us. Never mind what he said; what did he know?

He looked at his watch and said, "Look. I've got a stack of documents and a needy boss waiting for them. I hope you catch Mom's killer. She was batty, but she didn't deserve to be shot."

He got up from his chair and put on his windbreaker jacket.

"If you catch the guy, let me know, okay?"

Conklin said, "Of course," and walked Michael Dunn out to the elevator. I sat for a moment and stared at the wall.

I thought about Michael Dunn's glancing looks. Like he wanted to study me yet avoid my eyes.

But I had looked at him, and now I was thinking that I'd seen him before.

It would drive me crazy until I figured out when and where.

CHAPTER 84

BACK AT OUR desks, I said to Conklin, "Does Michael Dunn look familiar to you?"

"Reminds me a little of Jimmy Fallon, maybe."

"You think?"

The feeling I was having that I'd seen Dunn before intensified. I kept comparing him in my mind with his sister and mother, but even though they all had hazel eyes, I just didn't feel that was it.

And then something clicked.

I opened the folder on my computer where I'd filed the shots I'd snapped of the crowd behind the tape on that rainy night on Geary Street. I scrutinized all of them before I stabbed my finger at the face of a man who strongly resembled Michael Dunn. Millie had looked startled when I showed these same photos to her. Had she seen her son in that crowd?

"Come over here, Richie."

"Yes, boss."

He came around, looked at where I was pointing.

"Is this Michael?"

The man at the end of a row of bystanders wore a knit cap and a charcoal-gray ski jacket. His right hand was in his pocket, and he was holding an umbrella handle with his gloveless left hand.

Water dripped from the umbrella spokes.

"Could be him, Boxer. The picture is awful grainy, and it's hard to really see his face with that hat pulled down over his eyebrows. But I see what you mean."

I zoomed in on the hand gripping the handle and focused in on the man's wedding ring.

I said to Richie, "You noticed his ring, right?"

"Silver with gold on the edges."

"Correct," I said. "Is this the same ring?"

"It's possible," my partner said. "But with this lighting? The shadows, the headlights, a lot of contrast for a phone shot. I want to look at his face again."

I adjusted the picture on the screen and said, "Well?"

"Let's go to the videotape," Rich said.

He went to his desk, picked up the phone, and tapped in a couple of numbers, saying, "Maybe we'll catch Benny."

Benny is our interview room AV tech, among other roles.

"Benny," Conklin said into the mouthpiece. "This is urgent. I need a still shot of the dude Boxer and I just talked to in Interview 1. Find me the best frontal face shot and a profile if you've got one. You mind? I'll wait."

He hung up and drummed his fingers on the desk.

I knew he and I were both having the same thought. The lab could do a little facial-recognition magic on the two images, compare the Michael

Dunn we'd just interviewed with the unknown man under the umbrella on Geary.

While we waited for Benny, I did a database search for everything related to Michael Dunn. I didn't find much. He had no arrest sheet, no prints on file, not even a traffic violation.

And then I got a hit.

I said, "Holy moly," and rotated my monitor so Rich could read a line of type in the database. Michael Dunn of Union Street, San Francisco, had a registered 9mm Kimber handgun.

"Good catch," said Rich.

"Thanks, bud."

It was a good catch. Michael Dunn had purchased a gun of the same caliber as the one that had killed several homeless people, including Dunn's mother, Millie Cushing.

The lab had kept the bullets taken from the bodies of Jimmy Dolan, Laura Russell, Lou Doe, and Millie Cushing. Ballistics had logged them all as cold hits. All had been fired from the same gun, a gun that had not been used in a crime or otherwise entered into our system.

It wasn't a gotcha—yet. But if the mystery man on Geary Street was our Michael Dunn, and he had a weapon that matched the type that had fired bullets into his mother's body, that would be enough probable cause to arrest him on suspicion of murder.

Had those bullets come from Michael Dunn's Kimber?

We really needed to get his gun.

CHAPTER 85

IT WAS 8:30 A.M. the morning after our interview with Michael Dunn.

Conklin and I sat together in a parked squad car near the intersection of Leidesdorff and Commercial Streets in the Financial District. The Transamerica building was directly behind us, and we were within shouting distance of the red-and-white-brick three-story office building where Dunn worked as a paralegal.

We had confirmation from the lab that the man in our interview room was the same as the one I'd snapped standing across the street from the body of that poor dead woman on Geary.

Michael Dunn hadn't said a word to us about the scene on Geary. Why wouldn't he mention that he'd seen the body, as similar as it was to what he now knew about his mother's death?

We could ask him and hold him as a material witness for forty-eight hours while we got an ADA to get us a search warrant for his apartment.

But neither Rich nor I could bear to sit at our desks while waiting for an ADA to find a judge to sign a warrant. Not while our one suspect, Michael Dunn, was walking around with a gun.

Our plan was simple and entirely legal. We would pick Dunn up and bring him back to the Hall for questioning about the shooting of Lou Doe at 77 Geary.

That would buy a little time, and maybe Dunn would give up information we could use to arrest him for murder.

Dunn had told us that he was a creature of habit. Every morning he got to his office by nine, he spent his day doing legal research, and at the close of business he went home. What he'd called his "*Groundhog Day* life."

I hoped today would be just another Groundhog Day for Michael Dunn.

I turned the police radio down to a hiss and watched the early-morning traffic on Leidesdorff, a charming street a few blocks from Sydney G. Walton Square, eight or nine blocks from both 77 Geary and the spot on Mission Street where Millie Cushing had been gunned down a week ago.

It had been very loud on Mission after Millie died. I remembered every minute of that night with high-definition clarity. I had stood there in the fog, surrounded by flashing red and blue lights, with the shrieks of law enforcement vehicle sirens speeding toward the murder scene from all points.

If he was strolling around the area at that time, Michael could have seen the light show. Hell, he could have called dispatch himself.

CHAPTER 86

I FELT THE adrenaline rush before my brain made the connection.

Michael Dunn was walking toward his office building right on time.

I said to Richie, "There. See him?"

The man who more or less resembled Jimmy Fallon was passing the intersection at Commercial Street, heading toward us on Leidesdorff in the direction of the three-story building where he worked nine to six, five days a week.

He wore a knit cap over his brow, and both hands were shoved into the pockets of his windbreaker. He looked straight ahead and passed our backup team without noticing them.

I grabbed the radio mike and said to Nardone, "Bob. Suspect is on foot walking north on Leidesdorff, just passed you, wearing a black jacket, black knit hat."

"Copy that," Nardone said.

"Stay in your car until I need you."

Conklin and I got out of the squad car and walked toward Dunn, stopping him on the sidewalk.

I said, "Mr. Dunn. Glad we found you. We need to ask you some more questions."

"I have a meeting at nine fifteen," he said. "Why don't I get back to you?"

He started to walk past us, but Conklin put out a hand to block his passage.

"I'm sorry, Mr. Dunn," Conklin said. "This is very important. We have some photos to show you, and we need you to help us clear up a few questions. Has to be right now. This just can't wait."

"Am I under arrest?"

"Why would you ask that?" I asked.

"Because you're coming at me like I'm a suspect."

"Mr. Dunn. Michael," I said. "We need your help. The longer it takes to find whoever shot your mother, the greater the likelihood that the case will go cold or that the shooter will kill someone else."

Dunn planted his feet, and from the rage on his face, I thought he was going to punch me or run.

"Get away from me," he said. "Get the hell away from me."

There was a blur as his arm shot out and connected with my shoulder. The shock of the blow knocked me off balance. I staggered back but managed to keep my footing.

I unclipped my cuffs from my belt and shouted, "Put your hands behind your back. Michael Dunn, you're under arrest for assaulting a police officer."

Dunn switched his eyes to the cuffs and started babbling at me. He made no sense. I didn't know what he was thinking or saying, but one thing I did know. The gun that I wanted so badly?

It was in his hand and it was pointed at me.

I rushed him and yelled, "GUN!"

CHAPTER 87

CARS WERE SPEEDING past him—Michael heard them—but his vision was breaking into choppy split seconds, like old-fashioned film caught in the cogs of a projector.

One moment the cop called Boxer was coming at him. He hated her. She was just like his mother. She should be punished, so no one would have to suffer like he had.

But the other cop was blocking his way.

Get away from me. Get away.

He gave her a shove as he clasped the butt of his beloved gun.

Everything became blurred in his mind. *Mother. Why? Why don't you love me?*

She was coming back at him, so he aimed at her.

She shouted, "GUN!"—and he squeezed the trigger. He felt the shock in his hand travel up to his shoulder and ring the bell of his heart. Her partner came toward him with his gun out, shouting, "Drop the gun!"

Michael laughed and fired again. Brakes squealed. The shot rang out, metal against metal. His thoughts were fleeting images. His mother.

Why don't you love me? Why didn't you love me?

He was down on his back. Someone stepped on his hand. His gun spun away. He rolled and reached for it. He couldn't. Quite. Get it.

Mom. Where are you now?

Loud words came at him. He didn't understand. Faces were huge in front of his eyes. His cheek was against the pavement. Someone shouted his name. A kick landed on the side of his head. Another in his gut. His wrists were clamped and pinched behind him. He was dragged up to his feet. He saw someone he knew.

Roger Duncan. The boss.

He heard Duncan say, "Hey. What's going on here?"

Michael called out, "I did it, Roger. I killed my mother. I don't need a lawyer."

His true self was coming out. He had never felt so free, so alive. There was a hand on his head. Pushing him down. *You bitch. You've always been a bitch.* He said it to HER. *Motherrrrr.*

A car door slammed.

Duncan knocked on the window, his face as big as the moon, saying in a muffled voice, "Michael. I'll meet you at booking. Don't say anything to anyone."

He was living in real time, with real sound and images. Michael saw it all clearly now. He said, "It's okay, Duncan. I killed my mother. I shot them all."

Michael was thrown back against the seat. He welcomed it. He started to hum a song about a puppy with a waggly tail.

He was free at last. Life was good.

PART THREE

CHAPTER 88

I WAS AT my desk in the squad room when I opened the little shopping bag and took out the note and the foil-wrapped packet.

Conklin was putting on his windbreaker. He said, "Cappy and I are running across the street for lunch. Come with us."

"Rain check," I said.

"Prime rib special. All you can eat. Seven bucks."

I peeled back the aluminum foil and peeked between the slices of bread. Meat loaf. The note read, "Eat. Love, Joe."

That was priceless.

When I had come home last night, Joe had taken one look at me, hugged me, pulled off my outerwear and gun, and sat me down. Then he pulled off my shoes and poured me a drink.

"Talk to me," he said.

Once I started talking, I couldn't stop. Joe listened to every word about the Michael Dunn takedown that morning: His discombobulated name-calling as I confronted him. The wild shots

he'd fired, one of which put a new part in Sergeant
Nardone's scalp. And his confession to everything
but the Kennedy assassination as we locked him in
the squad car.

"Dunn is in a cell by himself, under close guard,
pending his arraignment," I concluded. "People on
the street can breathe a little more easily tonight.
Me, too."

Joe dished up the meat loaf and fixings, and as
I ate, he told me about his Mr. Mom day: ducks in
the park; Julie's new word, *panda;* a playdate for
Martha. And a haircut for him that I admired. I
got up from the table to run my fingers through the
thick new growth of hair that hid the long, bumpy
scar at the back of his head.

"Good haircut," I said.

"It's for my interview," he said.

Even as Joe was excited at the prospect of getting back to work himself, I knew some part of him
wanted me to take a desk job, have another baby,
stop mixing it up with crazy people with guns.

I'd tried to imagine it, but the picture just
wouldn't gel.

That night I ate dinner with two glasses of a
nice Chianti. I slept without moving all night, like
a rock or a log or a candle that had been burned at
both ends.

Now, at my desk, I saw that the meat loaf Joe
had made with loving hands was making an en-
core.

"I'm in brown-bag mode," I said to my partner.
"Thanks anyway."

As Conklin made his exit, he passed Yuki coming through the gate. Normally tightly wrapped

and focused, she looked frazzled. She pulled out Conklin's now-empty desk chair and dropped into the seat.

"Brady's in a meeting upstairs," I told her.

"I know," Yuki said. "I came to see you."

CHAPTER 89

"EXCELLENT TIMING," I said to Yuki. "I'm lunching at my desk. What's going on?"

Yuki ran her hands through her hair and gladly accepted half of my sandwich.

Then she said, "My case is going sideways, Linds. I'm starting to think that my star witness is a big fat liar. If that's true, the whole case against Briana Hill might be a lie, and if so, I have to jam on the brakes, and I mean right now."

"Back up a little," I said. "What lies are you talking about?"

Yuki leaned across Conklin's desk and spilled her fears: that Marc had added fabricated details to his original story of the assault while he was under oath.

"But then it got worse," Yuki said. "James Giftos turned up some old phone messages from Marc to Briana that sounded like he could have been *blackmailing* her."

"*Really?* You're serious?"

Yuki went on, saying, "Lindsay, do you remember what I told you about Paul Yates?"

I said, "He's the one that had a bedroom encounter with Briana Hill and claimed that she threatened him with a gun."

"Right. Not quite a corroboration, but Yates's testimony of attempted rape with a gun validated Marc's story. Now I'm questioning Yates's story, too," Yuki said. "I want to talk with him again, drill down hard on his story, and either debunk it or settle down the questions in my mind."

"Sounds right."

Yuki said, "I've called Paul at home and at work. I've left messages and I've texted him, but he hasn't gotten back to me. Why not? So before I turn nothing into something, can you run Marc Christopher and Paul Yates through NCIC for me? Both of them."

I said, "Yeats like the poet?"

"Y-a-t-e-s," she said. "Paul G."

I accessed NCIC, the FBI's National Crime Information Center, and typed in *Marc Christopher*. It took only a few minutes to assure myself that Marc Christopher wasn't in it. He was clean.

"I've found nothing on Marc," I told Yuki.

"Okay. Good," she said. She got to work on the meat loaf on rye.

I typed in *Paul G. Yates* and let the software run. I was about to say, "Nothing on him, either," when *Paul Gentry Yates* popped up in the Supervised Release file. It was an arrest sheet from ten years ago, when Paul Yates was a college kid of nineteen.

"Yuki. I found something you're going to want to see."

I pressed keys and the printer chugged out the

arrest report. I wheeled my chair around, took the report out of the tray, and handed it to Yuki.

She read it, then looked up at me with shock on her face. "I've got to get this to Red Dog," she said. "Fast."

CHAPTER 90

YUKI SHOVED HER chair back from Conklin's desk and ran, calling back to Lindsay, "I have to be back in court in thirty minutes."

Lindsay yelled, "Good luck," as Yuki made for the fire exit and ran down one flight to the third floor.

It was a short dash along the corridor to Parisi's office.

The DA was in a closed-door meeting, but Yuki couldn't wait and Len wouldn't want her to. She announced to his gatekeeper, "It's urgent," and, without waiting for a reply, swept past Toni's desk and barged into her boss's office, announcing, "I've got to speak with you right now."

Parisi told the two men in his office to hang on a minute, stepped out into the corridor, and asked Yuki what was wrong.

"Paul Yates," she said. "He tried to extort a professor when he was in college."

"And? Where does that go?" Parisi asked.

"Okay," Yuki said. "Ten years ago, when he was at UCLA, Yates threatened to expose his sociology professor for using inappropriate language unless he gave him a passing grade. The professor addressed it head-on and took it to the dean, who called the cops. Yates was arrested. Judge gave him a year of probation, and Yates was kicked out of school."

The spur of the hallway outside Len's office was starting to fill up. Yuki turned her back and continued.

"Len, I would never have believed Paul Yates was capable of extortion. He's…timid."

Len said, "It's a red flag, I agree, but it doesn't mean that he perjured himself against Hill."

"I'm connecting the dots this way," Yuki said. "Paul knows Marc and he tells him about his UCLA escapade. Briana has testified that she was starting to lose interest and Marc got the message. He feels aggrieved and also greedy. Paul's extortion gives him an idea. So he sets Briana up and tries to blackmail her. Hill tells him to bug off."

Parisi said, "So now Marc is mad."

"Correct. He's warned her and she's not going for it, so it's time to make her 'pay up.' Marc takes the sex video to the cops. He's emotional. He's got faded ligature marks on his wrists and ankles. He's got a *video*. Of course they buy it, and so do we. We charge Briana."

"Theoretically."

"Len, my theory that Marc and Paul colluded is speculative. This thought occurred to me when Marc told his new and improved story on the stand. Were old memories just coming to him? Or was he lying? And if he was lying, I have to ask. Is his whole story a lie?"

Len looked perturbed, but he was hanging in with her.

Yuki said, "In sum, we've got a witness with a history of extortion. I can't prove that Marc was untruthful, but I'm questioning his veracity. As for the defendant, her testimony was heartbreaking."

"Heartbreaking as in good acting? Or heartbreaking, she's been framed?"

Yuki shrugged. "I'm on the fence. I want some evidence before we ditch."

The prosecution had a legal obligation to withdraw charges if the case against Briana Hill was wrong. If Yuki proceeded without confidence in the defendant's guilt, she could get disbarred.

She said, "I need to talk to Yates again. If he changes his story, says he made up what he said happened between him and Briana, I'll go back to Marc and squeeze him until he yelps.

"Can you ask Rathburn for a continuance?"

"I'll give it a shot," Len said.

Parisi used Toni's desk phone and called Judge Rathburn. In twenty-five words or less he explained the new situation to the judge, who agreed to recess court until tomorrow morning.

"It's a gift," Parisi said to Yuki. "Make the most of it."

CHAPTER 91

AS YUKI HEADED toward her office, she phoned Arthur and left him a message, updating him on the situation, including that court was adjourned until morning. She had just gotten back to her desk when her phone rang.

She said into the mouthpiece, "Art?"

"It's Cindy."

There were very few people Yuki would be willing to talk to in the middle of this mess, but Cindy was on the short list.

Yuki said, "I'm kinda in a rush."

Cindy said, "Me, too. Did you hear?"

"Maybe not," said Yuki. "Tell me."

"This is a girlfriend-to-girlfriend heads-up," Cindy said. "I got it off the police scanner and I made a couple of follow-up calls to confirm. Paul Yates. He's your witness, right?"

"Right. What about him?"

"He committed suicide this morning. He hanged himself."

Yuki sat down hard behind her desk.

"Noooo. That can't be true."

Cindy assured her that her sources were good.

"I'm posting a cloaked version of this story to my crime blog in about ten minutes," Cindy said. "Claire should have Yates's body by now, so talk to her."

Yuki sat for a moment, trying to put this news flash in the context of her meeting with Parisi and her past meetings with Yates, and to consider the impact of his death on her case, which was coming apart at high speed, the wheels flying off and littering the roadway.

Cindy said, "Yuki? Yuki?"

"I'm here. I'm just stunned, that's all. Thanks, Cindy."

Yuki hung up with Cindy, phoned Claire's office, and was told that Claire wasn't available. She asked to speak with Claire's lab assistant, Bunny Ellis. After several crazy-making minutes of '80s Muzak, Bunny got on the line.

"Bunny. This is ADA Castellano. Do you have the body of Paul Yates?"

"Uh-huh. Claire's with him now."

Yuki had to know for sure. Was Paul's death a homicide, a suicide, an accident, or undetermined? She said to Bunny, "He was a witness in my case. How long before we have a determination in manner and cause of death?"

"I'll have Claire call you, okay?"

"*Wait.* Bunny, do you have the name of the officer or officers who called it in?"

Once Yuki had the names of the first officers, she called Lindsay and asked her to look up the report.

"Okay. I've got the file," said Lindsay. "What it says is that Paul Yates was found dead in his apartment this morning by his girlfriend, who was worried when he didn't answer his phone. He used a clothesline tied to his bedroom doorknob, strung over the top of the door, knotted around his neck. It's written up as an apparent suicide."

Yuki texted Parisi and then called Arthur again. After she briefed him, he asked, "What do we do now?"

"I want to speak with Marc Christopher."

"How can I help?"

"Go to the ME's office and wait for Yates's death certificate. I'll leave word that you're there."

CHAPTER 92

SOMETHING WAS HAPPENING to me that I didn't understand.

I was swimming in darkness, surrounded by garbled voices. I was both numb and cold, and my head hurt.

Is this a really bad dream?

Hands plucked at me. Someone slapped my cheek. I wanted to sink back into the swirl of underwater, but consciousness intruded. Whatever was happening was too real to be a dream.

I opened my eyes.

A patch of the floor came into focus and I recognized the pattern of the ceramic tiles. A row of half doors filled my peripheral view. And then there were the shoes. Pale-colored shoes with sponge soles. Red ballet flats. I knew then that I was in the ladies' room at the end of the hall from the squad room. I was lying half under a sink, but I didn't remember coming here.

Brenda, our PA, yelled into my face. Her expression scared me.

"Lindsay, can you hear me?" she shouted. "What the heck happened?"

She was terrified. Had I been shot?

I said, "I don't know." That was the whole truth and nothing but.

I wasn't ready to move, but I lifted my head and tried to make sense of the clamor. Paramedics had crammed into the small bathroom and were attempting to lift me onto a stretcher. I fought back. What had happened to me?

A man stooped down. His name was stitched above his pocket: A. MURPHY.

"I'm Andy," he told me. "Can you remember what happened to you?" He had other questions, and I tried to answer them.

"In the ladies' room....Lindsay Boxer....Two fingers....Wednesday....George Washington.... I'm fine."

"I'll be the judge of that, Lindsay. Now tell me the last thing you remember."

This was the second time I said this and it was still the truth. "I don't know what happened."

Another paramedic pricked my finger. Someone put a stethoscope to my chest. Andy shined a light into one eye, then the other.

"That's good, Lindsay," he said.

Fingers pressed across my wrist as Andy asked me more questions about my health—history of heart disease, previous episodes of blacking out, name of GP, last time I'd had a checkup. I struggled to sit up. I had pain in my shoulder and my forehead.

"I remember now. I came in here to wash my hands before having lunch. I must have passed out."

Andy said, "That sounds right. Syncope. Your blood glucose is about normal. Your blood pressure is within normal range," and he asked me to help him out by getting onto the stretcher. There was no way they could carry me out the narrow doorway on that thing.

My strength was coming back and so was my mind. I was feeling madder.

I said, "I'm fine, Andy. Please let me up. I've fainted once or twice before when I haven't eaten. I haven't eaten today. I've been busy. Look. Will someone just help me the fuck up?"

Hands went under my armpits. I was hoisted onto my feet. I felt woozy, but with the support of strong hands and a counter of sinks, I stood steady as a rock.

"I'm okay, see?"

Andy Murphy said, "There's a pretty big knot coming up on your forehead. Emergency docs should check you out at Metro, give you a CT scan. If you were my sister, I'd insist on that. It's the right thing to do, Lindsay."

"Thanks. No. I'll call my husband. He'll drive me home."

"We can't make you come with us, but you do have to sign this," said the paramedic, handing me a release. I signed it with a flourish. I thanked everyone. Brenda walked with me to my desk and I called Joe. I was scared, but I tried not to let him hear the throbbing freak-out in my voice.

I still hadn't made an appointment to see Dr. Glenn Arpino, but I had to do it. I couldn't justify putting it off any longer. Problem was, I was pretty sure that I now knew what was wrong with me.

It was a terrifying thought, and I couldn't bear it. So I shoved it to the back burner.

I would deal with it tomorrow.

CHAPTER 93

YUKI WATCHED MARC Christopher squirm in one of the two metal-frame chairs across from her desk.

He leaned his crutch against the second chair. She moved her lamp a few inches, placed her phone where Marc could see it, and pressed Record.

"I'm recording our meeting."

"Why?"

"You have a problem speaking on the record, Marc?"

"I guess not. But why do you want to do it?"

"I want to ask you some questions about Paul Yates," Yuki said. "I've seen his death certificate. It's official. Suicide by hanging. Do you have any idea why he killed himself?"

Marc's defiance withered, and it looked like tears were about to spring out of his eyes. Yuki really didn't care.

Marc cleared his throat a couple of times and said, "I just heard. It's horrible. I haven't spoken with Paul since, I don't know. A week. I don't know what to say."

Yuki asked him again. "Marc. Do you have any thoughts why he would have hanged himself?"

"You're asking if it's about what happened during the trial?"

Yuki didn't answer, just kept her eyes on Marc.

Marc said, "Maybe you're right. Oh, man. He's a pretty sensitive guy. Was. I shouldn't have even told you about him. You would never have even heard his name if it weren't for me. Oh, my God. I don't know what to do or say. I want it all to stop."

"Did you know that when Paul was in college, he was arrested for trying to blackmail a professor?"

Marc looked at her as if she were pointing a gun at him.

He said, "No. Of course not."

Yuki slapped her desk. "*Stop lying* to me."

He recoiled, then said, "Okay, okay, Paul told me about what he did in college. I don't see what that has to do with anything. It was harmless. Look. Yuki. I want you to drop the charges against Briana. This has gotten out of hand. Can we just draw this whole thing to a close?"

"Drop the charges? You mean I should tell the judge what, Marc? The prosecution changed its mind?"

"Can you do that?"

"Tell me what happened with you, Paul, and Briana," she said.

"What more is there to tell?" he asked her.

"Plenty. Feel free to fill in the blanks."

Yuki took a sheet of paper out of a folder on her desk and flashed it at Marc.

"This is Paul's suicide note."

"*No.* Please. Please don't read it to me."

"I'll skip around," Yuki said. "Paul said that he's sorry. He didn't mean to lie about Briana. He wishes he'd never met you, Marc. He wishes he'd aimed higher when he shot you, at your request."

Marc was saying, "Oh, God. Oh, God," and crying now, hands over his eyes. Compared with the tears he had shed on the witness stand, this was a very ugly cry.

Yuki went on. "Here's a quote: 'Please tell Briana I know what I did was wrong and I am more sorry than she can ever know or believe for hurting her. I hope one day she can forgive me.' That's about it, Marc. And he wrote an apology to his girlfriend and his parents for taking his life."

She gave the criminal liar sitting across from her direct eye contact. "Marc. Was this accusation that Briana Hill raped you a lie?"

He nodded.

"Speak up, Marc. Is that a yes?" Yuki asked.

"Yes. It was what she said it was. A game."

"You and Paul cooked this up together? To frame her for rape and blackmail her?"

"It was my idea," Marc said, his voice just barely audible. "Paul helped me."

"Helped you plan?" Yuki asked.

"Yes."

"And he shot you?"

"I asked him to do it."

"But you were going to cut him in?"

"Yes to all of that," Marc told Yuki. He looked broken, and Yuki felt that he was finally telling the truth.

"Why, Marc? Why did you do this?"

He grabbed the arms of the chair and lunged toward her, shouting, "Can't you see what a ball-buster she is?"

There it was—his anger and his venom. His dark side that he'd used to bring down Briana Hill. It would now fuel his own reversal of fortune.

Yuki drew back and said, "Oh, my God."

Marc sagged in the chair. His voice was breaking when he asked, "What's going to happen to me?"

"I'll let you know. Stay here."

Marc said, "I'm going to be sick."

"That makes two of us."

Yuki reached under her desk, pulled out the trash can, and walked it over to where Marc was slumped over his knees. She handed him the wastebasket and said, "You're despicable."

She picked her phone up off the desk, left the room, and walked down the hall to Red Dog's office.

He was waiting for her.

CHAPTER 94

YUKI PARKED HER car on Clayton Street in front of the pretty, shingled condo building where Briana Hill lived.

She grabbed her car keys and stepped out onto the tree-shaded residential block, walked up stone steps and under a trellis. She paused for a moment, checking her anxiety level, and then rang the doorbell.

She heard footsteps, the click of the peephole, followed by the clack of the lock. And there was Briana in her pink-and-blue-striped pajamas, smelling of liquor at three in the afternoon.

"What are you doing here?" Briana asked her.

"Hi, Briana. May I come in?"

"I can't speak with you without my lawyer present. You know that."

"Mr. Giftos is with DA Parisi right now," Yuki told her. "He knows that I'm here and he knows why. It's okay with him, but of course you should call him if you like."

Briana stepped back and let Yuki in.

The place was a mess—clothes tossed on the furniture, coffee cups and bowls of half-eaten cereal on tables and counters, dried-out potted palms. An open bottle of vodka was centered on the coffee table.

Briana threw herself into a basket chair. Yuki sat on the edge of a facing sectional.

Briana said, "So, why are you here?"

"I've got good news and bad news."

"For God's sake. What next? A knock-knock joke?"

Yuki could do nothing but press on.

"Paul Yates committed suicide, Briana. His body was found this morning."

Briana's expression was one of sheer disbelief. She shouted, "No way. Paul is dead? Why? Why did that creep kill himself?"

"According to his suicide note, it's because he regretted what he'd done to you."

Briana got up and paced around the room. When she had completed the circuit, she came back to Yuki and said, "Bad news and good news, you said?"

"The DA is dropping the case against you. It's over."

"*Are you serious?*"

"Absolutely," Yuki said.

Briana said, "You're *dropping* the case? I'm free?"

"That's right."

"Oh, my God. Oh, my God. I might have a heart attack."

Briana's phone rang from under a throw blanket on the couch. She found it, looked at the caller ID, said, "Mom? I can't talk. The DA is here.... Yes. In my fucking apartment."

Briana clicked off the call and said to Yuki, "I'll be right back."

She went down the hallway and into another room out of Yuki's view, but Yuki heard the door slam closed.

Right after that Yuki heard Briana screaming a loud, wordless howl, then came cursing, more screaming.

There was the sound of running water.

A moment later Briana came back into the living room with a towel around her neck, hair dripping, like she had put her head under the faucet.

She dropped back into the basket chair and said, "Okay, Yuki. Tell me everything. The good, the bad, the ugly, and any other damned thing you've got."

CHAPTER 95

YUKI PRESSED ON, past her own tremendous discomfort in the face of the shock Briana was clearly feeling.

She folded her hands in her lap and told Briana about confronting Marc with Paul Yates's suicide note, and the subsequent confession from Marc two hours ago.

"He committed crimes against you and he manipulated the justice system. We're working up charges against him now," Yuki told her. "Extortion, perjury, criminal libel, and maybe a few other things we can throw at him once we get his signed confession."

Briana shot out of her chair, lit up all over again. She stood over Yuki and shouted, "Throw *everything* at him. Do not spare him. Do you know what that *maniac* has done to me? He's wrecked my career, my reputation. Even my friends have lost faith in me. I can't leave the house without people taking pictures of me. Pointing. 'She raped that cute guy. She had a gun.'

"My privacy is gone. My dignity—destroyed. My poor mother, a proud woman, is now an object of pity."

Briana clambered back into the basket chair. She scowled, curled up, and hugged her knees, her face radiating hurt and anger. She turned her head and pinned Yuki with a hard glare.

"Do you understand? Marc took everything from me. I want to write hate mail to him in jail."

Yuki said, "Briana, I do understand. I feel terrible. Please, hear me out. I came to tell you that I'm sorry for my part in what you've had to go through."

"Oh. You're *sorry*. Thanks."

"I believed Marc," said Yuki. "The police believed Marc. His story was convincing, and if he'd been raped, as our office believed, he would have needed justice. I thought other male victims of rape would also be vindicated once this crime was exposed."

"You mean *I* had to be exposed."

"Not exactly. I'm a prosecutor. My intention was to prosecute a rapist. Briana, I only started to suspect Marc when he testified. Even then I thought he was making up things to make himself look better, not that the whole story was a complete fabrication."

Briana said, "Am I getting this right? Did Marc and Paul *collude* in this disgusting scam?"

"Yes," Yuki said. "Marc admitted it was his idea and Paul helped him. Paul apologized to you in his suicide note."

Briana scoffed, shook her head. "Sick. Both of them. I really don't have words."

She put her feet on the floor, grabbed the Stoli from the table, put the mouth of the bottle up to her lips, then stopped. She offered the bottle to Yuki.

"Can't," Yuki said, "I'm driving."

"Okay," Briana said. She took a few slugs of vodka and sighed loudly.

When she turned back to Yuki, her expression had softened.

She said, "You don't have to justify yourself, Yuki. You were doing your job. I respect that. I never felt that you were attacking me personally. I didn't think you were mean. If you want my forgiveness, you've got it."

"I do," said Yuki. "Thank you very much."

"If Paul hadn't pulled the plug, do you think you would have won?"

Yuki shrugged. "You never know with juries."

Briana said, "That horrible video. What a piece of work." She held out the bottle to Yuki. "You're sure?"

Yuki took the bottle, tipped it up, swallowed twice, and handed the bottle back. "That's my limit," she said.

Briana smiled. "So, what happens next?"

"You'll be hearing from James any minute now. He'll have a plan."

"That's good. Jesus. I still can't believe this. Talk about having your entire life turned inside out and then outside in. I've got to call my mom."

The two women stood up and walked to the front door. Briana said, "Thanks for coming. Really."

"Thank *you,* Briana."

Spontaneously they embraced and held each other for a good long minute in the doorway.

Then Yuki left the apartment and walked out to her car. When she was sitting behind the wheel, she called Parisi.

"How'd it go?" he asked.

"I told Briana that I was sorry. She forgave me. We both know that she'll never really get over this. It's sad."

Yuki knew that Len hadn't believed in this case, but he had believed in her. And she had absolutely misjudged Marc Christopher. *She* was never going to get over *that*.

Len said, "You know what the great pitcher Satchel Paige once said?"

"Tell me. I'm ready," she said.

"'You win a few, you lose a few. Some are rained out. But you got to dress for all of them.' That's what you do and have always done. You dress for all of them. This is what rain feels like."

"Thank you, Len. I appreciate that."

"See you in the morning, Yuki."

CHAPTER 96

THEIR APARTMENT WAS empty when Yuki came through the door.

No surprise. It was still early. She thought of calling Brady but didn't want him to blow her off. *I'm tied up here. Can I call you right back?*

She kicked off her heels and dropped into her favorite chair. She called Arthur, Cindy, Lindsay, and Claire, then she turned off the ringer on her phone.

She wasn't hungry or tired, so she took a bath, refilling the tub with hot water and bubble bath until she was finally just done.

She dried off with the plushest towel she owned, pulled on a white cotton nightgown with buttons at the neckline and a sprinkling of lace at the hem, and got into bed. It was almost seven o'clock.

She woke up to a weight at the side of the bed. Brady. He put his hand on her shoulder and said, "Darlin', are you sick?"

"I'm wrung out. Unbelievable day. What time is it?" she asked.

"Eleven fifteen, something like that."

"Oh, man," Yuki said, "I only meant to take a nap."

"You need anything? Hot dogs? Ice cream?"

She smiled at him in the dark. "No. I'm good," she said.

She heard Brady unbuckling his belt, throwing clothes over a chair, saying he was "gonna hose off the day." When he came back, naked and damp, he said, "Scooch over a few," and got under the covers. He took Yuki into his arms.

"You smell good," he said.

"I soaked for an hour in lemongrass and citrus. I have to do that more often."

Brady said, "I heard a rumor that your case collapsed. Lindsay told me. Don't be mad at her."

"It's okay. I was going to call you but figured I'd catch you in the middle of something."

"I deserve that. But you know how it is."

"Not really, Brady."

She pushed away from him, creating a foot of distance between them. "I don't know. So why don't you fuckin' tell me?"

"I will. You go first," he said. "Your case. What happened? Are you going to be all right with it?"

"Nope, no way, no chance. I've reached the end of my patience, Brady. Tell me what's going on with you or hit the couch until further notice."

He rolled onto his back, thumped the pillows into his desired support level, and said, "I'm sorry, Yuki. I couldn't tell you anything. I was under a mayor-mandated Chinese wall. Politics played a part in this. And the immediate future of my job and the direction of the SFPD are under scrutiny, and have been for the last three months."

He turned to face her. "You understand where I'm going?"

"Not at all," she said. "I lost my decoder ring."

"Ice cream," he said. "If I'm going to break my solemn oath to the brass, I'm doing it while eating butter pecan."

CHAPTER 97

BRADY ROLLED OUT of bed, and Yuki's mood dramatically shifted, from fear of a broken marriage to alarm for her husband.

What could have affected his job as well as the entire police department?

Was Brady in trouble? Had he gotten embroiled in some kind of scandal? Was he being tried by the deep state of Internal Affairs? Beyond that, she just couldn't imagine.

Brady returned to their bedroom with a bowl of ice cream, handed her one of the two spoons, and got under the covers.

Yuki gripped his forearm with her free hand. "What's going on?" she asked.

"Okay," he sighed. "Here it is. The whole ugly mess. Remember last year when a half dozen cops in Robbery disgraced the department?"

"Sure," Yuki said. "A gang of them were holding up check-cashing places and Western Union outlets."

"That's right. Citizens were killed, bunch of them. And while these dirtbags were robbing cash stores, they also robbed a major drug kingpin's distribution depot."

"Kingfisher. I remember all of it, but how does this figure into your job?"

"It figures into Jacobi's job."

"Jacobi?"

"That Robbery crew was a scandal. God punished most of them, but that's really not enough. Someone in the hierarchy of the SFPD has to take the fall for a division full of corrupt cops. Head of the crew is locked up for life. Head of Robbery was let go, but that's not really enough."

"So you're saying that this is going to fall on the chief?"

Brady said, "He's not going to be *officially* blamed, but he's going to be retired out. And everyone in the department will know why."

He pushed ice cream around with his spoon. Then he said, "I had to testify about all those bodies at the OK Corral. Made me sick to have to talk about that, knowing I was making the case against Jacobi. I really love the guy."

"What does he know?"

"He knows it all. Every day, after the day shift punched out, I'd go up to his office," Brady told her. "We'd talk about every case in all the squads, go over personnel, and discuss plans for how things are going to go forward. He wants me to take his job."

"He wants you to take over as chief of police?"

"He doesn't get a vote. He can make a recommendation, maybe."

Yuki felt closer to her husband than she had in months, and she even understood how badly he'd been feeling, how overworked, the weight he'd been carrying. What her hurt and anger hadn't allowed her to see before. And she understood finally that Brady's distance didn't have to do with her. With them. And why he had had to keep it to himself.

Their arms were tightly around each other. There was no distance between them now.

"How is he taking this?" she asked.

"He says he wants to retire, but I'm sure this isn't how he wants to do it."

Yuki asked, "Brady, if they put you up for the job, will you take it?"

"I don't know, darlin'. I like the job I have. But who would come in as chief? Levant? Or some new sheriff comes into town. That would be a game changer. I'm standing in for Jacobi while they figure out who's going to replace him."

"Starting when?"

"Any minute. Could be tomorrow or next week at the latest. Hon?"

"Uh-huh."

"I'm sorry," he said. "I'm sorry I've been so out of it. I've been working two jobs and depressed beyond belief. I've been dying to talk to you."

She said, "It's okay, love. I understand now. I feel so bad for what you've been going through."

After Brady put the bowl on the floor, Yuki reached her arms up and put them around her husband's neck.

He held her close, kissing her deeply, then pulled away to fumble with the little buttons at the collar of her nightgown. When the buttons frustrated him, he pulled the slip of cotton up to her waist. She put her hands between his legs.

Brady's breathing was loud in her ears and she

was burning up when he said, "Are you going to tell me about your day?"

"No, and you can't make me."

He grinned at her as he tugged off her panties and said, "I could just eat you up."

"Say please."

He laughed and said, "Please, please, please, baby, please." He pulled her legs over his hips, telling her how much he missed her and loved her.

Their lovemaking was fierce and touching. It brought Yuki all the way back from anger and fear and grief to the only man she had ever really loved. She felt, as she always did in his arms, protected and adored. Connecting with Brady sent her to a place where she didn't have to be in control. She could just let go.

She hoped he felt as she did—loved, understood, and safe. She was surprised when they were lying together in the afterglow and Brady began to cry in her arms.

CHAPTER 98

IT WAS THE day after my dramatic and embarrassing faint in the ladies' room, and I was feeling pretty good. So I called a meeting of the Women's Murder Club.

I was so glad everyone was available, because I truly needed an evening out with my best buds.

Susie's Café is a mad scene on the weekend, filled with regulars and tourists and passersby drawn in by the smell of curry coming through the vents, the rhythmic plink of the steel drums, the bright-ocher walls, and the jollity seen through the windows.

But tonight, a Thursday, Susie's was only half filled. There were a dozen locals at the long bar, the vacant barstools like missing teeth in an otherwise broad smile, and there was a smattering of diners in the main room. And no drums.

I waved at Lorraine and took the short walk down the corridor past the take-out window to the back room. I was last to arrive at our table.

Cindy stood up to let me into the booth, putting a steadying hand around my arm as I edged in, asking me if I was okay.

"I need a drink," I said.

"Hear, hear," said Claire. Her hand was in the air, and Lorraine materialized with a glass for me and a refill on the pitcher of brew.

"What'd I miss?" I asked the girls.

Claire said, "I was just talking about my little one."

"Keep talking," I said. Ruby Rose was four, a child with a big personality.

"We were at Target," Claire said. "I am looking for new soft-tread shoes, and Rosie is right next to me. Then she's not. I start screaming, 'Rosie, Rosie, Rosie!' I'm picturing the posters on the telephone poles, and I am well on my way to pure freaking panic.

"Then, there she is. I see her one aisle over. Rosie has seen a dress she just has to have. She has pulled off aaaall her clothes in the middle of the store except for panties that say 'Momma's Girl.'"

"There's a big relief," I said, feeling it. Julie is younger than Rosie, but she has shown potential to live up to a frightening public display like that one.

Claire went on.

"I say, 'Rosie, no. You can't get naked in public.'

"She says, 'God likes naked kids.' I say, 'Please, Rosie. Put your clothes on, please.'

"She says, *loud,* so everyone in the whole store can hear, 'Mom, how many times do I have to tell you. *I hate it when you beg.*'"

Yuki's infectious peal of laughter carried across the back room, and we all were swept up in it when Lorraine appeared and said, "Sorry to interrupt, but we're about to run out of shrimp."

When our orders were on the way to the

kitchen, I said to Yuki, "Spill, girlfriend. Last I heard, the DA dropped the charges against Briana Hill."

She said, "That's correct. And for the cherry on top, the Ad Shop is giving Briana her old job back."

A chorus of "Yahoo"s and "Thank God"s rose up around the table, and Yuki said, "I'll drink to that."

We all did. And then Claire turned to me and asked, "How're you doing, Linds? What did the doctor say?"

"Nothing just yet. Dr. Arpino gave me a hell of a workup this morning. Pulled a whole lot of blood. So now we're waiting for test results. I'm scared, guys. I have to admit it. I'm afraid it could be aplastic anemia."

"But you kicked it," Cindy said. "Didn't you?"

I'd had aplastic anemia years before I married Joe, years before Julie. Back then, when I was diagnosed with that wretched and often fatal disease, I actually put my gun into my mouth before common sense and survival instinct pulled me back.

I had so much more to live for now.

I said, "Even if the symptoms disappear, it can come back. I haven't told Joe what's freaking me out. He thinks I'm just working too hard. I don't want to scare him unless I'm sure. I don't want to break his heart."

Yuki had grabbed a paper napkin and was weeping into it.

"I'm sorry," she blubbered. "Take the booze away from me."

Cindy put an arm around Yuki and drained her

glass. She said to me, "You're not scared alone, Lindsay. We're all here."

Claire added, "Call us as soon as you hear."

I promised.

Yuki said, "Tell Joe. You have to tell him. He needs to go through this with you, and you need him, too."

"Group hug," I said.

We all stood up awkwardly in our booth and hugged across the table. I hoped this love and friendship would steady me until I saw Dr. Arpino again.

CHAPTER 99

THE NEXT DAY, early in the morning, I drove up Lake Street to Twelfth, but instead of heading to the Hall, I took a right onto Tenth, turned again onto California Street, and kept going.

Dr. Arpino's office was on a tidy block of houses on Broderick Street, many of which doubled as doctor's offices. I didn't have to check the house numbers. I knew the place—a gray-shingled Victorian with dormers and white trim and a mailbox painted with flowers.

I stopped the car at the curb and sat there with the motor running. I thought about how when I'd gotten home last night, Joe had been almost glowing with good news.

"I got the job, Blondie."

"And it's the job you want?" I asked him.

"Turns out that dick Benjamin Rollins and I have some friends in common."

"Wow. No kidding, Joe. This is amazing."

I'd hugged and kissed him, thinking this new job had come through at just the right time. If the worst happened—the stuff of my nightmares—the

Molinari family would have one income, anyway. And probably a good one.

I was due in Doc Arpino's office in ten minutes, and he was usually on time. I turned on the radio to Jazz 91 and listened to something by the late, great Miles Davis. While "Blue in Green" carried the seconds along, I took out my phone and checked my incoming mail.

There was nothing but spam to distract me. I opened the junk mail folder and imagined no more snoring, considered an urgent request for money to get my friend safely back from Europe, and imagined a trip to the Bahamas for only $77 a night, all expenses included.

The Bahamas. If only.

I dropped my phone back into my bag and watched a school bus stop on the opposite side of the street to pick up a kiddo, who dashed off his front steps and climbed up into the big yellow bus. Then the bus was on the move, and as it passed me, I put my car in gear and drove up the street to the intersection at Union.

I slowed for the stop sign and came to a full stop. I watched an old man clipping his doorstep hedges. A calico cat trotted across the street, and when it was safely home, I revved my engine.

I was running away. This was not my usual style and I knew that I was being crazy. I had to go to see the doc. I drummed my fingers on the wheel.

Not going. Going. Not going.

A car honked behind me and I put my foot on the gas. My hands spun the wheel to the right and I turned onto Union, then I took another right onto Divisadero. I took two more right turns in this pretty neighborhood that looked as though it had been ripped from a storybook tale ending with "And they lived happily ever after."

Having circled Doc Arpino's block, I parked again beside the pansy-painted mailbox.

I sighed. I dragged myself out of my car and put one foot in front of the other until I'd reached the top of the doctor's front steps.

I rang the bell and opened the door.

CHAPTER 100

I PUT THE doctor's office in my rearview and drove to the Hall on autopilot.

I parked on Harriet Street under the rumbling roof of Interstate 80, and in a few minutes Brady crossed the alley and got into my passenger seat. He looked at me, did a double take, and said, "You're scaring me, Boxer."

I nodded as if I knew what I was going to say or do.

One option was to go for the weekly B_{12} shots and, at the same time, go to work as usual and hope for the best. That meant no all-night stakeouts, firefights, or hand-to-hand combat with insane gunmen. In other words, I could not safely do what I called my job.

Or I could get the weekly shots and take a medical leave, as directed by my doctor. During that time Conklin would get a new partner, and I would lose my place in Homicide. I just *hated* that thought. It was roughly equivalent to closing my eyes and jumping into a sinkhole.

I said, "Brady, my condition is…how can I say this? It's serious. I have something called pernicious anemia."

"You're saying you're anemic?"

"It's a form of anemia. The causes are various and so are the symptoms, but it has to do with my blood being unable to absorb vitamin B_{12}. If I don't deal with this situation pronto, it could damage organs and nerves, or could become something worse. Years back I had aplastic anemia, and that really could have killed me."

Brady kept his eyes fixed on me. He was reading me.

"This pernicious kind. You're heading it off right now, right? And so you say it's treatable? Reversible?"

"I've got a good doctor. I need shots every week for a while. And Doc wants me to take time off."

"Please, Boxer. Do what you're supposed to do. Take whatever time you need."

"He says a couple of months. He said I have to do a whole mind and body reset. Sleep, you know, whatever *that* is. Meditation would be good. See him on schedule. Get better."

Brady smiled. "You. Lying around the house."

I tried to smile back, then I shook my head. Brady put his hand on my arm.

"Be a good girl, will you, Boxer?"

"Yes. I will. I have no choice."

Brady said, "I might as well tell you something you're going to hear soon anyway."

"Shoot," I said.

Brady checked his phone, sent someone a reply, then came back to me. He told me that Jacobi was being retired out, as a result of a case Conklin and I had worked about a year ago involving a crew of dirty cops. After the fallout, the body count had been, all told, about nineteen guilty and innocent souls.

I said to Brady, "IAD is hanging it on Jacobi?"

"Accountability goes with the job," he said.

I felt tears welling up. Not only was I at a personal low, I was taking this blame-Jacobi news personally.

"Who is replacing him?" I asked.

Brady shrugged. "To be decided."

Then he said, "Go home, Lindsay. Fight this pernicious anemia. It's something you have control over. Other than that, don't worry about a thing. It'll all work out somehow. You get better, and when you get a green light from your doctor, come back. Not a second before."

He leaned over, kissed my cheek, said, "Love you, Linds. Be good to yourself. I'll talk to you soon."

Then he got out of my car. I sat there and watched him cross Harriet Street and disappear behind a line of parked cars on his way up to the squad room.

"Don't worry about a thing," he'd said.

What, me worry?

But he was right. I counseled myself to get a grip on the one thing I might be able to use to save myself. I had to stay home. Spend more time with Julie and Joe and Martha. It would be quite interesting to find out who I was when not working a homicide case.

I couldn't put it off any longer. I had to go home and give Joe the news.

CHAPTER 101

I HADNT SEEN Jacobi since the hammer came down, but I'd called him the day after he walked out of the Hall for the last time to ask how he was doing.

"You know how it is, Boxer. Sometimes you're the dog. Sometimes you're the tree."

I commiserated. For different reasons, we were both feeling like trees.

We had a breakfast date this morning. Not in the break room with passed-over donuts, but at an actual eatery in Jacobi's section of town.

He lives in Hayes Valley. Gentrified not long ago, it has shaken off the rough edges and is now littered with cute little restaurants and bars and boutiques; a nice place to visit. Jacobi's house holds down the end of a block on Ivy Street and is one of many single-family and multifamily wood-frame houses, built closely together, facing sidewalks lined with young red-flowering gum trees.

I parked my Explorer behind my old friend's Hyundai SUV and called him on my phone.

"Lindsay?"

"Who else?"

"You're not the only woman I know," he said, laughing. "I'll be right down."

A couple of minutes later he came down the zigzag of wooden steps from his living quarters over his wide-body garage. He looked the same as always: gray haired, with hooded eyes, walking with a limp, and wearing a leather flight jacket handed down to him from an uncle who'd fought in the Korean War.

But he looked different to me now. He hadn't aged. It was nothing as obvious as that. He didn't even look depressed.

He looked lighter. Like a man who had been retired before he was ready to go, but was glad that the load was off his back. He was grinning when he crossed the street and I crossed the street toward him.

We opened our arms and hugged in the middle of Ivy, and man, it felt good.

Jacobi had stood in for my awful father before, and he was doing it now, even as I had come to comfort him.

He might have heard my strangled sob.

"Do not go wobbly on me, Boxer. I may be fat, I may be pushing sixty, but here I am."

"Let's get out of the road," I said, "so that those aren't your last words."

Playa del Oro was a little Mexican joint sandwiched between a shoe repair shop and an art gallery. We ordered huevos rancheros and tea and talked about how we'd come to this unexpected place in our lives.

He said, "Boxer, I'm not an innocent party. I didn't know Ted Swanson had assembled a robbery crew, but I should have known. I have to be accountable. If I were the mayor, jeez, Louise—someone had to pay. Obviously the buck stopped at my door. And hey, it came with full retirement pay."

"That part is awesome," I said.

"And pretty soon, Medicare." Jacobi grinned broadly, looking lighter and younger by the minute. He said, "But enough about me. Tell me how you're doing. Don't leave anything out."

I told him, "I feel pretty good but like I'm playing hooky. I'm supposed to be on the job. I mean, shit happens and then you die, right? But this is a case of shit happens and you get to stay home, watch movies, and collect a paycheck."

"Go figure," said Jacobi. "We've got the same deal. But there's an upside for both of us. Your job is to rest up and heal. Mine is to get back to my fighting weight. My doctor told me to lose the bowling ball or else, and when he described 'or else,' I definitely didn't want it."

I pointed to the dish of chocolate chili cake with a side of churros our waitress had put down in front of us, and he laughed. "I know, I know, but this is a special occasion, old friend. I'm going to cut down on the carbs and start walking. I might get a dog."

"How about this, Chief? Why don't we get together to walk my dog every week or so. Or our dogs. We could go to a museum once in a while, take in a ball game. Fight back against enforced home confinement."

"I like the sound of that, Boxer."

We grinned at each other, reached across the small round table laden with sweets, and shook on it.

I said, "We're both fighters."

Jacobi said, "And fighters win."

ACKNOWLEDGMENTS

Our thanks to those who shared their time and expertise with us in the creation of this book: Judge Kevin Rathburn of Suamico, Wisconsin, Northeast Wisconsin Technical College; Attorney Steven Rabinowitz, Pryor Cashman, New York City, for his wise counsel; and Captain Richard Conklin, BCI commander, Stamford, Connecticut, Police Department. And gratitude to the home team, Mary Jordan, John A. Duffy, and our amazing researcher, Ingrid Taylar, West Coast, USA.

ABOUT THE AUTHORS

James Patterson received the Literarian Award for Outstanding Service to the American Literary Community from the National Book Foundation. He holds the Guinness World Record for the most #1 *New York Times* bestsellers, and his books have sold more than 380 million copies worldwide. A tireless champion of the power of books and reading, Patterson created a children's book imprint, JIMMY Patterson, whose mission is simple: "We want every kid who finishes a JIMMY Book to say, 'PLEASE GIVE ME ANOTHER BOOK.'" He has donated more than one million books to students and soldiers and funds over four hundred Teacher Education Scholarships at twenty-four colleges and universities. He has also donated millions of dollars to independent bookstores and school libraries. Patterson invests proceeds from the sales of JIMMY Patterson Books in pro-reading initiatives.

Maxine Paetro has collaborated with James Patterson on the bestselling Women's Murder Club, Private, and Confessions series. She lives with her husband in New York State.

BOOKS BY JAMES PATTERSON

FEATURING ALEX CROSS

Target: Alex Cross • *The People vs. Alex Cross* • *Cross the Line* • *Cross Justice* • *Hope to Die* • *Cross My Heart* • *Alex Cross, Run* • *Merry Christmas, Alex Cross* • *Kill Alex Cross* • *Cross Fire* • *I, Alex Cross* • *Alex Cross's Trial* (with Richard DiLallo) • *Cross Country* • *Double Cross* • *Cross* (also published as *Alex Cross*) • *Mary, Mary* • *London Bridges* • *The Big Bad Wolf* • *Four Blind Mice* • *Violets Are Blue* • *Roses Are Red* • *Pop Goes the Weasel* • *Cat & Mouse* • *Jack & Jill* • *Kiss the Girls* • *Along Came a Spider*

THE WOMEN'S MURDER CLUB

The 17th Suspect (with Maxine Paetro) • *16th Seduction* (with Maxine Paetro) • *15th Affair* (with Maxine Paetro) • *14th Deadly Sin* (with Maxine Paetro) • *Unlucky 13* (with Maxine Paetro) • *12th of Never* (with Maxine Paetro) • *11th Hour* (with Maxine Paetro) • *10th Anniversary* (with Maxine Paetro) • *The 9th Judgment* (with Maxine Paetro) • *The 8th Confession* (with Maxine Paetro) • *7th Heaven* (with Maxine Paetro) • *The 6th Target* (with Maxine Paetro) • *The 5th Horseman* (with Maxine Paetro) • *4th of July* (with Maxine Paetro) • *3rd Degree* (with Andrew Gross) • *2nd Chance* (with Andrew Gross) • *1st to Die*

FEATURING MICHAEL BENNETT

Ambush (with James O. Born) • *Haunted* (with James O. Born) • *Bullseye* (with Michael Ledwidge) • *Alert* (with Michael Ledwidge) • *Burn* (with Michael Ledwidge) • *Gone* (with Michael Ledwidge) • *I, Michael Bennett* (with Michael Ledwidge) • *Tick Tock* (with Michael Ledwidge) • *Worst Case* (with Michael Ledwidge) • *Run for Your Life* (with Michael Ledwidge) • *Step on a Crack* (with Michael Ledwidge)

FEATURING HARRIET BLUE

Liar Liar (with Candice Fox) • *Fifty Fifty* (with Candice Fox) • *Never Never* (with Candice Fox)

FEATURING TRAVIS MCKINLEY

Miracle at Augusta (with Peter de Jonge) • *Miracle on the 17th Green* (with Peter de Jonge)

THE PRIVATE NOVELS

Princess (with Rees Jones) • *Count to Ten* (with Ashwin Sanghi) • *Missing* (with Kathryn Fox) • *The Games* (with Mark Sullivan) • *Private Paris* (with Mark Sullivan) • *Private Vegas* (with Maxine Paetro) • *Private India: City on Fire* (with Ashwin Sanghi) • *Private Down Under* (with Michael White) • *Private L.A.* (with Mark Sullivan) • *Private Berlin* (with Mark Sullivan) • *Private London* (with Mark Pearson) • *Private Games* (with Mark Sullivan) • *Private: #1 Suspect* (with Maxine Paetro) • *Private* (with Maxine Paetro)

NYPD RED NOVELS

Red Alert (with Marshall Karp) • *NYPD Red 4* (with Marshall Karp) • *NYPD Red 3* (with Marshall Karp) • *NYPD Red 2* (with Marshall Karp) • *NYPD Red* (with Marshall Karp)

SUMMER NOVELS

Second Honeymoon (with Howard Roughan) • *Now You See Her* (with Michael Ledwidge) • *Swimsuit* (with Maxine Paetro) • *Sail* (with Howard Roughan) • *Beach Road* (with Peter de Jonge) • *Lifeguard* (with Andrew Gross) • *Honeymoon* (with Howard Roughan) • *The Beach House* (with Peter de Jonge)

STAND-ALONE BOOKS

The Cornwalls Are Gone (with Brendan DuBois) • *The First Lady* (with Brendan DuBois) • *The Chef* (with Max DiLallo) • *The House Next Door* • *Juror #3* (with Nancy Allen) • *Texas Ranger* (with Andrew Bourelle) • *Triple Homicide* (with Maxine Paetro and James O. Born) • *The President Is Missing* (with Bill Clinton) • *Murder in Paradise* (with Doug Allyn, Connor Hyde, Duane Swierczynski) • *Murder Beyond the Grave* (with Andrew Bourelle and Christopher Charles) • *Home Sweet Murder* (with Andrew Bourelle and Scott Slaven) • *Murder, Interrupted* (with Alex Abramovich and Christopher Charles) • *All-American Murder* (with Alex Abramovich and Mike Harvkey) • *The Family Lawyer* (with Robert Rotstein, Christopher Charles, Rachel Howzell

Hall) • *The Store* (with Richard DiLallo) • *The Moores Are Missing* (with Loren D. Estleman, Sam Hawken, Ed Chatterton) • *Triple Threat* (with Max DiLallo, Andrew Bourelle) • *Murder Games* (with Howard Roughan) • *Penguins of America* (with Jack Patterson with Florence Yue) • *Two from the Heart* (with Frank Constantini, Emily Raymond, Brian Sitts) • *The Black Book* (with David Ellis) • *Humans, Bow Down* (with Emily Raymond) • *Woman of God* (with Maxine Paetro) • *Filthy Rich* (with John Connolly and Timothy Malloy) • *The Murder House* (with David Ellis) • *Truth or Die* (with Howard Roughan) • *Invisible* (with David Ellis) • *First Love* (with Emily Raymond) • *Mistress* (with David Ellis) • *Zoo* (with Michael Ledwidge) • *Guilty Wives* (with David Ellis) • *The Christmas Wedding* (with Richard DiLallo) • *Kill Me If You Can* (with Marshall Karp) • *Toys* (with Neil McMahon) • *Don't Blink* (with Howard Roughan) • *The Postcard Killers* (with Liza Marklund) • *The Murder of King Tut* (with Martin Dugard) • *Against Medical Advice* (with Hal Friedman) • *Sundays at Tiffany's* (with Gabrielle Charbonnet) • *You've Been Warned* (with Howard Roughan) • *The Quickie* (with Michael Ledwidge) • *Judge & Jury* (with Andrew Gross) • *Sam's Letters to Jennifer* • *The Lake House* • *The Jester* (with Andrew Gross) • *Suzanne's Diary for Nicholas* • *Cradle and All* • *When the Wind Blows* • *Hide & Seek* • *The Midnight Club* • *Black Friday* (originally published as *Black Market*) • *See How They Run* • *Season of the Machete* • *The Thomas Berryman Number*

BOOK**SHOTS**

The Exile (with Alison Joseph) • *The Medical Examiner* (with Maxine Paetro) • *Black Dress Affair* (with Susan DiLallo) • *The Killer's Wife* (with Max DiLallo) • *Scott Free* (with Rob Hart) • *The Dolls* (with Kecia Bal) • *Detective Cross* • *Nooners* (with Tim Arnold) • *Stealing Gulfstreams* (with Max DiLallo) • *Diary of a Succubus* (with Derek Nikitas) • *Night Sniper* (with Christopher Charles) • *Juror #3* (with Nancy Allen) • *The Shut-In* (with Duane Swierczynski) • *French Twist* (with Richard DiLallo) • *Malicious* (with James O. Born) • *Hidden* (with James O. Born) • *The House Husband* (with Duane Swierczynski) • *The Christmas Mystery* (with Richard DiLallo) • *Black & Blue* (with Candice Fox) • *Come and Get Us* (with Shan Serafin) • *Private: The Royals* (with Rees Jones) • *Taking the Titanic* (with Scott Slaven) • *Killer Chef* (with Jeffrey J. Keyes) • *French Kiss* (with Richard DiLallo) • *$10,000,000 Marriage Proposal* (with Hilary Liftin) • *Hunted* (with Andrew Holmes) • *113 Minutes* (with Max DiLallo) • *Chase* (with Michael Ledwidge) • *Let's Play Make-Believe* (with James O. Born) • *The Trial* (with Maxine Paetro) • *Little Black Dress* (with Emily Raymond) • *Cross Kill* • *Zoo II* (with Max DiLallo)

Sabotage: An Under Covers Story by Jessica Linden • *Love Me Tender* by Laurie Horowitz • *Bedding*

the Highlander by Sabrina York • *The Wedding Florist* by T.J. Kline • *A Wedding in Maine* by Jen McLaughlin • *Radiant* by Elizabeth Hayley • *Hot Winter Nights* by Codi Gray • *Bodyguard* by Jessica Linden • *Dazzling* by Elizabeth Hayley • *The Mating Season* by Laurie Horowitz • *Sacking the Quarterback* by Samantha Towle • *Learning to Ride* by Erin Knightley • *The McCullagh Inn in Maine* by Jen McLaughlin

FOR READERS OF ALL AGES

MAXIMUM RIDE
Maximum Ride Forever • Nevermore: The Final Maximum Ride Adventure • Angel: A Maximum Ride Novel • Fang: A Maximum Ride Novel • Max: A Maximum Ride Novel • The Final Warning: A Maximum Ride Novel • Saving the World and Other Extreme Sports: A Maximum Ride Novel • School's Out—Forever: A Maximum Ride Novel • The Angel Experiment: A Maximum Ride Novel

DANIEL X
Daniel X: Lights Out (with Chris Grabenstein) • *Daniel X: Armageddon* (with Chris Grabenstein) • *Daniel X: Game Over* (with Ned Rust) • *Daniel X: Demons and Druids* (with Adam Sadler) • *Daniel X: Watch the Skies* (with Ned Rust) • *The Dangerous Days of Daniel X* (with Michael Ledwidge)

WITCH & WIZARD
Witch & Wizard: The Lost (with Emily Raymond) • *Witch & Wizard: The Kiss* (with Jill Dembowski) • *Witch & Wizard: The Fire* (with Jill Dembowski)

• *Witch & Wizard: The Gift* (with Ned Rust) •
Witch & Wizard (with Gabrielle Charbonnet)

CONFESSIONS

Confessions: The Murder of an Angel (with Maxine
Paetro) • *Confessions: The Paris Mysteries* (with
Maxine Paetro) • *Confessions: The Private School
Murders* (with Maxine Paetro) • *Confessions of a
Murder Suspect* (with Maxine Paetro)

MIDDLE SCHOOL

Middle School: Born to Rock (with Chris
Tebbetts, illustrated by Neil Swaab) • *Dog
Diaries: A Middle School Story* (with Steven
Butler, illustrated by Richard Watson) • *Middle
School: Escape to Australia* (with Martin
Chatterton, illustrated by Daniel Griffo) •
Middle School: Dog's Best Friend (with Chris
Tebbetts, illustrated by Jomike Tejido) • *Middle
School: Just My Rotten Luck* (with Chris
Tebbetts, illustrated by Laura Park) • *Middle
School: Save Rafe!* (with Chris Tebbetts,
illustrated by Laura Park) • *Middle School:
Ultimate Showdown* (with Julia Bergen,
illustrated by Alec Longstreth) • *Middle School:
How I Survived Bullies, Broccoli, and Snake Hill*
(with Chris Tebbetts, illustrated by Laura Park)
• *Middle School: My Brother Is a Big, Fat Liar*
(with Lisa Papademetriou, illustrated by Neil
Swaab) • *Middle School: Get Me Out of Here!*
(with Chris Tebbetts, illustrated by Laura Park)
• *Middle School, The Worst Years of My Life*
(with Chris Tebbetts, illustrated by Laura Park)

I FUNNY

I Funny: Around the World (with Chris Grabenstein) • *I Funny: School of Laughs* (with Chris Grabenstein, illustrated by Jomike Tejido) • *I Funny TV* (with Chris Grabenstein, illustrated by Laura Park) • *I Totally Funniest: A Middle School Story* (with Chris Grabenstein, illustrated by Laura Park) • *I Even Funnier: A Middle School Story* (with Chris Grabenstein, illustrated by Laura Park) • *I Funny: A Middle School Story* (with Chris Grabenstein, illustrated by Laura Park)

TREASURE HUNTERS

Treasure Hunters: Quest for the City of Gold (with Chris Grabenstein, illustrated by Juliana Neufeld) • *Treasure Hunters: Peril at the Top of the World* (with Chris Grabenstein, illustrated by Juliana Neufeld) • *Treasure Hunters: Secret of the Forbidden City* (with Chris Grabenstein, illustrated by Juliana Neufeld) • *Treasure Hunters: Danger Down the Nile* (with Chris Grabenstein, illustrated by Juliana Neufeld) • *Treasure Hunters* (with Chris Grabenstein, illustrated by Juliana Neufeld)

OTHER BOOKS FOR READERS OF ALL AGES

Max Einstein: The Genius Experiment (with Chris Grabenstein, illustrated by Beverly Johnson) • *Cuddly Critters for Little Geniuses* (with Susan Patterson, illustrated by Hsinping Pan) • *Unbelievably Boring Bart* (with Duane Swierczynski, illustrated by Xavier Bonet) • *Not So Normal Norbert* (with Joey Green, illustrated by Hatem Aly) • *The Candies' Easter Party* (illustrated by Andy Elkerton) • *Jacky Ha-Ha: My Life is a Joke* (with Chris Grabenstein, illustrated by Kerascoët) • *Give Thank You a Try* (with Bill O'Reilly) • *The Injustice* (previously published as *Expelled*, with Emily Raymond) • *The Candies Save Christmas* (illustrated by Andy Elkerton) • *Big Words for Little Geniuses* (with Susan Patterson, illustrated by Hsinping Pan) • *Laugh Out Loud* (with Chris Grabenstein) • *Pottymouth and Stoopid* (with Chris Grabenstein) • *Crazy House* (with Gabrielle Charbonnet) • *House of Robots: Robot Revolution* (with Chris Grabenstein, illustrated by Juliana Neufeld) • *Word of Mouse* (with Chris Grabenstein, illustrated by Joe Sutphin) • *Give Please a Chance* (with Bill O'Reilly) • *Jacky Ha-Ha* (with Chris Grabenstein, illustrated by Kerascoët) • *House of Robots: Robots Go Wild!* (with Chris Grabenstein, illustrated by Juliana Neufeld) • *Public School Superhero* (with Chris Tebbetts, illustrated by Cory Thomas) • *House of Robots* (with Chris Grabenstein, illustrated by Juliana Neufeld) • *Homeroom Diaries* (with Lisa Papademetriou, illustrated by Keino) • *Med Head* (with Hal Friedman) • *santaKid* (illustrated by Michael Garland)

For previews and information about the author, visit JamesPatterson.com or find him on Facebook or at your app store.

JAMES
PATTERSON
RECOMMENDS

Don't tell Alex Cross and Michael Bennett this, but I might have a bit of a soft spot for Lindsay Boxer and the Women's Murder Club. Why? Because Lindsay, Cindy, Claire, and Jill always get their man. And by "man," I mean the criminal they're hunting. As some of the most respected professionals in the San Francisco justice system, they were sick and tired of tip-toeing around their male bosses to get the job done. So they banded together, shared information, and closed more cases.

Meet the first ladies of crime fighting: the Women's Murder Club.

JAMES
PATTERSON

1ST
TO DIE

A WOMEN'S MURDER CLUB NOVEL

1ST TO DIE

Three sets of murdered newlyweds, bureaucratic red tape, and a truly terrible diagnosis from the doctor—Detective Lindsay Boxer has her hands full in 1ST TO DIE, the book that launched the Women's Murder Club series. She's one tough cookie, though, and a heck of a character to get to know: fierce, determined, smart, and unstoppable. In short, she's my kind of woman. She'll need to keep her wits—and her WMC friends—about her, though, because the killer is the last person anyone would ever see coming.

"Unquestionably the best book in the series."
—BookReporter.com

JAMES PATTERSON

and Maxine Paetro

#1
NEW YORK TIMES BESTSELLER

4TH OF JULY

A WOMEN'S MURDER CLUB NOVEL

4TH OF JULY

As an author, I love shaking things up and seeing how characters grow—or, in my books, if they even make it to the end of the story. The most interesting thing to test? Loyalty. Lindsay Boxer has dedicated her life to upholding the law. But after a routine arrest goes terribly wrong, she finds herself facing judge, jury, a very public trial, and a brutal murderer slashing through her sister's once-peaceful hometown. I turned Lindsay's life upside down in this book. And that's not all of it. Read what happens because I put a twist in this book that's pretty killer.

JAMES
PATTERSON

AND MAXINE PAETRO

"Patterson's books might as
well come with movie tickets
as a bonus feature."
—*New York Times*

7

#**1**
NEW YORK
TIMES
BESTSELLING
AUTHOR

7TH
HEAVEN

A WOMEN'S MURDER CLUB NOVEL

7TH HEAVEN

San Francisco. Beautiful weather. Beautiful people. Beautiful architecture. It's the perfect setting for everything to go wrong. And, boy, does everything go terribly wrong. Lindsay and the WMC face two of their biggest cases yet: the politically charged disappearance of the mayor's son and a string of devastating fires that destroy some of the city's most iconic homes—with their wealthy owners inside. When the pressure is on, the WMC is at its best, and that's what they need to be in this book. Because when everything converges in 7TH HEAVEN, it's nothing short of explosive.

THE WORLD'S #1 BESTSELLING WRITER

JAMES PATTERSON

& MAXINE PAETRO

The new
WOMEN'S
MURDER
CLUB
novel

12TH
OF NEVER

12TH OF NEVER

When I think of a newborn baby, I think "nesting" and desperately trying to sneak in a few moments of precious sleep. Lindsay Boxer, detective and newly minted mom, doesn't experience any of those in 12TH OF NEVER. After only a week of baby bliss, a string of murders pulls Lindsay out of the nursery and onto the streets of San Francisco. I've always been amazed at how working moms juggle families and careers. But on top of finding lost socks, Lindsay also has to find a missing body from the morgue. And that's just the beginning. The shocker I have lined up at the end? Mind-blowing.

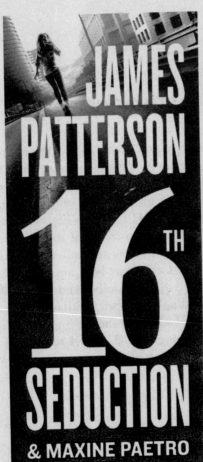

THE
WORLD'S
#1
BEST-
SELLING
WRITER

A horrific
crime.

One
suspect.

No
evidence.

THE
NEW
WOMEN'S
MURDER
CLUB
NOVEL

JAMES
PATTERSON
16TH
SEDUCTION
& MAXINE PAETRO

16TH SEDUCTION

Fierce. Determined. Smart. Unstoppable. That's Detective Lindsay Boxer in a nutshell. As the leader of the Women's Murder Club solving crimes in San Francisco, she's been tested time and time again. Now I've put even more pressure on her—as everyone she's ever relied on turns their back on her.

After her husband Joe's double life shattered their family, Lindsay is finally ready to welcome him back with open arms. And when their beloved hometown faces a threat unlike any the country has ever seen, Lindsay and Joe find a common cause and spring into action.

But what at first seems like an open-and-shut case quickly explodes. Undermined by a suspect with a brilliant mind, Lindsay's investigation is scrutinized and her motives are called into question. In a desperate fight for her career—and her life—Lindsay must connect the dots of a deadly conspiracy before *she's* put on trial and a criminal walks free with blood on his hands.